How Dare He Show Up At One in the Morning!

She flung the door open, accusations on her lips. The words never materialized as she took in the picture Gard made, standing in the doorway, his hands thrust in the back pockets of his jeans. His shoulders slumped, and his hair looked as if he'd been running his fingers through it. Dark circles were smudged beneath his eyes. The silence stretched as they stared at each other.

"I need you," he said at last.

Season didn't analyze how it had happened but she knew she loved him. Wordlessly, she moved aside, allowing him entrance to her home and heart.

SANDI SHAYNE is a wife, mother and full-time writer of romance. She's also an animal lover and shares her North Louisiana home with three smug cats, numerous dogs, and thoroughbred horses. She likes rain. And autumn. And she loves stories that make you cry.

Dear Reader:

There is an electricity between two people in love that makes everything they do magic, larger than life. This is what we bring you in SILHOUETTE INTIMATE MOMENTS.

SILHOUETTE INTIMATE MOMENTS are longer, more sensuous romance novels filled with adventure, suspense, glamor or melodrama. These books have an element no one else has tapped: excitement.

We are proud to present the very best romance has to offer from the very best romance writers. In the coming months look for some of your favorite authors such as Elizabeth Lowell, Nora Roberts, Erin St. Claire and Brooke Hastings.

SILHOUETTE INTIMATE MOMENTS are for the woman who wants more than she has ever had before. These books are for you.

Karen Solem
Editor-in-Chief
Silhouette Books

No Perfect Season

Sandi Shane

Silhouette Intimate Moments

Published by Silhouette Books New York

America's Publisher of Contemporary Romance

Silhouette Books by Sandi Shane

No Perfect Season (IM #91)

SILHOUETTE BOOKS
300 E. 42nd St., New York, N.Y. 10017

Distributed by Pocket Books

ISBN: 0-373-07091-8

First Silhouette Books printing April, 1985

10 9 8 7 6 5 4 3 2 1

America's Publisher of Contemporary Romance

Printed in the U.S.A.

To Marian M. Poe,
who believed in us.

Chapter 1

"SEASON, SEASON," THE VOICE CHANTED, "WHEN ARE you going to give up this ridiculous notion of independence and come back to me?" Clayton Ashford waited for the mirrored reflection of the tall, slender woman standing behind him to answer.

Season Ashford's dark, almost black, eyes stared over the top of her ex-husband's attractive white head, meeting the irritated, azure gaze of the man to whom she had been married for two years and divorced for slightly more than six months. Unable to hold the eye contact, she carefully combed a wet lock of his hair to its proper position between her index and middle fingers and snipped off the ends with the tiny scissors she held in her right hand.

"Clay, do we have to go over all this again?" she asked, wishing for the hundredth time that he would find another stylist to do his hair. "You know I can't." Her hands moved mechanically and with an instinctive expertise, sectioning hair, combining it in with another section, and cutting off the longer ends.

"In God's name, why?" he asked. "I thought we had a workable arrangement." His frowning eyes roamed restlessly over her reflection, studying the classic perfection of her bronze-tinted beauty. At twenty-six, the woman was exactly half his age, though at the moment her composure bespoke that of a much older woman.

Season sighed, letting her capable hands drop to the back of his chair. Sloe eyes stared emotionlessly at him, the perfect oval of her face enhanced by the severe style of her hair, which was drawn sleekly back from a center part and coiled in an intricate figure eight at the back of her head. Its seal-black sheen held a blue tint in the glow of the harsh overhead lights that gilded the high cheekbones blushed with delicate rose and caused shadows to nestle in the hollows of her cheeks.

"Yes . . . in the beginning." Season placed slender fingers to the sides of his head and tilted it, combing through the recently cut hair and checking for any missed strands. "I was nothing when you walked into that exclusive Oklahoma styling salon three years ago. Nothing. A half-white, half-Indian born of an alcoholic father and a Kiowa mother. All I had was a cosmetologist's license." She smiled wryly.

"I was good at my profession, and I'm smart enough to know, and truthful enough to admit that I'm more than pretty. That's why I was working for Jeff Marsden. Only the most talented and lovely were good enough for his wealthy clientele. Then you walked in. Clayton Ashford. One of *the* Ashfords. Pillars of society. Old family. Old money. You were handsome, wealthy, and you swept me off my feet. You petted and pampered me and gave me a confidence in myself as a person and as a woman that I'd never had before. You lavished gifts and attention on me, and I loved you in return. For a while, I was the happiest woman in Tulsa."

"So what happened?" Clay asked gruffly.

Season's astonished eyes met his. "Come on, Clay. Are you getting senile?"

At the slight slur against his age, Clay's face suffused with angry color. Season smiled sweetly. Too sweetly. "For one thing," she said, "you drank too much. I didn't like it, but I could handle it. And then there's Holly. Surely you remember Holly? I remember Holly, and I only saw her for about ten seconds. You were in bed with her. Our bed," she added succinctly.

Clay swore.

"Good God, Clay! Did you really think I'd smile and say 'Carry on . . . so sorry I got back sooner than I expected?' I'm afraid that sort of thing just doesn't go with me. Besides, I'm certain that Holly wasn't the first."

Clay's handsome features held no guilt or chagrin. "Grow up, Season! This is the twentieth century. I'll lay odds that ninety-five percent of the men out there in the big, wide world sleep around."

"Maybe so, Clay, but not *my* husband. Maybe it's because I never had any toys when I was growing up, but I don't intend to share. Especially not with an entire regiment!"

"Now, Season . . ."

"All I wanted was for you to love me."

"Season, you know I cared for you."

"I said love, Clay. I can get care from the Salvation Army."

"Dammit, there's no such thing as love. There are good times and good sex—which we had, if you'll remember— but love is a highly overrated emotion that young girls use as a salve to their guilt when they go to bed with a man for that sex I was talking about. Trust me, Season. The only place you're going to find love is in a romantic novel. And as far as your loving me, that's a joke, too. You can't tell me that my money and the things it bought you weren't a big part of that love."

"I'm not sure of anything anymore, Clay," she told him, weary of the whole conversation. One in a long series that invariably followed the same lines. "Let's just drop it. Forget trying to get me back and find yourself a new play-pretty."

"I want you," the attractive fifty-two-year-old growled.

"Only because you can't have me," Season argued. "It's your pride that's hurt, not your heart. I was a possession to you. Maybe you did buy me with gifts—pay for the use of my body—and show me off. You were very good to me in your own way, but I'm just not sophisticated enough to sanction an open marriage. There should be more to marriage than some sort of bargain that benefits both parties."

"There's another man, isn't there? That's what all this is about." Another flash of anger flitted across his face.

"No, Clay! I divorced you for a woman, not a man. And that woman was myself. I had to see if I could salvage the ego your cheating had destroyed." She waved her arms to point out the modern, beautifully decorated room. "I'm the owner of Season's, the most exclusive styling salon in the entire state of Oklahoma, thanks to your very generous divorce settlement. They tell me that having your hair done by Season is the ultimate to the oil-rich Tulsa society ladies . . . and men. That does wonders for my damaged ego. That and the fact that I'm in demand as a lecturer all over the country. I love my job, Clay, and success does smell sweet." She didn't tell him of her lonely nights and the sometimes almost unbearable need to have someone to talk to when she got home, someone to love . . . if there was such an emotion. Instead, she reached for the styling brush and blow dryer. The sound of the forced hot air put a welcome end to the conversation.

She had been married just three weeks when she realized that Clay drank too much. It was a year before she began to suspect there was another woman—or women—and several months more until she caught him with Holly What's-her-name. That scene had given her the courage to ask Clay for a divorce. That had been six months ago. Their relationship now fell somewhere just short of friendly and a bit more than civilized. He still visited her at the house they'd once shared in an exclusive neighborhood on the outskirts of Tulsa. Season had even fixed dinner for him once or twice, but she hadn't let him stay the night, though he'd tried to persuade her to. Poor Clay, she thought, suppressing a smile. She was probably the first woman to refuse him.

It wasn't that she wouldn't have welcomed him in her bed. Their sex had always been good, and Season, though she'd divorced a husband, had been unable to divorce herself from the physical needs that still plagued her with an annoying regularity. She couldn't, however, give in to his demands because the love she'd once felt had been lost in the pain of his infidelity. She simply couldn't make love without some warm emotion, and she felt no warmth toward him.

At first the divorce had brought a sense of guilt, a sense of failure. Maybe it was her fault. Maybe if she'd loved Clay more, she could have endured their less than perfect life together. As her mother had endured the imperfect life Season's father had offered her.

Daniel Clark had been a terrible father, a terrible husband, a terrible human being. He wasn't really bad, only weak, Season's mother, Mary, often said with a sweet smile. They had been so much in love when Daniel married the beautiful Kiowa girl, but he couldn't cope with the innuendos, the jokes, the constant slurs about his Indian wife, and he had begun to drink.

Season remembered him as vile and abusive in both language and actions, humiliating her mother time after time. She also remembered the tears she herself had cried when he'd physically abused her mother, and she remembered her own determined lack of tears when he had turned his rage on her. Season soon learned to hide her fear and anger behind a blank expression. She'd heard whispers behind her back that her reticence and her impassive looks were attributed to her ancestry. ''Cold, uncaring heathen'' she'd heard herself called. Yet the rich now flocked to her salon. They paid for her exclusive services and bragged to their friends that they were able to. They watched her and judged her, none of them suspecting that the emotionless face she presented to the world had been adopted early in her life. She had seldom dropped the mask in her youth . . . and never in front of her father. It had been firmly in place on her twelve-year-old face when Daniel Clark had died. Only her mother, desolate with grief, had cried. In spite of everything, she'd loved her husband. Season had felt only relief.

''You look as if you're a million miles away,'' Clay observed as the blow dryer came to a stop.

''Years. A million years,'' she corrected.

''Season, you know there has never been a divorce in the Ashford family before. It doesn't look good . . .''

''Clay! No more! You should have thought of that when you were out sleeping around.'' She combed his hair in silence for a moment, hating herself for the shortness of her voice, a shortness that stemmed from her bitterness at Clay's self-centered attitude. She cast about in her mind for a neutral topic of conversation that might last until she finished his hair. ''Beth's coming back,'' she said at last. ''I saw some servants milling around yesterday.''

''I'd heard through the grapevine that she was back from Europe,'' Clay said, though his face still held a sullen frown.

Elizabeth Galbraith, the recent widow of Victor Galbraith, Oklahoma's most popular and colorful state senator, owned the house that stood on the two acres adjoining the house where Season and Clay had lived. Though they had been neighbors for two years, Season had seen little of either of them. Most of the couple's time had been spent in the capital, at their condominium in town, or cruising around the world. The house next to the Ashfords' served only as their retreat from the political pressures accompanying Victor's position.

"I've heard Elizabeth is planning on vying for a seat in the House next election," Clay said.

Season's hands stopped their movement. "How could she, after Victor's death?"

"Murder, Season. Victor Galbraith was murdered. Every politician is a sitting duck for the nuts in his constituency. Unfortunately, one of the nuts took an intense dislike to the best senator Oklahoma has had in a hundred years."

"They never caught anyone, did they?"

"They never even had a decent suspect," Clay replied. "The whole thing was so damned senseless."

Both were quiet for a moment before Season asked, "How can Beth put herself, if you'll pardon the pun, back in the line of fire?"

"I've known her for a lot of years. She's a strong, gutsy woman."

Season ripped open the Velcro fastener of the cape covering Clay's impeccable gray suit. "She'd have to be," she commented, easing the plastic covering from him and shaking it free of the damp strands of hair. "All finished."

"Season, Jim Nighthawk is on line two," the soft voice of Lisa Paden, the salon manager, announced over the intercom.

"Thanks, Lisa," Season said, a delighted smile curving her lips. She pressed a button and picked up the ivory phone. "Jim! How's it going?"

As she listened to the young Cherokee artist, she noticed the suspicion lurking in Clay's blue eyes. She fought to suppress a smile. Clay thought she was interested in Jim Nighthawk. Hadn't he already asked her about another man in her life? He found it easier to believe that she had left him for someone else, despite her protestations to the contrary. And if she were having an affair with someone, Clay would reason, why not Jim?

Season frowned. Why not Jim? Wasn't he the proverbial answer to a maiden's prayers? He stood well over six feet tall, towering inches above her own five feet eight. He was slender, yet boasted a physique to turn any woman's head. His pure Indian ancestry was etched in the bone structure of his copper face, from the chiseled angle of cheek and jaw to the eaglelike nose and dark eyes that always held a hint of laughter. His was a mobile face that expressed his every emotion. A bundle of irrepressible nervous energy, he paced a lot, eating up the ground with his long-legged stride. Just watching him made Season tired.

So, she asked herself for the dozenth time, if he's so perfect why doesn't he make your heart go pitter-pat? She didn't know why; she just knew that he didn't. Was it because she was afraid to try another relationship after Clay? Possibly. No, probably. Part of her reason for not getting involved with Jim was fear of another failure, but mostly it was because he just didn't set her pulses racing.

She was fond of Jim, nothing more. It had taken her a long time to convince him that there could be nothing but friendship between them, but finally he had ceased his pursuit of her and settled for a platonic relationship. Now if only she could stop Clay's regularly scheduled pleas for her to return to him, she would be happy . . . almost.

"You aren't listening, Season," Jim Nighthawk accused, jolting her out of her thoughts.

"Sorry. Guess I'm not."

"I said, are we still on for Saturday night?"

"Sure. Nothing's changed that I know of," Season answered. "Are you going to pick me up at my place?"

"Right. About seven-thirty sound okay?"

"Seven-thirty is fine."

The two said their good-byes, and Season hung up, meeting Clay's questioning gaze as she did so. "Jim

Nighthawk," she said, in what was an unnecessary admission.

"That artist you're sponsoring?" Clay's tone was accusatory.

Season's chin tilted a fraction. "Yes."

"I see." Clayton rose from the chair and regarded her silently for a moment. "Be sure and give Beth a call, will you? I'm sure she'd like an invitation to that show you're planning for your young artist friend."

"I will. You should call her, too. You've known her a long time, and it's probably pretty lonely for her." Season quickly stored the loose items at her station in their appropriate and hygienic places. "Does she have any family?" she asked idly, suddenly realizing she knew very little about the woman's personal life. "I've never heard you mention anyone."

Clay's eyes narrowed. Of course! Beth's family. Why hadn't he thought of it before? Beth's half brother. Gardner Kincannon could find out anything and everything about this Jim Nighthawk . . . and his relationship with Season. Realizing his ex-wife was waiting for an answer, he replied, just short of a lie, "No family to speak of."

Clay settled himself in the splitting green vinyl chair across from the desk in the small office the Tulsa Police Department had supplied its best detective after he'd received his first citation for bravery during a $750,000-drug bust.

Gard Kincannon, who leaned back in the swivel chair, his feet propped on the battered desk, his mind engrossed in the manila folder he held in his left hand, had barely acknowledged Clay's entrance—much to the latter's irritation. In the quiet that filled the room, Clay noted with disgust that Gard's shoes were not the usual kind he'd seen on the other detectives' feet, but rather scruffy, battered Adidas. As Clay watched, Gard raised a Hershey bar to his mouth and polished off the remains. Then with nothing more than a cursory glance at the chipped metal wastebasket, he crushed the candy wrapper with strong fingers and tossed it with unerring accuracy.

His pale blue eyes alight with pleasure, he smiled up at Clay over the top of the folder, chewed a couple of times, and proudly announced, "Twenty-seven."

"Twenty-seven?" Clay questioned.

"Twenty-seven tosses with no misses," the younger man replied. Seeing the incredulity on Clay's face, that he was actually keeping count of how many times he hit the wastebasket, Detective Kincannon said, "Lighten up, Ashford. There are few pleasures left in life. Learn to enjoy, huh?" He swung his long legs to the floor and dropped the folder on the desktop, his expression suddenly serious. What on earth could Clayton Ashford want with him? They were certainly less than friends, though their acquaintance had been a lengthy one. "What can I do for you?"

Clay, who had known the younger man for most of his thirty-six years, marveled anew at his ability to approach life with such ease. Still, Clay knew that Gard was no fool. Beth's young half brother had gone to serve time in Vietnam a carefree boy, and had returned, his chest full of ribbons and medals, a grim, reserved man. But after a while Gard's personality had reasserted itself and, with remarkable determination, he'd put that portion of his life behind him and gone back to college to get a degree in criminology. He'd then gone through the police academy and eventually had become the youngest detective ever in the Tulsa Police Department.

Even Gard's marriage and subsequent disastrous divorce, rumored to be because of his job, had left no visible scars on him. He had the uncommon and enviable ability to put problems behind him and go on with his life. As Season urged him to do, Clayton mused. That thought prompted him to speak.

"I'd like you to keep an eye on my ex-wife."

One of Gard's brown brows was raised a tad higher than the other. "'Keep an eye on' as in surveillance?"

"Exactly."

"I'm not a private detective, Clay. And besides, why do you want to watch Autumn or Spring or whatever the hell her name is if you're already divorced?"

"Season," Clay corrected in a peevish tone.

Gard's white teeth flashed briefly beneath the thick darkness of his mustache. He gave a nonchalant shrug of his massive shoulders. "Close."

"To answer your question," Clayton continued, "I want her to come back to me, but she keeps refusing. I think there's another man. She says there isn't anyone else, but I'm not so sure. There's a guy called Jim Nighthawk she seems pretty chummy with."

She probably got sick of you, ole boy, and I can't blame her, Gard thought, but said, "I appreciate the problem, Clay, but I can't help you." He sat back in his chair and ran a hand through his slightly wavy, chocolate-brown hair. "I'm that close"—he held up a thumb and index finger with only scant space showing between the two—"to taking a leave of absence. Beth is back from Europe."

"I know," Clay said, his tone suggesting that he didn't quite understand the connection between Beth's being back and Gard's taking a leave of absence.

"She's having a rough time getting over Victor, and I thought my company might help. Besides, I've been wanting to write a book on criminal law." He couldn't tell Clay about the threatening phone calls Beth had received, calls that hinted that if she ran for Congress, she'd wind up like Victor. He couldn't tell him that the real reason for his moving in with her was to offer her protection until they could figure out who the maniac was and if he meant what he said. He and his partner, Rick Riccitello, were going to do all they could to flush him out.

Clay sat silently, digesting the information Gard had just revealed. Gard felt a moment's uneasiness as the man's face broke into a sudden, sly smile. "You wouldn't by any chance be staying at the house outside of town, would you?"

"Why do I suddenly wish I could say no?" Gard asked with a frown that turned down the corners of his mustache.

"You are," Clay stated.

"Yeah."

"Great!" Clay suddenly oozed with the charm that made him such a successful and dangerous businessman. "As I'm sure you remember, my house is right next door."

"So?"

"So I let Season have that house."

"What are you getting at?"

"You can watch Season. It'll be easy, Gard. You'll be right there."

"No."

"All you have to do is watch and see if she has any male callers . . ."

"No."

". . . and who they are and how long they stay," Clay finished.

"Dammit, Clay! What you're asking me to do is to infringe on the lady's privacy. It's disgusting." He picked up a folder from his desk and unconsciously slammed it back down in the same spot. "What can you do if she is playing footsy with someone? Nothing. C'mon, Clay, let her go."

"I can't, Gard. I'm not used to being ditched." There was a sudden, almost pathetic vulnerability on the older man's face. "I guess it's been a blow to my ego. We weren't in love, but we were happy. I won't leave her alone until I know that she's made a commitment to someone else. That's the only way I'll walk out of her life. Surely you can relate to that."

Gard pushed his chair away from the desk and rose. His plaid shirt was rolled up to the elbows, partially unbuttoned, and hung free of the gray slacks he wore. As he started to stuff the shirt into the waistband of the pants that hugged his muscular thighs, a look of pain momentarily contorted his features. "Yeah, I can relate to that."

Clay watched as Gard finished tucking in his shirt, his eyes absently focused on an object across the room. Then with the same willful determination that underscored everything in his life, Gard pushed aside his soul-hurting memories, whatever they were, and said reasonably, "Look, Clay, I really don't think I'm your man."

"Remember the big campaign donation I gave to Victor?" Clay asked. "My endorsement of Beth can sway a lot of votes. Let's just say you'd be repaying a favor."

Gard's head swung sharply toward the older man. "Do I detect the fine hand of blackmail?"

Clay shrugged, one white brow lifted in a look of near insolence. "It would be so easy. You don't have to make a big deal of it. Just give me a call every few days and let me know what's going on."

The man was powerful, Gard thought, powerful as in oil rich, powerful as in big bucks in the bank, powerful as in knows all the right people. And he was telling the truth. Though Beth wasn't exactly pleading for votes, no politician could afford to turn his or her back on proffered support. What the man was suggesting was distasteful, but, as Clay had pointed out, it was no big deal. Especially weighed against the alternative of withdrawing, or failing to give political support.

Planting his hands on his lean hips, Gard shook his head in resignation. "Okay, Clay. Why the hell not? I'll do it, but only if it's convenient at the moment," he qualified.

"Fine. I'll make it worth your while."

"No, thanks," Gard said, rolling his shirt sleeves down over muscular forearms that were liberally sprinkled with dark hair. He just wanted the man to leave. He didn't like the way he operated. "Now get out of here, Ashford," he said with more civility than he felt. "I have a meeting with the chief in five minutes, and I don't dare be late."

"Let me write you a check for your trouble," Clay said, drawing his checkbook out of his breast pocket.

"Keep your money," Gard protested. "Just support Beth as you promised."

"Nonsense. This will be for you," Clay insisted as he wrote out the check with bold strokes, and then signed his name with a flourish. He held out the check to Gard, who made no move to take it. A smile curved Clay's mouth. "You'll change your mind when you see the amount." Dropping the negotiable piece of paper so that it glided onto the desktop, he added, "Call me soon, huh, Kincannon?"

Gard watched as Clayton Ashford left the office and disappeared down the hallway. What had he gotten himself into? he wondered. Spying on some poor, unsuspecting woman! *I never thought you'd sink so low, Kincannon,* he chided under his breath as he picked up the check and ran his eyes over it. A long, low whistle escaped his pursed lips. Almost a half year's salary. *It's a good thing you like the simple life, Gard, ole boy,* he thought as he tore the check into so many pieces it resembled confetti. He tossed the shredded paper into the wastebasket where it sprinkled the top of the crumpled candy wrapper. A smile of self-satisfaction curved his lips as he left the office for his meeting with the chief.

Two days later, a bright yellow Corvette barreled down the gray highway. Long, ebony hair escaped the clasp at Season's nape and whipped about her face, partially obscuring the countryside. Barely out of the city limits, they started—the steel mule heads whose slow, almost lazy nodding pumped up the very soul and lifeblood of Tulsa. Season was accustomed to them; they'd been a part of her horizons all her life, as had the sight of rusty, long-forgotten machinery and rickety, collapsing derricks. And the smell. Oil. Black gold. The very scent of wealth that hung in the air almost all the time. Except today, Season thought as she geared down to make the turn into the familiar subdivision. Today she could delight in the fresh scent of wet earth that followed the short April afternoon shower and overrode the haunting smell of oil.

It was Friday, and she'd left the salon a little early to go to her weekly golf lesson. She was improving, she thought with a small smile, but none of the women pro golfers had anything to fear from her for a while.

Slowing her pace through the neighborhood streets, she reveled in the fact that the weekend was here. At last. She loved her work, but it was tiring to be on her feet all day, and by Friday her legs and feet ached unbearably. She had to admit that the low golf shoes were a vast improvement over her high heels.

Hmmm, it looked as if Beth had moved in. There were boxes stacked outside, and a telephone truck was just pulling away. Whose car? she wondered, eyeing the bright red '57 Thunderbird that sat in front of the house. Even as she pondered the car's ownership, the front door of the Galbraith house opened and a man jogged across the flagstone portico and down the shallow steps to the car. His movements were smooth and graceful, she acknowledged as she slowly drove past the modern, two-story cedar and brick structure, and pulled into her own driveway.

Allowing her eyes to roam in typical feminine appreciation over the man's tall, muscular body, she wondered who he was. At the same time, she rated him a 15 out of 10 on the GMB—Great Male Bods—scale that Lisa Paden and the other girls at the salon frequently used. Long legs were sheathed in faded Levi's that rode low on his slim hips. A faded, short-sleeved chambray shirt hung free and open to the waist, revealing a wide chest covered with dark hair that trailed in an inviting line down the flat planes of his stomach, jumped the small indentation of his navel, and disappeared into the waistband of his jeans.

Season felt a sudden, irrational urge to trace that line with her fingertips. Startled by her turn of thought, she pulled her eyes away. What on earth was the matter with her? No man, not even Jim Nighthawk, had as much as marginally aroused her for months, and here this stranger in Levi's, who wasn't even trying, was stirring her hormones into a mild whirlwind. It made no sense. Or did it? Okay, she admitted with a sigh, it's been a while. Six months of abstinence translates into roughly 180 long nights spent alone in a bed. She threw open the car door, mentally cursing her body for taking this moment to remind her she was a healthy woman.

As she uncoiled her long, bronze legs, she quickly cast another glance in the direction of the Galbraith house. Oh, God! He was looking at her. At her legs. She suddenly wished she'd worn jeans instead of the brief white shorts for her golf game. Though the two houses were well-distanced from each other, as were all the twenty or so houses in the exclusive, elite neighborhood, Season could sense the man's interest.

There was no denying it, she admitted, her thoughts betraying her once again. He was attractive. She'd always been a sucker for dark hair and mustaches. Though she'd never dated a man with a mustache, it was a recurring wonder in her mind just what all that hair felt like during a kiss. For instance, would the dark hair framing this man's upper lip be abrasive, or slightly tickling, or perhaps delectably sensuous in a way she'd never experienced? *For God's sake, Season*, she chastised herself once more. *Get hold of yourself.* Tucking a recalcitrant strand of hair behind her ear, she turned to get her purse from the seat. As she bent to reach it, she was unaware of two things. She was unaware that the shorts rode higher, exposing a glimpse of white, lacy panties. She was also unaware that the man gave a low whistle of appreciation.

As she straightened, she saw him unloading two suitcases from the Thunderbird's interior. Suddenly, his eyes caught hers, and just as suddenly he waved—a spontaneous, friendly, even neighborly, gesture. Neighborly? The thought caused her to hesitate long enough so that her reflexive and reciprocal wave never materialized. Instead, she watched as Beth bounded out of the house and, her lips moving in low conversation, moved to join the man. She then reached up and kissed him on the cheek before relieving him of an armload of books and a reading lamp.

Season frowned. Was the man moving in? Why would a younger man be moving in with an older woman whose husband had been dead less than a year? Unless . . . Season suddenly felt slightly ill. Young, attractive man. Older woman with money. Suitcases. Kissy-kissy in the April afternoon. It all added up. Beth had found someone to share her bed. And Season would wager every dime she had that this man had not committed himself to Beth in a wedding ceremony. Season shook her head in utter disbelief. The cool, serene, graciously lovely Elizabeth Galbraith was shacking up with a man a good twenty years younger than she! The always proper Beth had bought herself a gigolo!

Chapter 2

Barefoot and bare-chested, Gard took the steps of the wide, carpeted staircase with an easy nonchalance that had fooled more than one member of society's criminal element. Actually, as he always touted, his brain was its sharpest in the morning, following a reasonably good night of sleep, a cup of strong, black coffee, and a two-mile jog. The latter he would forego this morning due to the unusually late hour at which he had gotten up. He and Beth, seldom together, had talked and laughed long into the night, mostly over a continuing series of "Do you remember the time . . . ?" Both carefully avoided the topic that had brought their lives back into such close proximity.

Ambling into the modern, oversize kitchen, decorated in yellow and cornflower blue and hung with copper pans, Gard perched his hand at the waist of his faded Levi's and looked about for the coffee that he could smell perking. Locating it on the island in the middle of the kitchen, he poured a mugful, at the same time scanning the note the maid had left, advising the reader that she had gone into town for groceries to restock the skeletal pantry. Gard took a cautious slurp of the hot brew, snatched up the morning newspaper where it had been thoughtfully laid next to the coffeepot, and pulled out a chair at the table.

Twenty minutes and a second cup of coffee later, he folded the *Tulsa World,* content that he was fairly abreast of the current news. Someone had robbed one of Tulsa's leading banks—ought to keep the boys downtown busy, he mused. Unemployment was slightly below what it had been last month, and some super jock had signed a football contract for a sum of money that had more figures than a group of Hollywood starlets. Life as usual, he thought, relinquishing the empty mug to the porcelain sink.

He was about to walk from the room when a sudden movement outside the kitchen window caught his eye. He watched as the red, white, and blue mail truck pulled even with the brick-encased mailbox, situated just at the edge of the portico, and saw an anonymous hand deposit a fistful of postal goodies. Gard headed for the front door as the vehicle sailed on down the circular drive. So much for keeping Beth's whereabouts quiet for a while, he thought in mild irritation. Half the world was already sending her mail at the new location. But then he'd been in the police department long enough to know you couldn't keep anything a secret—especially if it was important.

The same ten o'clock Saturday sun that was nourishing the two enormous pots of juniper that graced either side of the double doors had heated the portico stone a toasty warm, a fact that Gard noted as his bare feet walked the distance. Hand poised on the lid of the mailbox, his attention quickly shifted to the low, sprawling, cream stucco and glass house on the right. Season Ashford hadn't been what he'd expected. Of course, he'd seen her for only a couple of minutes at the most. He had heard she was pretty, real pretty, but he hadn't expected her stunning, classic beauty, nor had he expected to find such heavenly long legs, legs that seemed to go on forever, shapely, tanned legs that put only one thing on a man's mind. Sorry about that, Clay, he apologized insincerely.

He gave a tiny frown that tugged his full lips downward. Actually, the only other thing he'd heard about Season Ashford seemed to be true, and in spades. Remembering how she had ignored his friendly wave, he could believe her to be the cool lady rumor had her. Cool and lovely. A combination some men couldn't resist. Hell! The woman probably had so many suitors it would take a full squad of private detectives working overtime to keep a tally.

You're a fool, Gardner Kincannon, he railed at himself as he reached for the mail. How did you ever let Clayton Ashford talk you into this?

From sheer habit, he riffled through the envelopes he had just drawn from the box—a couple of advertisements, an equal number of bills, some campaign material. . . . Gard's face broke into a smile—a letter from their dad, addressed to them jointly. He pulled this piece of correspondence from its companions, intent on opening it, when his eyes fell to the following letter. Suddenly his hand froze, as did his feet. His stomach muscles tensed in a literal gut reaction, the same instinctive coiling that had brought him home from Vietnam and saved his hide more than once on the police force.

It was a plain, white, inexpensive envelope on which had been typed, a little too high to be centered, Beth's name and address. The postmark read Tulsa, the day before. Gard flipped the envelope over onto its back. No return address. There was nothing about the letter to distinguish it, and that very fact alarmed him.

With quick, resolute steps, he entered the house, headed for the den, and, grabbed a letter opener from the desk that still smelled of recently applied furniture polish. After slitting open the top of the letter, he yanked a Kleenex from its square box and carefully slipped out the envelope's contents. He'd apologize to Beth for opening her mail should his actions prove to be paranoid, but deep in his heart he knew an apology wouldn't be necessary.

The message consisted of three words, cut from a magazine, he suspected, and pasted in the middle of a white sheet of paper, three terse, to-the-point, heart-chilling words. *Murderers must die!*

"Sh—!" Gard swore on a deep, agonized sigh. So as not to interfere with any fingerprints, he cautiously replaced the sheet of paper in the envelope and, with a frown pinching his mouth, reached for the phone and punched in a number. A span of time equal to two rings passed.

"Police department."

"Hey, doll, Kincannon here." The "doll" was sixty-two-year-old, gray-haired Sarah Woodruff, grandmother of three of the world's cutest and smartest children—if Mrs. Woodruff's claims could be believed.

"Well, well, *Sincannon,* how are you?" She had dubbed him Sincannon three years before when, only half a day into her new job as dispatcher for the TPD, she'd told him he had a sinfully handsome body, and that the only thing sparing him was that she was happily married to Ralph Woodruff. Since then the two had shared lunches, laughs, and a love of poetry.

Deep in the throes of preoccupation, Gard ignored her inquiry into his health, instead commanding, "Put me through to Riccitello, will you?"

"Sure thing, hon," she answered, recognizing the no-nonsense tone that told her his ever-quick mind was onto something.

Another few seconds passed, during which Gard once again turned over the envelope, as if hoping a return address would magically appear. It didn't.

"Riccitello," a strong voice with a Brooklyn accent suddenly boomed on the line.

"Riccitello . . ." Gard began, but was cut short.

"Hey, guys, it's Kincannon," the voice announced. Gard heard wisecracking in the background, some of which would have been a strain on delicate, naive ears should any have been around to hear. "Settle a bet for us, Kincannon," Riccitello taunted good-naturedly. "Did you or did you not sleep late this morning?"

"We've got a problem," Gard threw into the middle of the teasing banter.

Instantly the voice at the other end sobered. "What kind of problem?" At the end of Gard's explanation, Riccitello uttered the same four-letter expletive Gard had used minutes before. "The jerk's trying a new approach, huh?"

"Yeah, guess he got tired of dialing."

"I'll be out to get the letter," the transplanted Brooklynite said. "I'll tell the guys down at the lab to go over it with a fine-tooth comb. Maybe they can lift some fingerprints. Hell, maybe the guy is even crying out to get caught and signed his name in invisible ink."

"You watch too much TV," Gard returned.

"That's the problem, friend. I don't get to watch it at all. I'm too busy rounding up the weirdos of the world." There was a pause that could only be called contemplative. "Have you told her?"

Unconsciously, Gard's head turned in the direction of his sister's upstairs bedroom. "No," he answered, his voice flat. He'd done a lot of things that he hadn't wanted to do in his thirty-six years, he thought, but few could hold a candle to his going up there and telling Beth that some crazy had threatened her life again. Though she was putting up a brave enough front, she was scared. And he was scared for her.

As if reading his partner's mind, Rick Riccitello said, "Tell her we're going to get the creep."

"Yeah," Gard answered, dragging the phone from his ear and lowering it back into place. The pale blue eyes that stared down at the malignant letter were a sharp contrast to the tanned face and dark hair. They would get him. He just hoped to hell it was before he got the woman upstairs.

Gard leveled one bold rap on the dark wood of his half sister's bedroom door. At her soft-voiced "Come in," he took a deep breath, squared his still-bare shoulders, and twisted the doorknob. He found her propped up in the middle of the bed, paperwork strewn all about her in something just short of chaos.

"Good morning," she said, a sweet smile on her lips. "Been up long?" As she spoke, she slipped a pair of silver-framed glasses from gray eyes that were almost a perfect color match and lightly tossed them on a pile of papers.

"Not long. Thirty, forty minutes," he answered. Nodding in the direction of her cluttered bed, he added, "Don't tell me you're working."

Beth Galbraith threaded unringed fingers through the full, dark brown hair that was feathered back from her face, hair that showed not the slightest betraying sign of her age. In fact, nothing about the woman revealed her fifty-four years, not her well-kept figure, not her wrinkle-free face, and certainly not the girlish laugh she now gave Gard. "I'm afraid so. Campaigning politicians are busy people. I haven't touched my mail for two days, and there's probably more downstairs this very minute."

"There is," Gard admitted, trying to screw up his courage, but not quite making it. "We had a letter from Dad."

Another smile, this time wider, danced on Beth's lips. "We did? What did he say?"

"I haven't read it."

"Haven't read it?" Her eyes fell to the envelope he held in his hand. "Well, bring it here," she said, shoving papers aside and fluffing the pillows behind her, "and we'll read it together."

Gard made no move to comply with his sister's request. His bare feet planted firmly in the gray-green carpet, his eyes studied her, a hint of an apology somewhere in the pale blue irises.

After a few seconds, she asked, "What's wrong, Gard?"

He glanced at the floor, closed his eyes briefly, then, raising his head, said without any further preamble, "There's been another threat." *Good boy,* he congratulated himself. It was best to say it right out.

"This morning?"

He nodded.

"But I didn't hear the phone."

"It came through the mail."

"The mail?" she asked disbelievingly, as if the idea had never once occurred to her. She swallowed deep in her throat. "I see. Is that it?" Her eyes dropped to the paper clutched in his hand.

"Yeah." Gard's long, slim legs crossed to the bedside, where he eased himself next to his half sister. She held out her hand for the letter. Hesitating only slightly, he passed it to her.

Holding it between thumb and fingers, she perused the front of the envelope for long, quiet moments, her eyes at last finding his. "It seems so real now," she said, her voice low and tinged with shock. "For the first time, I feel it's real."

"It's always been real, Beth."

"I know, but it was only a male voice on the phone . . . nothing I could touch." She looked again at the letter and, with fingers that Gard thought trembled, started to remove the paper from within.

"Don't take it out. We don't want to smear any possible fingerprints."

"Oh, of course. How stupid of me." She gave a weak smile, contenting herself with passing the envelope back to him. "What does it say?"

He avoided her eyes. "The usual tripe."

As he started to rise from the bed, her hand tightened around his upper arm, forcing him to stay and, just as naturally, forcing his eyes to hers. "What does it say, Gard? I have a right to know."

He watched her, wishing he could come up with a logical denial of what she'd just said. The truth was, however— and they both knew it—that she did have a right to know. "'Murderers must die,'" he finally said. Though the anonymous voice on the phone had hinted and implied a great deal during the past weeks, the threat had never been quite so specific.

Only someone who knew Beth Galbraith well, very well indeed, would have been able to discern any break in her composure. There was an infinitesimal tightening around her mouth, as if her teeth were clamped tightly together, and her eyes, normally a silver gray, blanched to a near-crystal color. There was a slight haze to them, but Gard knew his sister wouldn't cry. She never had . . . at least not in front of him.

"But I'm not a murderer," Beth said, appalled at the accusation. "And neither was Victor."

"Don't expect logic from him."

"No, I suppose I shouldn't." Her eyes found his and held them for countless moments. "Oh, Gard, what am I going to do?"

Pulling her toward him, he settled his arms about her in a protective, brotherly fashion. Her arms grasped him with a fierceness that betrayed her real emotion. "You're going to let the police do their job. We'll get him, Beth. I make you that promise." He closed his eyes in a silent prayer that he had not exaggerated his and the department's abilities.

For long moments they remained in a quiet embrace. Suddenly, as if nothing had ever happened, Beth pulled away and, with a small, shallow smile, said, "Go get Dad's letter."

Gard studied his sister in open admiration before finally placing a kiss on her forehead and rising from the bed. He was halfway to the bedroom door when the three musical notes of the door chimes sounded. Both pairs of eyes sought and questioned each other.

"Are we expecting anyone?" Beth asked.

"Riccitello's coming by for the letter, but it can't be him this soon." He started for the door. "I'll see who it is."

"Nancy will get it."

"She's gone shopping," he called over his shoulder. The knob of the now-opened door in his hand, he turned once more to his sister. "Not a word about our arrangement. Because of the age difference and our differing life-styles, few people know about our relationship. Let's keep it that way. No one's to know I'm your brother. No one's to know I'm a cop. No one's to know anything."

Beth frowned slightly. "What am I going to tell people?"

"That I'm Gardner Kincannon and that I'm living here."

A shocked expression crossed Beth's features. "What will people think?"

A grin slashed Gard's face, lifting the corners of his well-tended, dark brown mustache. "Damned if that isn't just like a woman . . . someone's threatening your life, and you're worried about your reputation."

"But I'm running for election."

"The voters love colorful, slightly naughty politicians."

"But . . ."

"Let people believe what they choose, Beth. They always do anyway." With that, he disappeared through the door, leaving his sister wearing a resigned expression.

Maybe she had been mistaken, Season reasoned, her fingers grazing over the heavy turquoise and silver necklace at her throat as she stood waiting for the Galbraith door to be opened. Maybe she had jumped to a wrong conclusion. There could be a dozen reasons why a handsome, younger man was carrying suitcases, books, and other personal belongings into an older woman's house, right? Right.

Maybe she had been too quick to judge. Maybe being married to Clay had made her too cynical. Maybe . . .

As the door swung open, Season's eyes met those of Gard Kincannon, then lowered to take in the naked, brown-furred chest, low-riding denims, and bare feet. Then again, she thought, smugness tilting her chin, maybe she hadn't been mistaken at all.

"Is Mrs. Galbraith in?" she asked, not even attempting to keep the disapproval from her voice.

Gard's eyes had not been idle either. They'd started with her midnight-black hair, plaited into a single braid that draped over one shoulder and hung almost to her waist, and stopped at the white, beaded, obviously expensive moccasins on her feet. In between they noted black eyes, cheekbones reaching for the heavens, and skin so bronzed that it was the perfect foil for the white knit top and white slacks she wore. In short, Gard's eyes sent a one-word message to his brain: Indian! Season Ashford was an Indian, a fact she was doing nothing to hide and everything to accentuate. Why had he never heard that Clay's ex was an Indian? Hold it. Another word was finding its way into Gard's cerebrum: beautiful. Even more beautiful than he'd believed after yesterday's distant view. Suddenly, Clay's wanting to hold onto her made a lot more sense.

"Is Mrs. Galbraith in?" she repeated with a chill to her tone. For God's sake, Beth, she thought, you could have at least gotten one with his hearing intact; though Season was certain his hearing ability was not the reason he had been moved in.

"Yeah, sure, she's in," Gard said, moving aside to allow Season's entrance. "I'll just call her."

As she walked past him, her sensitive nostrils picked up the faint smell of a woman's perfume. Season was reminded of the times she had smelled another woman's fragrance on Clay . . . and the fights that had always followed.

"There's no need to call," came Beth's soft, cultured

voice from the direction of the stairs. The woman, who had covered her pink gown with a matching silk robe, negotiated the last of the carpeted steps and crossed to her guest with her hand extended. "Season, how lovely of you to call on me."

"It's good to have you back in the neighborhood," Season returned. Though comfortable in Beth's presence the few times she'd been around her, Season couldn't squelch a feeling of awkwardness now. "I apologize," she continued, "for getting you out of bed."

"No apology is necessary," Beth assured her. "We" —she glanced toward Gard—"were up late last night and slept in this morning. But we were certainly awake."

Yes, and she'd just bet she knew what they'd been doing, Season thought. Both of them near states of undress and the perfume lingering about him left little room for doubt.

"Gard"—it was Beth's voice again—"I'd like for you to meet Season Ashford, my neighbor. Season, this is my"—her eyes briefly met those of her half brother—"this is Gardner Kincannon."

Season deliberately did not extend her hand, but forced herself, in what she viewed as an act of civil politeness, to turn her full attention on Gard. That proved to be a mistake; she found that his eyes, of the palest blue she'd ever seen, were already, and disconcertingly, glued to her. She watched with growing disbelief as his gaze lowered from her own and moved to the turquoise necklace, where it meandered lazily about the intricate design, then dipped brazenly beyond to the full swell of her breasts. My God, what boldness! she thought, and with Beth standing only a few feet away; though from the look on her face, she was blissfully unaware of her lover's wandering attention. Season felt her former disapproval of the man before her turn to out-and-out anger. He could at least show some loyalty to Beth, if nothing more than the loyalty of an employee to an employer. God, how she hated faithlessness!

"Nice to meet you," Gard spoke at last, shattering a silence that was becoming embarrassingly long.

"Mr. Kincannon," Season returned in a cool voice.

"Gard, please," he corrected. In an unconscious gesture, his hand began to rake through the spirals of hair that thickly carpeted his bare chest.

Season watched as his fingers rustled the curly sprigs of hair that covered at least two thirds of his deep chest in a brown, wiry cloud. She saw two darker brown buttons of flesh peeping through on either side. While she had seen Clay perform this same distracted gesture on more than one occasion, she had never seen it done with quite the same results to her senses. She momentarily felt the ice thawing in the slow heat of her body's instinctive reaction. Okay, she thought, she'd be the first to admit that Beth was spending her money well. The man had a primitive sensuality that she, in all fairness, couldn't deny.

Suddenly a hint of a frown appeared as her eyes strayed to a spot on Gard's left shoulder. Well above the hairline and angled diagonally from his collarbone, a slight scar marred the deep tan of his skin. Though Season couldn't be certain, she nonetheless felt that it had all the characteristics of a gunshot wound. Her mind ran rampant at the possibilities that opened up, deciding, in a somewhat malicious vein, that if the man before her had been shot, it had probably been by some irate husband.

When Gard noted that Season's attention was riveted on his chest, his hand abruptly stopped its trailing, rubbing motion and settled at his hip. Their eyes met briefly, his clearly telling her that she had been caught surveying his anatomy. Season's reaction to his silent message was a freeze of even colder proportions than before.

"If you ladies will excuse me, I think I'll go get decent." With these words and a slight smile, he moved off toward the stairs, his legs taking the sloping steps with clipped precision.

Season watched his ascent, his trim derriere finally disappearing at the top of the landing.

"Season?"

The sound of Beth's well-modulated voice finally dragged her attention from the stairway. "Yes?"

"I said, why don't we sit in the living room? I think we'll be comfortable there." As the woman spoke, she led the way toward the large, modernly furnished room to their right. Season followed, once again channeling her delinquent thoughts back to her reason for calling on her neighbor.

After a conversation that covered the delights of Europe versus the pleasures of being home, condolences regarding Victor Galbraith's untimely and tragic demise, and Beth Galbraith's political aspirations, Season gave a slightly sheepish grin. "To be honest, I had an ulterior motive for calling on you today. Although I am glad you're home," she hastened to add. At the interest expressed on Beth's face, she went on. "The Cloverdale Gallery is having a special exhibition the end of this month, featuring the paintings of Jim Nighthawk. Jim is making his home here in Tulsa now, and we all think he has an exciting future ahead of him. Since I've been actively sponsoring him, I've been put in charge of the guest list for the evening. It will be a formal, champagne gala, and well, to be blunt, the more outstanding the Tulsa citizenry we have in attendance, the more credibility Jim has." She gave a smile. "But the evening wouldn't be a total waste for you. We already have quite an impressive list of the who's who of the city attending. It would be a wonderful opportunity for you to advance your campaign. Although there won't be any babies to kiss, I can promise you lots of hands to shake."

Beth laughed. "You sound like my campaign manager."

"I take it she'd be allowed an escort?" came Gard's suddenly intrusive voice. The look he gave his sister clearly said he wished she wouldn't go at all, not with this nut loose, but that she certainly wasn't going if he couldn't.

Season had jumped slightly at Gard's question. She hadn't even known that he'd been in the room. Her eyes now followed him as he deftly moved to the coffee table, bent from the waist, and poured himself a cup of coffee from the silver pot that Beth had brought in earlier. He then took the chair next to Season's and squared ankle to knee. Season made two quick and idle observations—he looked more the mug than the cup and saucer type and he had covered his bare chest with a blue shirt carelessly tucked into his Levi's.

"Of course," she replied, her voice coolly formal. "Beth may bring whomever she wishes."

The older woman glanced in her brother's direction. "Well, I think it's settled then. We'd love to attend the exhibition."

"Wonderful," Season responded, her voice warm with pleasure.

"Are you an artist, too?" Gard asked conversationally, easing his gaze to Season as he drew the cup to his lips.

"No, I'm not." Her voice was once again politely cool and rigid, as rigid as the spine holding her back and shoulders in a correct, unapproachable posture.

Gard briefly wondered what had happened to the warm voice of seconds before.

"Actually, Season *is* an artist, from what I hear," Beth Galbraith slipped in, "though she works in the unexpected medium of hair."

"Hair?" Gard asked with a puzzled look. "Oh, you're a beautician?" Seemed as though he had heard something about that, he thought. Something about some ritzy beauty shop.

"A hair stylist, Mr. Kincannon. I'm a hair stylist." This time there was a definite disdain in her answer that no conscious person could have missed.

"Close," he added, feeling a prickling of irritation.

"Not close enough," she returned. "Stylists have more training."

Beth Galbraith looked from one to the other as if trying to size up the reason for the sudden tension in the atmosphere. Then in true diplomatic style, she changed the subject entirely. "I spoke with Clay last night."

"Did you? He said he would try to call or stop by, but with his busy schedule you can't always count on it."

"Ashford Oil always did keep him busy," Beth agreed. "He said he still sees you occasionally."

"Occasionally," Season confirmed, taking the final swallow of her coffee and placing the cup and saucer on the table. Gard immediately reached for it.

"More coffee?" he offered, once again striving to be pleasant. Maybe it was just his imagination that she was being perversely rude to him. Maybe there was nothing personal in her attitude.

"No, thank you," she quickly refused, settling back in the chair and crossing one long leg over the other. "Tell me, Mr. Kincannon," she said, a wicked gleam in her black eyes, "what business are you in?" Season noted with satisfaction the quick, conspiratorial look that passed between Beth and Gard. She could hardly wait to hear his answer. Ten to one he'd say he was between jobs, maybe even that he was in the entertainment business, which wouldn't be too far from the truth, she guessed. Or maybe he'd come up with something really creative.

"Actually, I'm a writer," Gard answered.

"A writer? How interesting," Season replied, "and creative. Is it likely that I've read any of your books?" She knew she wouldn't have for one good reason: There weren't any.

Though her sarcasm was subtle, Gard did not fail to pick up on it. "Probably not," he replied, "since this is my first."

"Ah, I see. Well, how fortunate that Beth has supplied you with this nice, quiet retreat to work in."

"Yes, it is fortunate, isn't it?" he concurred, poorly

concealing his renewed irritation. He suddenly felt as if he was being given the third degree that he was so famous for handing out himself.

Long, quiet moments ensued, the silence of which was broken only by the ringing of the telephone. Gard pulled his tall, near six-feet-three-inch frame from the chair and moved to the room's extension, where he picked up the receiver to still the shrill ringing. After a few low words were exchanged, he turned to his sister and announced, "It's Fred. He says it's important."

Beth gave her guest an apologetic look. "It's my campaign manager."

"By all means, take the call," Season urged, coming to her feet. "I really must go."

After thanking her neighbor for stopping by and assuring her she would see her at the exhibition later that month, Beth said, "Gard, please show Season out."

"Sure," he said, moving after Season's already retreating form. As the two stepped out into the large entryway, he called out to her, "I want to talk to you." She never slowed her pace. "Ms. Ashford, I'd like to speak with you." If anything, Season's stride quickened. At the same time her hand was about to close around the front-door knob, Gard's fingers grabbed the black braid rhythmically swaying back and forth across Season's spine. Her head snapped backward as she gave a muffled gasp.

Turning around with a speed that made spinning look slow, she hissed, "What do you think you're doing?" Her jet-black eyes shone with that thin film of moisture that always comes from having the scalp yanked.

"Getting your attention," he drawled, both hands now resting on his hips.

For countless seconds, they stared at each other, her chest heaving up and down with anger, his eyes icy blue.

"Well, you've got it," she said at last. "What do you want?"

"I want to know why the instant dislike of me."

"Don't be ridiculous," she snipped back. "I don't even know you." With that, she swirled on her heels, intent once again on opening the door—which she did, a fraction.

Gard's left hand shoved the door shut with a thud and remained positioned on it at a level approximately even with Season's head. She whirled to find herself nearly pinned against the hard surface by the length of his firm, male body. Suddenly her heart speeded up, but she wasn't certain whether it was from his nearness or the menacing scowl on his face. Perhaps it was from both.

"My point precisely," he said. "You don't know me from Adam's holy hell, yet you sashay in here with dislike smeared all over your pretty face. Why?" His own face was so close Season thought she could count the hairs of his dark mustache were she so inclined, and inclined or not, his spicy after-shave was wafting to her nostrils in full strength. "You're not leaving here until you answer me," he added.

Season's eyes locked with his in a combat of wills. "Okay," she finally said. "You're right. I don't like you. Your hair is a mess."

Her words so stunned Gard that he dropped his hand from the door and stepped back. His face clearly registered his confusion. "My hair is a mess? Yeah, well," he said with first-degree sarcasm, "that certainly clears up the issue to everyone's satisfaction, doesn't it? And, of course, it's a perfect reason to carry a grudge."

Season said nothing.

"I'll have you know," he suddenly said, as if just remembering something and taking offense at the recollection, "that I had my hair cut just this week."

"Yeah, well, you need to change butchers. The man can't see."

"I suppose you could do better?"

"In my sleep . . . with my feet." The two of them continued to stare at each other until finally Season said with saccharine sweetness, "I've just loved our little talk, but I've got to run." She turned toward the door.

"I'm going to ask you one more time, Ms. Ashford," he said quietly, seriously, "and I expect a reasonable facsimile of the truth. Why the rude treatment?"

Season stopped. For long moments her thoughts skittered around the question he'd just asked and lighted on an uncomfortable comparison. Clay had told her that there was no such thing as love, that she had married him for good times, good sex, and the monetary things he could give her, things she'd never had before. If he had in essence bought her, she was no better than the man standing before her. No, she rejected the thought, she had loved Clay, as purely as she had known how, until he had destroyed that tender feeling. She had nothing, nothing, in common with this Gard Kincannon. Suddenly she whirled around and her words tore through the silence, their venom divided equally between Gard for selling himself and Clay for even suggesting she had done the same. "Okay, Mr. Kincannon, I'll tell you why I don't like you. I don't like what you do for a living."

Gard tilted his head to one side. "You don't like writing?"

"You're no more a writer than I am," she sneered.

His dark eyebrow rose in question. "Then what am I, Ms. Ashford?"

"Older woman, monied and with a lovely estate, moves in handsome man nearly half her age. At ten-thirty in the morning, he is practically naked, she's wearing only a peignoir. Her hair is disheveled, he smells of her perfume. What would any intelligent person think, Mr. Kincannon? That he's her 'writer'?"

Gard, his left thumb hooked in the front pocket of his jeans, watched the smug, righteous expression settle on Season's features. In a startling contrast, his own face was a blank that couldn't have been read by the most astute of observers. In fact, only a momentary darkening of his blue eyes indicated that he'd heard her accusation at all.

"Well," she repeated, pressing the issue, "what would any intelligent person think?"

His eyes never leaving her face, he replied, "How about that he's her brother?"

Chapter 3

THEIR EYES HELD FOR SECONDS THAT SEEMED SUSPENDED in time.

"I stopped believing in fairy tales a very long time ago," she said at last, her voice edged with disbelief. Even as she spoke, she realized that she wished she could believe his explanation. She would love to believe that this man was Beth's brother. In fact, she would love to believe he was anything but her lover.

"Somehow I didn't think you'd buy it," he returned with a cynical smile. And he truly hadn't thought she would believe him. But he couldn't explain, even to himself, that it had been important that he at least offer her the truth, though it went entirely contrary to what he had just cautioned his sister about doing. For some reason, foreign and faint in his thinking, he hadn't wanted Season Ashford to think the worst of him. But, of course, she was standing here doing precisely that. He might have found her accusation amusing if he hadn't found it so damned annoying. He also found the coldness she'd exhibited since walking in the front door a challenge he couldn't resist. Especially in view of what she thought him.

Reaching out a hand, Gard dragged the lone braid of Season's hair from her back over her shoulder, trailing his fingers slowly, sensuously down its long, nearly endless length. At the plaited braid's tip, held closed with a gold band, he crushed the silky black hair in a soft fist. Season felt a tugging that skittered up the ropelike braid. She also felt something tugging at her emotions, the same something she'd experienced as she'd watched him unconsciously rub his chest earlier, and the same something that had tripped her feminine alarm when she'd first seen him unpacking his car the day before.

"Tell me something, Ms. Ashford . . . Season," he crooned her name. "Did you come over here this morning believing I was Beth's lover?"

"I suspected it," she returned, attempting to sound scathing, but finding that the blue eyes fastened to hers reduced the sting somewhat.

An amused smile tweaked the corners of his mouth, making his mustache crawl slightly upward. At the subtle action, Season's gaze left the clear blue eyes, traveled to the mesmerizing mustache, then hastened back to his eyes.

"Did you come over out of curiosity?" he asked. "Were you eager to see just what Beth had caught herself? Or I guess more appropriately, bought herself? You are giving me professional status, aren't you?"

Season ignored the last question. "I came over to invite Beth to the art exhibition."

Releasing her hair, he let it fall over one breast, his eyes blatantly following its trail, then watched as it cascaded to her waist. He leaned forward, placing the flat of his hand on the door beside her head, a position he had held earlier. Season immediately had a whiff of his after-shave . . . plus Beth's perfume.

"C'mon, be honest. Weren't you the slightest bit curious to see what money could buy?"

"You're insufferable," she said into the face now only inches from her own.

"I saw the way you looked at me when you first came in. Didn't you feel a tiny sexual thrill at knowing what I do for a living? Didn't you then, and don't you now, wonder just how good I am at it?"

"You could use a lesson in humility," she spat out, but somewhere in the back of her mind she did wonder exactly what he had suggested. A man of his experience must know every trick of pleasing a woman. And it had been a long time since she had been pleased. A long time that was growing longer by the moment.

"And you could use a lesson in honesty," he drawled back.

His gaze traveled over her face even as hers, against her will, traveled over his. Thick lashes lined the blue eyes, expressive and glinting with a dangerous warmth, that were studying her. High cheekbones, tanned and hollowed as with the skill of a master sculptor, begged for the soft skin of a woman's hand to caress them. And his mustache . . . heaven help her, it drew her like a magnet, making her wonder, imagine, and burn with curiosity. What would it be like to kiss those lips peeking so boldly beneath the brown brush of hair? Damn! She knew what this man was and yet . . .

"I see the pulse throbbing in your throat, Season," he spoke softly as he stretched out a hand and rested a finger at the slightly fluttering point in the bronze-skinned column of her neck. He felt an instant acceleration in her pulse, an acceleration she felt as well, but tried to deny. "Your breathing is growing shallow. Your eyes are softening. You're becoming excited at the thought of what I could do to you."

He ignored, or tried to, the similar feelings building in himself.

"You're tacky . . ." she whispered.

"You're aroused," he accused, gripping her throat tenderly with his splayed hand at the same time as his head unconsciously lowered toward hers.

". . . and crude . . ." she added.

"You're curious," he charged as his head began to turn to accommodate her mouth.

". . . and probably grossly overpaid," she finished, her voice barely audible.

His lips hovered and smiled above hers. "Want to find out for yourself?"

Time stopped. For endless moments they stood locked in eternity. Gradually his smile faded; just as gradually her lips unconsciously parted, preparing for the touch of his mouth. Their breathing blended; their heartbeats merged into one strong, fast cadence. Both waited for the insanity of the moment to pass or to consume them completely.

Suddenly Gard sobered and, releasing his hold on her neck, stepped back. The hand plastered to the door near her head fell away, too. Season took a deep breath as reality returned. They watched each other closely, neither speaking, both assessing what had almost happened. Season swallowed low in her throat. In dead silence, she turned, opened the door, and fled out into the April morning.

Gard often said that Rick Riccitello's life could be summed up in one word. Renunciation. Five years before, at the age of thirty-three, the man had renounced everything that up to then had shaped his life. From a staunch Catholic family, he turned to Protestantism, moved from Brooklyn to Tulsa, divorced his wife of eight years, and gave up custody of his then four-month-old son. Gard never asked the whys, Rick never volunteered them, but Gard suspected it had something to do with a wife who couldn't cope with police pressures, the same kinds of hellish problems that he'd lived through himself. All Gard knew for sure was that Rick Riccitello was a helluva good cop and as good a friend as he had.

Watching the dark-haired, dark-eyed Italian unwind his

medium-height frame from the unmarked squad car, Gard silently praised the man's timely arrival. Only moments after Season had stormed from the house, leaving him to wonder just what had happened between them—or, more importantly, what had *almost* happened between them— Rick pulled into the circular drive. All thoughts of Season were from necessity shoved to a back burner to make way for the more pressing problem of who was trying to kill his sister.

"Got held up," Rick apologized, his feet carrying him around the front of the dark green Chevy, up the shallow front steps with a couple of leaps, and onto the portico to join Gard. Nodding his head in the direction of Season's rigid retreating back, he asked, "Who's that?"

"Just a neighbor," Gard responded, deliberately not following his partner's gaze and just as deliberately not elaborating further on the question.

"How come we never get neighbors like that?" the man returned in obvious appreciation of what he could see of Season's physical beauty.

"Because we're poorly paid cops who can't afford this kind of neighborhood," Gard said, moving on into the house.

"Why didn't I think of that?" Rick said as a teasing frown claimed his expression. Following Gard, he closed the door behind him.

For the next twenty minutes, the two men lived up to their reputation as the hardest-working team of detectives on the Tulsa Police Department.

When the two once more stepped through the front door and onto the brownish-gray stone of the portico, Rick was carrying a plastic bag that contained the threatening letter. Indicating it, he said, "I'll get this to the guys in the lab right away."

Gard nodded, slipping a hand into the back pocket of his jeans. "Tell them we need something bad."

"Yeah," Rick agreed in the same somber tone of his

partner. "The wiretap is going to be useless if he switches to the mail."

"It's going to be useless, anyway," Gard added, "if we can't keep him on the phone longer. The creep is smart enough to know it takes a while to trace a call."

"Ever feel the bad guys are getting smarter than the good?"

"Only every day," Gard replied, his voice suddenly sounding world-weary.

The two men stood talking for several minutes longer.

"Look, what do you think about having the patrol cars in the area swing by several times during the night?" Gard asked. "You know, just drive by and see if everything looks okay?"

"Good idea," Rick Riccitello agreed. "I'll take care of setting it up." Moving on down the steps, he added, "Well, let me get to work. The bad guys may not be taking a coffee break."

Gard watched as Rick opened the car door and started to slip inside. At the last minute, he turned and called over the top of the car, "Next time *I* get to hole up in a house with a classy dame next door." As he spoke, he jerked his head in the direction of Season's house. "She isn't too bad on the eyes."

Gard's stomach tightened at the reference to Season. "You can't buy enough thermal underwear to insulate yourself against that one," he said, instantly wishing he'd kept his comment to himself.

The Italian's dark eyebrows rose in obvious speculation. "I don't suppose you want to tell me anything?"

Gard smiled lightly. "Go earn a buck, Riccitello."

As the Chevy slid from the drive and out into the street, the nearly noonday sun caught a blinding reflection that caused Gard to squint at the momentary flash of brightness. He looked away and turned toward the house, but his gaze was pulled, almost beyond his control, to the rambling stucco house next door. Season. He felt his stomach knot again. He had just told Rick she was cold. That was no lie, he admitted, still smarting from the frostbite she'd given him earlier that morning. She was as cold as a subzero winter in Alaska, but, and here his breathing quickened, he suspected she could also be as hot as a sizzling summer in Arizona. He had taken her, he had taken them, he corrected, from cold to hot in a matter of minutes. He had gone from teasing to promising, she from anger to far less in the span of seconds, and for a moment he had seen her coldness melt with the promise of a consuming heat.

He felt a momentary sense of confusion. He was supposed to be watching Season, not putting the make on her.

The confusion turned to anger. And damn Season's hide; she thought he was selling himself to Beth.

His anger turned to arousal. And damn his hide, he wanted nothing more than to thaw her chill until it burst into flames that burned them both with their blazing passion. The tightening in his stomach traveled lower to settle in the most masculine part of him in a way that was borderline painful.

He swore an oath and stormed into the house.

Season was angry with herself at the realization that she had spent more time in the bathroom putting on her makeup than she'd planned. The clock on the rough-hewn oak mantel of the bedroom's corner fireplace said 7:20 P.M.; she had ten minutes to throw on some clothes for her date with Jim Nighthawk. Actually, she knew she had less than ten minutes. Fast-paced in everything he did, Jim was one of life's early people.

She quickly pulled off her robe and threw it across the arm of a chair. Tall, stately, and totally naked, she crossed the hardwood floor to the dresser. Removing a pair of white, lacy, and very brief panties, she bent and slipped one foot, then the other into them, drawing them up her slim, shapely legs. She did not reach for a bra. The deerskin halter top she had chosen to wear did not allow room for any underwear beneath it. Recrossing the room, she opened the door of the massive, Spanish-style armoire and searched inside for the top and its matching, fringe-edged skirt, both in a peach color that complimented her golden skin. Easing into the skirt, which hit her at midcalf, she picked up the halter. She carefully maneuvered the top over her head so as not to muss the hair that was simply but stylishly piled on her head. Then she tied the midriff strings in a bow at her back. Because it had a tendency to slip, she gave the bow an extra check. Satisfied, she next worked her feet into beige sandals that raised her height to just under six feet.

Moving with a gentle, unconscious sway of her hips to the mirror of the vanity table, she checked her appearance. Her mouth arched downward. *Not bad,* she thought. She ruffled the beige feathers speckled in brown that lined the neck of the halter and decided not to detract from their simple beauty by adorning her throat with jewelry. Instead, she bent from the waist to select more gold bracelets than the average woman could wear without appearing gaudy and shoved them onto both arms. She fitted the small holes in her ears with large, gold, dangling hoops. She then bent forward once again for one of the bottles of perfume, a clean, woodsy fragrance.

She stopped just then. With each movement she had made since putting on the halter, the fabric, though soft enough, had rubbed against her bare breasts in a most disturbing way. She knew it wasn't the manufacturer she should blame, but *him.* Gard Kincannon. Ever since that morning, when he had almost kissed her, she had felt as tight as a war drum. Her entire body had become sensitive. Napping had been impossible; showering had been pure hell. Even laps in the backyard pool had done little to reduce her body heat or rechannel the single bent of her thoughts. Dammit, the fantasies racing around in her mind were obscene! She stretched for the perfume, straightened, and watched as the peaks of her breasts boldly left their imprint in the soft fabric. She sighed, closed her eyes as she closed her hand around the cool bottle, and gave herself up to the feelings flooding her. She admitted her problem: She had been too long without a man. And Gard Kincannon's bold masculinity had reminded her of that. Of course it was nothing personal, she quickly told herself. Any good-looking, virile man could have pushed her thoughts into this sensual realm.

Season jumped at the sudden callous buzzing of the doorbell. Spraying on the fragrance and snatching up her handbag, she made her way to the foyer and the front door. There was a man, one who had made it clear before that he was willing, waiting for her right this moment. Why didn't she just open the door, say a few provocative nothings, and let nature take its course? Well, maybe she'd do just that, she thought in annoyance. Maybe that was precisely what she'd do to end this prickly, jump-out-of-her-skin feeling.

"Hi," Jim Nighthawk said as the door swung open.

"Hi," Season heard herself reply as her mind made several mental calculations that she seemed unable to stop. Jim Nighthawk was probably taller than Gard, he was possibly even more handsome. His profession was certainly more honorable. But this man in no way spoke to the sensual side of her nature. In fact, standing here watching him, she could only think of how hungry she was.

"You all right?" Jim Nighthawk asked, a curious look in his dark, hawklike eyes.

Season smiled wryly. "Sure. Let's go. I'm starved." As she stepped out into the dusky April evening that was striped with the remnants of the sunset, she wondered why her reaction to Gard Kincannon had been so strong but her reaction to Jim, as always, remained nonexistent. She also wondered, and for this she cursed herself, how Beth and her "friend" were spending the evening.

"This is disgusting!" Gard muttered into the can of light beer he held in his right hand as with his left he allowed the drape at the den window to settle back into place. Spying, for God's sake! He was reduced to spying like some sleazy sherlock! Suddenly he felt as if he should wash his hands. If he hadn't, for the sake of Beth's campaign, already promised Clay . . .

He glanced at the clock on the massive desk. Nearly seven-thirty. Clay had said Season had a date with some Indian, but so far he'd made no appearance. Clay had also said he wanted Gard to observe how late Season stayed out and if her date stayed over. That last thought coiled Gard's stomach, but he blamed it on the maid's broccoli and chicken casserole, definitely not his favorite.

One thing he knew, Gard sneered, taking another swallow of the brew: He wasn't about to stand here all night playing peekaboo out this window. With that personal promise still hot with conviction, he raked back the drape once more . . . just in time to see a new, expensive, two-seater sports car streak to a stop in front of Season's house. A tall, dark-skinned, ebony-haired man walked from the car to the house with a swiftness that was almost a blur in Gard's vision. *The brave arriveth!* Gard thought sarcastically, his already bad mood taking a tumble for the worse.

Letting the drape fall slightly forward to reduce his chances of being observed, Gard watched. Less than a minute passed before Season and the man reappeared. Even at this distance, Gard could tell they were talking, maybe even laughing. The man certainly had his hand at the small of Season's back . . . real cozy, real familiar. Gard frowned at the quick steps that Season's long legs had to take to keep up with the energized movements of the man. Insensitive clod! he thought. He could at least slow down for her.

With a loud gunning that traveled the distance to Gard's ears, the car burst into life and, with movements that characterized its owner, sped out into the street. Gard stood at the window long after the car disappeared from sight. For long moments he felt nothing, just a kind of emptiness he was hard pressed to put a reason or a name to, but slowly the emptiness gave way to a peevish anger that he took out on Season's date. It must be nice, he thought, to drive a new and expensive sports car. This Jim Nighthawk must have big money. For God's sake, didn't he know that as a member of a minority, he had a poverty-stricken image to maintain? To say nothing of his starving-artist image! Of course, what would he, Gard Kincannon, know about anything? He was just a dumb cop who put his life on the line every time he went to work, and all for a sum of money that meant more hamburger than steak. And never in his wildest dreams could he drive that kind of sports car. Hell, he thought he was fancy, restoring his classic '57 Thunderbird!

Gard sighed in self-disgust. This is insane, Kincannon. You've never begrudged anyone anything. You're just being petty. Frowning, he let the drape fall back into place and killed the can of beer. He didn't know what was wrong with him tonight, but it had to stop. And now! Seating himself at the desk, he opened up a textbook on criminology. He pulled a pad and pen closer, determined to take some notes for the book he himself planned to write. He'd just knock off a couple of hours of work before bedtime.

A little after ten, Beth stopped in to say good night. A little before ten-thirty, Gard closed the book with an annoyed sigh when he realized he'd read the same paragraph twice. He started to the kitchen for another beer, but decided against it. Looking at the clock, he moved to the window and peered out in the direction of Season's house. It was dark. They weren't back yet.

Finding a book of poetry, one of the few personal possessions he'd brought with him, he stretched out on the sofa and started to read. Periodically, he checked the clock . . . and the window. At 11:05 he checked. At 11:20 he checked. And again at 11:30 and 11:38. Where the hell was she? Simmer down, Kincannon. She's a grown woman. And what she does is none of Clay's business . . . or yours.

He forced himself back to the poetry, but ultimately discovered that to be a mistake. The poet's words grew more and more sensual, more and more provocative . . . and Gard's mind turned to Season. At last he threw down the book and once again checked the clock. Seven minutes to midnight. He was not going to look out that window. He was tired. He was going to bed. He was fed up with this ridiculous game. Drawing the drape aside even as he swore not to, he saw the bright shafts of car lights pull into Season's drive. *Well, it's about damn time!* he grumbled to himself. He figured five, okay, ten minutes to say good night and he'd have Jim Nighthawk out of his hair.

He figured wrong. Thirty minutes later the sports car still sat in front of Season's house, a mocking, goading sight to Gard, who was now pacing a restless trail back and forth on the den carpet. How long does it take to say good night? he raged. How long does it take to say you've had a wonderful evening and cash in on a kiss? Gard, one hand at his trim waist, snatched back the curtain for another look. The man was homesteading! Or cashing in on more than one kiss. Suddenly the thought of Season's lips parting for the taste of her date's kiss, just as her mouth had unconsciously parted in anticipation of his that morning, ripped through his mind and gut. Dear God, were her eyes softening, hazing for this Jim Nighthawk? Was her breath growing sensuously shallow? He groaned softly, then swore. What if she'd invited her brave to stay the night?

He was still watching out the window when another set of headlights pierced the night. A car, approaching at a snail's pace, swung into the Galbraith driveway. A patrol car, Gard instantly and correctly surmised. And just as instantly a thought occurred to him, a thought that put a devilish grin where a frown had been moments before. If he could just catch that patrol car . . .

"I'm going to yawn," Season warned a millisecond before she did.

Jim Nighthawk laughed. "That's all right. I'm almost through." Another few frenetic slashes of a charcoal pencil and he declared, "There, I'm finished. What do you think?"

Season slipped from the wooden stool where she had sat painfully motionless ever since returning from dinner some forty-five minutes before. Jim had insisted on sketching her despite the late hour, and she had bowed to his artistic temperament, the way she always bowed to his impromptu need to sketch, draw, paint, and otherwise capture on paper what he said was the most inspiring model any artist had ever had. Now, looking down at her charcoal image, she was once again struck by the genius of the man.

"It's beautiful, Jim," she said, studying the few lines that captured so much. With a few strokes of the pencil, he had created a woman of regal bearing whose lips were parted in promise and whose eyes were half closed with mystery. Tilting her head upward and rising to the balls of her bare feet, she placed her lips to his in a quick, appreciative kiss.

"It is good, isn't it?" Jim echoed, surveying the portrait once again, then Season. "Oh, it wasn't so much my skill as it was you this evening." His dark eyes narrowed in scrutiny. "There's something about you tonight. I noticed it when you first opened the door. There's a subtle, yet blatant . . ."—he searched for the right word— ". . . sensuality, yes, that's it, sensuality about you. I knew I had to sketch you when I saw you."

For a moment Season felt as if she stood naked before her friend. Had he sensed the sexual vibrations that had ravaged her body all day? Uncomfortable with the depth of his perception, she added, "Well, there or not, you've certainly captured a sensual woman on that pad."

"Believe me, the sensuality is there," Jim Nighthawk reassured her. Season might have imagined it, but for a fleeting second she thought she saw a flicker of wistful longing and regret that that sensuality would never be for him. "I want to hang it in the show," he added. "Okay?"

"Sure," Season agreed with a nod of her head.

"Well, let me get out of here," the handsome Indian said, "and let you get some sleep."

"I had a lovely . . ."

The loud buzzing of the doorbell stopped her in midsentence. She cut her eyes to Jim.

"Who could that be at this hour?" she asked, a puzzled frown creasing her forehead.

"Why don't you open it and see?" A grin nipped at his lips as he offered this bit of logic.

As Season moved toward the sound of the doorbell that was once again chiming, she promised herself that she was going to check about a peephole. God alone knew what kind of pervert might be standing on the other side of the door.

Slowly pulling it open, she peeked out.

"Hi, neighbor," Gard said, caught in the middle of tucking his plaid shirt into the back of his tight jeans.

The unexpected sight of the handsome man standing on her doorstep, the one she'd fought valiantly to get out of her mind all day, threw a cog in the normally rhythmic beat of her heart.

Holding up a glass measuring cup, he asked with a grin, "Could I borrow a cup of sugar?"

Season's eyes narrowed in disbelief. "You've got to be kidding."

"Honest Injun," Gard replied, then hastily added, "oops, sorry about that."

The sight of his smile, which could have easily fallen under the category of irresistible, caused her heart to go from skipping to racing, a fact that angered her, and she covered the emotion with a hostile tone of voice. "Do you have any idea what time it is?"

Gard checked the watch nestled in the dark hair above his wrist. "Twelve fifty-one," he announced. "Sweet-tooth attacks don't work on a schedule." Then he added as if this explained everything, "I'm making brownies."

Without waiting for an invitation, he edged himself past her. Season sighed in resignation.

Catching sight of Jim Nighthawk, Gard feigned surprise. "Hey, I'm not interrupting anything, am I?"

"Whatever gave you that idea?" she answered sarcastically.

Gard entered the room and approached the tall man with a social sureness that Season did not fail to note; but then, she reasoned, men in his profession had to be socially adept. "Hi. I'm Gard Kincannon," he said, extending his hand. "I'm Season's neighbor."

"Jim Nighthawk," the other man acknowledged, his own voice warm and friendly.

Gard waited for a clarification of the man's relationship to Season, but was disappointed. Jim Nighthawk added nothing.

"Oh, you're Season's artist friend?" Gard was finally reduced to saying.

The other man agreed.

"I'm looking forward to your exhibition at the end of the month," Gard added.

"Wonderful. Delighted you'll be there."

A quiet fell over the trio. Season was thinking that she had been right. Jim was a little taller, though viewed side by side, it was highly debatable if he was any more handsome. And no matter how hard she might want to ignore it, Gard Kincannon had an elemental sexuality that Jim had no chance of competing with. In short, Gard filled out a pair of jeans in a way Jim could only hope to. The loser in her comparison was at that exact moment wondering as to the identity of this neighbor whom he'd never heard Season speak of. He was also wondering why Season seemed so upset by his arrival, albeit at an unconventional hour. Gard's thoughts were centered on Season's bare feet and Jim Nighthawk's partially unbuttoned shirt. As unobtrusively as possible, he took in the discarded sport coat and tie that lay on the sofa. He also noted what he thought was a smear of lipstick on the man's lips. Obviously he'd gotten here just in the nick of time. That thought gave him immense satisfaction.

In the prolonged silence, Jim looked at Season, Season looked at Jim and shrugged slightly, and Gard looked about the room. Modern furniture in off-white and stucco walls of the same color acted as neutral backgrounds for the splashes of the bright and bold color of the countless pictures adorning the walls and the numerous Indian rugs, basically black and red, covering the hardwood floor. A cathedral ceiling was vaulted by heavy, dark-wooded beams. What part the tall, wooden stool in the middle of the room played in the decor, he had no idea.

"Nice," Gard commented, indicating the surroundings.

Season did not thank him.

"Well," Gard said, holding up the glass cup, "if I could just get some sugar."

Before Season could respond, Jim Nighthawk reached for his coat, tie, and sketch pad, and announced, "I'll let myself out, Season." Stretching once again to shake hands, he said, "Nice to have met you, Gard. I'll see you at the exhibition."

"Hey, I'm not running you off, am I?" Gard asked, looking as if the very thought scandalized him.

Jim shook his head. "No, I was just leaving." Bending to kiss Season's lips, he added, "I'll talk to you later."

"Good night," Season answered with a smile. "And thanks for the evening."

Seconds later, Season and Gard found themselves alone, she wondering what it would have felt like to have Gard's lips against hers instead of Jim's and he fantasizing about the softness of the mouth the artist had just tasted. It came as a double jolt when both realized they were staring at each other.

"Give me that," Season snapped as she snatched the cup from his hand and walked down the hall to the kitchen. Gard followed, watching and admiring the vast, bare expanse of her copper-skinned back. That she couldn't possibly be wearing a bra did not escape him, and he found the thought more than stimulating.

"Did I interrupt anything?" Gard asked sweetly, hoping that was precisely what he'd done.

"You've already asked that," Season shot over her back. Turning left into the kitchen, she moved unhesitatingly for the tin canisters lining the countertop, jerked off the lid of one, and began to scoop out the white granules of sugar.

"I mean, the lights were on and . . ."

"Drop it," she demanded.

Out of the corner of her eye, she saw Gard shrug. "Okay, it's dropped. But," he added in a few seconds, "I'd sure hate to know I screwed up your Saturday night."

She gave him a scathing look.

"Okay, okay," he said, holding up his hand as if to ward off her disapproval. "It's dropped."

Season finished filling the glass measuring cup and unceremoniously set the lid back on the canister. When she turned toward Gard, she found him wandering aimlessly about the kitchen, looking at her collection of cacti decorously placed to receive the full daytime sun through the bay window. He next browsed through the display of Indian pottery that she had so zealously bought over the years and arranged on the shelves of a turn-of-the-century breakfront. She watched with growing fascination at the gentle way his fingers traced the primitive designs. She wondered if his fingers were that gentle with a woman's body.

Calling herself up short and forcing herself to remember the reality of the situation, she asked, "Where did you leave Beth?"

His eyes coasted to her. "Sleeping."

"Do you always run off when she's sleeping?"

He set down the piece of pottery still in his hand, his eyes once again finding hers. "Only when there's sugar next door."

Season felt disgust ooze through every pore of her body. "You're crude," she accused.

"So you've told me."

Shoving the glass cup across the counter, she said, "Here's your sugar. Go home and make brownies."

Gard's eyes never wavered from hers as he stepped toward her and leaned against the counter. Only the width of the countertop separated them.

"Is this Jim Nighthawk your boyfriend?"

"He's the man I was out with tonight," she evaded.

"That doesn't answer my question."

She smiled coyly. "No, it doesn't, does it?"

"But it's all the answer I'm going to get, right?"

"Right," she agreed.

Her eyes were captivated by the slight twitching of his mustache, a twitching that suggested that a smile threatened. She'd give him one thing: He certainly spent a lot of his time amused by life.

"You can go out the back door," she said, nodding toward the curtained door behind him. "It's closer."

"Why do I have the feeling you're trying to get rid of me?"

"Because I am."

"Wonder why that is."

"Because I find you . . ."

"Crude," he finished.

"Crude," she confirmed.

For a moment neither spoke. "Is that all you find me, Season?" Suddenly the teasing light in his eyes vanished.

The sexual feelings that had plagued her all day surfaced. She made no attempt to answer his question; indeed, she doubted she could have answered any question coherently. She was sinking, drowning in the wonderfully blue depths of his eyes, and she had the same curious feeling that she'd had that morning, that somehow time was being suspended, that the two of them had just entered a new realm of reality.

"Are you sleeping with him?" Gard asked quietly, and in an almost desperate tone. Why had he asked her that? he wondered. He hadn't planned to, and it was really none of his business. And he certainly had no intention of relaying anything she said to Clay.

She tried to sound vexed at the question, but how could she sound vexed when her voice was nothing but a whisper? "Don't you think that's a little personal?"

"It's more than a little. It's damned personal," he returned. His eyes faded to a crystal blue. "Are you sleeping with him?"

Her own eyes were blacker than the night peeping through the windows and doing combat with the fluorescent lights of the kitchen.

"No," she whispered. She had no idea why she was answering his question.

"Why not?" he asked.

She shook her head slightly. "He's not my type."

His eyes traveled from her eyes to her soft, soft lips, then back to her ebony irises. "Who is your type, Season Ashford?"

She hesitated. "I don't know."

Reaching out, he lightly fingered the feathers that stylishly outlined the low cut of her halter top. The tip of his little finger gently brushed the swell of her full breast. At his touch, she felt and heard the air hiss from her lungs.

"It's a real shame you're not into crude men," he whispered, his eyes holding hers for a moment.

He then picked up the sugar, crossed the room, and disappeared through the door. He should have left her with a burning desire to tell him he'd never in a million years be her type. Instead, he just left her with a burning desire.

Chapter 4

AT EXACTLY 6:57 ON SUNDAY MORNING SEASON SIGHED deeply, bowing to the fact that she'd evidently slept all she was going to for the night. She gave a muffled groan of weariness and frustration. Damn Gardner Kincannon!

Never a morning person, she had always survived the two hours after awakening solely because there was absolutely no way to get around them. She could thank Beth's writer friend for the miserable night she'd just spent. Thoughts of him, his parting statement, and the way he had left her body aching for fulfillment had made sleep impossible. The restless night only added the extra dollop of anger to her usual morning fuzziness, disorientation, and general bad humor.

Making a supreme effort, Season gathered her diffuse energies and forced herself out of the relative comfort afforded by her gently rocking water bed. Her feet felt for and found the frivolous, high-heeled slippers that sat in readiness beside the bed. They were black satin, an exact match to the satin and lace teddy that clung lovingly to her slender curves. Unable to locate the short robe that went with the scandalously brief nightwear, she shrugged and groped her way to the bathroom, took care of Mother Nature, and proceeded to work her way through a brief brushing of her teeth and an even briefer brushing of her waist-length hair. She'd do better after her coffee.

Coffee. That's what she needed. It always took at least three cups to start her heart beating. She began the trek down the long hallway, the heels of her shoes clicking with annoying regularity against the tiles. She squelched a yawn and groaned as the first weak rays of morning sunshine attacked her through the French doors opening onto the Spanish-style courtyard that faced eastward.

Thoughts of the man who so obviously shared Beth Galbraith's bed edged aside a portion of Season's grogginess. Was the gigolo up yet? she wondered sourly. Or was he still in bed with Beth—holding her in those muscular arms, kissing her awake with that sinfully tempting mouth, tickling secret places with the erotic brush of his dark mustache? *For God's sake, Season Ashford! Stop it! The man isn't worth a sleepless night, nor your curiosity.* She ground her teeth and determinedly pushed his attractive face from her mind. *Maybe Lisa is right. Maybe it's high time you purged yourself of all these ungratified sexual fantasies you've been indulging yourself in by having a good, old-fashioned affair. Jim Nighthawk may not turn you on, but as Lisa says, all cats are gray in the dark.*

Jim! What on earth had he thought when Gard had so brashly ushered himself into the house to borrow sugar? She'd have to call Jim later and explain . . . if she could.

Her feet carried her through the elegant, understated living room she'd furnished so tastefully and expensively with the Indian artifacts and paintings she loved, on toward the kitchen and straight to the coffee, all her fortitude targeted toward one goal—waking up. She stopped dead in her tracks as her eyes came to rest on the cream-and-smoke-colored pot that sat gleaming and empty on the ceramic counter top.

"Oh, no!" she wailed. Filling the coffeepot and setting the automatic timer were part of the nighttime ritual she performed before going to bed. Gardner Kincannon's unheralded appearance, and his prolonged stay during which he roamed and rummaged through her kitchen while asking her personal questions about her relationship with Jim, had scattered her wits so that she had totally forgotten her normal routine.

Muttering a string of Kiowa curses beneath her breath, Season made the coffee and drew a reconditioned milk can that doubled as a bar stool up to the cabinet. Resting her elbow on the counter, she propped her rounded chin in her hand. Jet-black eyes, less than four feet from the dripping coffee maker, watched intently as the steady stream of umber liquid dribbled into the glass pot. The aroma of the freshly brewed beverage caused her stomach to rumble in mild protest at being forced to go so long without being filled. First things first. She had to get her eyes open before she could even think about cooking. Mornings were bad enough, for heaven's sake, without having to wait ten whole minutes for her coffee!

As she sat, an idea of utter brilliance seeped into her sleep-fogged mind. Attributing the thought to some latent sense of survival, Season grabbed a mug from the cedar cabinet. If only a cupful dripped into the mug, she might just make it until the rest was finished. She snatched the glass pot eagerly from under the descending drizzle. At that exact moment she heard a bold knock at the back door. Who on earth could that be at the ungodly hour of seven o'clock in the morning? She started to yell for whoever it was to come in, but realized that the door was locked.

Turning back to the countertop, she saw that coffee was pouring onto the clean, white-tile surface. Damn! She'd have to bleach the grout again! she realized as she rushed the container back under the dripping coffee.

The knock came again, accompanied by the shrill ringing of the doorbell. Obviously whoever it was had as little patience in the morning as she did, she thought, crossing the brick-red tiles in a most unladylike stomp. Clicking back the dead bolt, she wrenched open the door and snarled, "What do you want?"

The words were thrown at the broad back of the person who was aiding fate's attempt to make this the most miserably memorable Sunday of her entire life. Gardner Kincannon. Stud extraordinaire. The sight of his muscular legs and the curve of his buttocks in the tight, cutoff jeans he wore lessened Season's irritation and started a tingling in the heart of her femininity.

"Now is that any way," he began as he turned toward her with a disarming smile curving his lips, "to speak . . . to . . . a . . . neighbor?"

The smile faded from his face with comical rapidity, only to be replaced by typical masculine appreciation, tempered with a bit of disbelief, as he stared at the vision she made framed in the doorway.

Her right hand rested on the doorframe, her left poised on a curvaceous hip. Ridiculously high heels encased her slender feet and drew attention to shapely calves, dimpled knees, and slim thighs that extended beyond the lacy edging of the brief garment barely covering her fantastic body. Gard's gaze meandered from her rounded hips to the indentation of her waist, on up to her full, thrusting breasts. With each breath she drew, they strained against the lacy confines of the skimpy bodice held up, somewhat precariously, it seemed, by two sliplike straps.

Her jaw was held at a rigid angle while full lips thinned and her delicate nostrils flared. She seemed to be looking down her nose at him, almost as if the weight of the ebony hair that fell loose and flowing down her back was too

heavy for the slender column of her neck. Sloe eyes
smoldered with barely suppressed anger that seemed to
change into some unfathomable emotion even as he stared
at her.

Gard was astounded at his body's lightning response to
the primitive sensuality that exuded from every pore of
Season's voluptuous body. Blood pounded hotly, heavily
through his veins, and he felt the uncontrollable stirring of
his masculinity against the tightness of his jeans. *My God,
Kincannon*, he chided himself. *You're thirty-six years old,
not some teenager who just discovered the arousing power
of a woman's body. Get hold of yourself. You're not
interested, and even if you were, the ex-wife of Clayton
Ashford is strictly off limits.*

Season had forgotten that she hadn't been able to find her
robe, forgotten that she wore the sexy, black teddy until
Gard's scorching survey reminded her. She felt like running
and hiding from his hot gaze. She snapped the electrical
tension crackling between them by asking coldly, "What do
you want at this time of the morning?"

Gard smiled lazily. "I'm not sure I'd ask that if I were
dressed like you, lady."

Season gave him a withering look. "What do you
want?"

He held out a foil package. "I brought you some
brownies."

The words implied that the gesture was neighborly, but
Gard knew his action for what it was. He'd just wanted to
see her. It was that simple. He hadn't slept worth a damn all
night, thinking about her in the feathered halter top and
cursing himself for not kissing her as he'd wanted to. *Hell,
Kincannon! In one breath you say Season is off limits, in the
next you're wondering what all that black hair would feel
like wrapped around you in the heat of passion. You're
wondering if that sexy mouth of hers can murmur love
words as well as it does barbed comments.*

"Brownies?" those lips were saying now as she instinctively reached to take the package he offered her.

"Yeah. I told you I had a chocolate craving. After I borrowed the sugar, I went home and whipped up a double batch of brownies." He saw the disbelieving look on her face. "Ah," he smiled, "you didn't believe me. You didn't think I could really bake brownies."

Season couldn't help but notice that the announcement that he'd baked brownies was delivered without a hint of embarrassment, even though he looked as if he belonged on the front line of the Steelers instead of in a kitchen.

"I don't eat sweets," she informed him haughtily.

Somehow, just as he had the previous evening, Gard Kincannon was through the door before she could shut it in his handsome, arrogant face. Amazed at his temerity, she turned her back on him and strode across the kitchen.

"You never eat sweets?" he asked in a tone that wavered somewhere between amazement and disbelief.

"Never."

"Maybe that's why you're such a sourpuss in the morning," he said to her stiffly held back.

Season closed her eyes and mentally counted to ten before she pivoted with catlike speed. Her impassive black eyes met his. "If I am a sourpuss, Mr. Kincannon, it is because my neighbor's paid lover knocked on my door before I could drink my first cup of coffee . . . after a night of little sleep." She enunciated each word with icy clarity, and the term *paid lover* was delivered with an emphasis that was almost underscored. "Now if you'll excuse me, I'll go put on some clothes."

Deep grooves etched both cheeks as Gard drawled, "Don't bother on my account."

Season stared at him for several silent seconds. Feeling the threads of her composure unraveling in the heat of his gaze, she quickly made her escape.

In the haven of her room, she searched frantically

through her closet for something quick to put on. She decided on a deep-purple sun dress cinched at the waist with a wide, purple-and-white-striped belt that buckled in the back. As she dragged the dress from its hanger, she felt the faint stirrings of a headache. Lack of sleep and lack of coffee. It looked as though she was doomed to do without her morning sustenance unless she wanted to share a cup with the maddening man downstairs. Share! She'd take bets that he was already snooping around for a cup to help himself! Season sighed and eased full breasts into the lacy cups of a strapless bra. Surely she could be civil to him for the length of time it took to drink a cup of coffee. But darn it, he made her so angry!

The dress settled around her hips. *Face it, Season. You're angry with yourself as much as you are with him. If you're honest, you'll admit that he arouses you as no other man ever has. Everything he does turns you on. You love the sexual innuendos and undertones when he badgers you, even though you hate him for doing it and yourself for responding.*

Season tightened the belt around her small waist. "Okay," she admitted aloud, "I've got the hots for him." She looked at the woman in the mirror. "I said it. Now are you happy?" She sighed. Of course she wasn't happy. The man that Beth was paying to share her bed was the same man she, Season, couldn't get off her mind. She kept wondering what he would be like as a lover . . . her lover.

"No!" she cried into the room's silence. "He isn't what you want." If she kept reminding herself of that, maybe in time she'd believe it. Go give him a cup of coffee and get rid of him. He's no good for you.

Fortified by her decision, Season retraced her steps to the kitchen. As she'd expected, Gard was sitting at the round oak table, his forearms resting on its polished surface. His long, tanned fingers cradled a mug of coffee. Looking up as she entered the room, his eyes lit up with pleasure when he saw the gorgeous picture she made in the boldly colored dress.

A slow smile curved his lips. "Very pretty."

"Thank you. I see you helped yourself to the coffee."

The smile broadened. "Yeah. I didn't think you'd mind since I cleaned up the mess."

Season's eyes flew to the coffeepot and the now shining counter. "Thank you," she said again. She poured herself a cup of the much desired brew and lifted it eagerly to her lips. The coffee, straight from the pot, burned her mouth and loosened another string of Indian swear words.

"Tsk, tsk," Gard said with a shake of his head and a glint of laughter lurking in his blue eyes. "Ladies shouldn't say such things."

Her mouth still on fire, Season glared at him. The wretched man had not only jinxed her night, but her morning as well! "How do you know what I said? Do you speak Kiowa?"

Gard shook his head. "No. But a curse is a curse in any language. Come sit down and drink your coffee. You're obviously one of those people who has a hard time waking up in the morning."

Season carried her coffee to the table and sat down, determined to do whatever it took to rid herself of him. She cupped her chin in both palms, framing her oval face with slim fingers tipped with mauve polish. Her dark, brooding gaze roamed the pleasing bone structure of his face. "And you, Mr. Kincannon? Are you an early riser?"

Gard chuckled. "I'm afraid so. It always seems like a waste of daylight to sleep past dawn. I usually get up and either jog or exercise before I start to work."

Season's smile was almost a smirk as their eyes met. "Ah, yes, the book. How's it coming?"

"Slowly."

"Why don't you tell me about it."

Gard's eyes shifted from hers. He knew she didn't

believe that he was writing a book. He knew she believed he made his living being a plaything to wealthy women. He fought back a slight smile of amusement, but couldn't fight back a mildly flattered feeling. "Actually, I'd rather not. If you tell everything, sometimes it dries up the creative juices."

I'll bet! Season thought. She smiled with an artificial sweetness. "I see." Then, taking another try at backing him into a corner, she added, "And how is Beth this morning?"

"Still sleeping when I left."

"Ooh," Season cooed. "Did she have a rough night?"

Just keep it up, Season Ashford, he thought as his eyes boldly went to her lips, *and you'll get a good sampling of what you think Beth's been getting!* "Beth likes to sleep late."

Season noted the gleam of recklessness in Gard's blue eyes following her last sly comment and tried to get the conversation back on an even keel. "So do I," she confessed, "but I seldom get to since I opened the salon."

Gard leaned back in his chair and folded his arms across his chest. "According to Beth, your beauty shop is a great success."

She grimaced at the phrase *beauty shop.* "Fortunately, yes. I like the work, and it's always nice to be on top."

"Do you just take care of women?" he asked. His gaze shifted to her obviously capable hands, and he fought back the desire to feel them touching his body.

"No, men and women."

"Good. Then you won't mind cutting my hair this morning."

"What!" Season yelped, her friendliness of moments before fading into new anger.

"I said, you won't mind cutting my hair. Since you think it's in such terrible shape, it seems to me you're the person to straighten it out."

"If you want a haircut, Mr. Kincannon, you can call the

salon for an appointment,'' Season suggested smugly. ''And unless you can catch a cancellation, I'm booked solid into infinity.''

He shrugged. ''No problem. You can do it here.''

Her smugness disappeared, replaced by a look of incredulity. ''It's Sunday.''

''So? You aren't busy right now.''

''Right now?''

''Yeah. I can spare about thirty minutes.''

''*You* can spare? How do you know *I* can spare the time? I might have plans for this morning.''

''Well, do you?''

She eyed his head of wavy, chocolate-brown hair. He could use a good shaping, and the hair was entirely too long over the ears for today's style. It kicked up here and there, but curly hair had to be cut just so if it was to fall correctly. His hair was thick and healthy, and she'd like to see if the texture was as good as it looked from where she sat. Season felt herself weakening. She'd like to cut his hair. It was always a challenge to see how she could improve someone's looks. Not that Gard needed any improving. Besides, knowing him as she was beginning to, he would hound her until she agreed. Why not just give in gracefully to the inevitable?

''No, I don't have plans,'' she answered reluctantly and a tad sheepishly.

''You'll cut it then?''

''All right. I'll give you a haircut. But if I do,'' she hastened to add, ''you have to promise to leave me alone. This dropping by unexpectedly is driving me crazy. Besides, I'm sure that Beth can't possibly approve of your little visits.''

One corner of Gard's mouth drew up into a half smile. ''Oh, I think I can handle Beth.''

Season rose. ''I'll just bet you can,'' she said acidly, longing to get the haircut over with. ''Stay put while I get my scissors.''

He swallowed the remaining dregs in his cup. A smile that could only be described as innocent curved his lips. "I think I'll have another cup of coffee."

Season clenched her hands at her sides and stalked from the room at this maddening takeover of her kitchen and her morning. She returned moments later, a flowered cape hung over her arm and various tools of her trade clutched in her hand. "Pull your chair into the middle of the floor so I can walk around you."

Gard obeyed her command and settled back comfortably. The cape was whisked over his head and fastened around his neck. Then her hands were in his hair, sifting it through her sensitive fingers, holding out strands here and there, examining length and texture, resilience and body.

It felt good, she thought. *His hair was a good texture.*

It felt good, he thought. *Her touch felt good.*

"Wet it at the sink," she said at last, tossing a thick hand towel onto his lap.

Gard turned to look at her. "I thought you'd wash it for me."

"Don't push your luck, Mr. Kincannon."

"You might call me by my first name, Season, since we're neighbors."

She didn't want to call him by his first name, she thought. She wanted no familiarity to remind her of the feelings his nearness had aroused the night before. "Just wet your hair."

"I will if you call me Gard."

Her black eyes met his steadily. "All right," she said. "Will you wet your hair, Gard?"

With a satisfied grin, he pushed himself from the chair and did as he was told. Hair plastered to his shapely head, he sat back down, closed his eyes, and sighed. Someone working on his hair always made him sleepy. He leaned back and prepared for Season to administer her magic.

"Look up at me," she commanded as she lifted his chin. His eyes flew open and widened when he saw her standing over him with a single-edged razor in her hand. "I know you aren't crazy about me, but . . ." he quipped lightly as another of his infuriating grins spread across his face.

"If you don't be quiet, I will be tempted to use this someplace besides on your hair," she said, doing her best to hide the smile that teased the corners of her mouth. "You need a razor cut," she explained. "You'll have to look at me so I can get the front the right length."

She moved closer, enveloping him with the musky scent of her perfume. Her hands dragged the comb through his hair. He felt the slight tugging of the razor as it sliced through the damp strands, providing a rhythm that relaxed him totally. His eyes drifted shut.

God, his eyelashes were long, Season thought. And his hair was wonderful. The razor, as she had known it would, sculpted the hair into perfect layers, thinning and cutting in one process. A professional to the core, Season forgot whom she was working on and concentrated solely on giving the best haircut she could.

Gard never spoke. She knew from experience that working on some people's hair was a natural tranquilizer. She suspected that he was almost asleep. Turning his head at will, she sectioned and combed, cut and recut until she was finally satisfied that she had done her best.

She moved to the front of him and combed the hair over his ears to make certain that it fell naturally into place. His eyes opened, pale blue and drowsy. Something in their depths caused Season's heart to beat faster.

"You wouldn't want to trim my mustache, would you?" he asked in a husky whisper.

Season's eyes were drawn magnetically to the fringe of dark hair and the mobile mouth beneath it. Knowing it was insanity, yet unable to stop herself, she nodded. "I think I have some manicure scissors."

She rummaged through the kitchen catchall drawer, glad he was still in that state of semisleep. The silent rapport they'd shared while she'd cut his hair had gone a long way in softening her attitude toward him. The look in his eyes reminded her anew that he was a devastating male. A male who raised her hormone level considerably. Tiny scissors in hand, Season neared the chair where he sat. She stood at his side and said once more, "Look up."

Their eyes met. "I'll get a crick in my neck before you finish," he complained good-naturedly.

"I have to look you full in the face or you might come out lopsided."

"I certainly wouldn't want that." Before Season knew what was happening, she felt Gard's hands on her hips, pushing her back and relocating her between his long legs. Her mouth dropped open in surprise, and she gasped when she felt the slow slide of his hands down her thighs. "How's that?"

"Fine." The answer came out on a small puff of breath. She looked down at his upturned face. Deciding that his head wasn't just right, she grasped his chin between her thumb and forefinger and tilted it slightly. Her hand trembled. The stubble of his beard was curiously stimulating. She'd always thought a bit of a five o'clock shadow enhanced a man's ruggedness.

Resolutely, she raised the scissors and began to snip the dark mustache . . . almost one hair at a time. As she worked, she could feel his thighs brush against her dress. She was acutely aware of the rise and fall of his chest in the blue T-shirt he wore. She combed the mustache and smoothed it with her finger near the corner of his mouth, trying to tame a stubborn hair that refused to lie flat. The mustache was a revelation. It was more coarse than the hair on his head, yet somehow not as bristly as she had expected it to be. Deliberately avoiding any eye contact, she worked carefully at the job at hand.

His mouth twitched once. "It tickles," he mumbled, careful to hold his lips still.

"I'm sorry."

She cut her way from one side of his mouth to the other, noting the indentation of his top lip, the fullness of his bottom lip, and the sensuousness of them both. By the time she finished, her hands trembled so badly that she was certain he couldn't help but notice. She glanced into his eyes. Her breathing almost stopped when she saw that they were fastened on her breasts.

"Finished," she whispered.

He nodded, looking up at her with dark, sapphire eyes.

Tension coiled tightly inside her. Season longed to run, longed to stay. Her finger reached out automatically to brush away a hair that clung to his lower lip. It stuck. Using the edge of one long nail, she gently applied pressure and lifted it free. "There."

As her hand moved back toward her side, Gard's fingers closed around it and carried it back to his mouth. His lips touched each knuckle before he pried open her fist and pressed a kiss to her palm.

"I didn't sleep either," he confessed softly, huskily.

"No?" she whispered.

He shook his head, his arms enfolding her even as he pulled her onto his lap. "I couldn't sleep for thinking of you."

She closed her eyes, shaking her head slowly in negation of what he was saying and doing. "You shouldn't."

"I know." His hands came up to cup her face. Her lashes fluttered open as his thumbs brushed with unbelievable lightness over her high cheekbones and traced the dark wings of her brows. "I know," he repeated.

His hands filtered out every sound except the wild beating of her heart. Who would have ever thought he could be so gentle? Even as she thought it, he feathered her eyes closed with a butterfly touch. Her tongue darted out to moisten her lips.

Gard groaned, his thumb slicking over the wetness of her lips, forcing them open with subtle insistence. His head lowered to claim the honeyed treasure. His mouth met hers

tentatively, lightly, his tongue making a preliminary foray
into her mouth. Season parted her lips to his gentle probing
and answered his groan with something that sounded like a
whimper. The mustache added an extra sensual jolt to the
kiss and, lost in the moment, her hand slid to the back of his
head.

The action was all Gard needed for encouragement. His
mouth ground against hers in a kiss that might have hurt had
it not been for the other sensations it created. Mouths fused
in a passion that was almost unbelievable. His tongue thrust
into the void of her mouth with increasingly faster, deeper
movements. She felt the hardness of his arousal against her
hip, felt him press her against it. Oh, God, she wanted him!
The need was a pain inside her that threatened to burst the
dam of emotion so long held in check. No wonder Beth . . .
the thought of the older woman was like a bucket of cold
water thrown in Season's face. She was sitting on Beth's
lover's lap, letting him kiss her . . . wanting him to make
love to her, no *needing* it as she never had before.

She lowered her hands and began to push against his
shoulders, wrenching her mouth free. "No!"

Gard was slower to surface from the depths of his desire.
He regarded her swollen mouth and anguished eyes, unable
to make any sense of the contradiction on her face.
"Season?" he questioned, his own eyes a silver-blue haze
of passion and confusion.

She pushed free of his embrace and got to her feet,
staggering slightly.

His hands reached out to steady her. "Season . . ." he
began as he tried to pull her down once more.

"No!" she almost screamed. He wasn't what she wanted
from life. She didn't want a man who could be bought and
sold. And she'd bet a pretty penny that Beth Galbraith was
paying a premium price for him.

Season acknowledged the fact that she wanted this man
more than any she'd ever met, but she was going to do
herself a favor and refuse to indulge herself by having him.

Gard thought he saw a shimmer of tears in the darkness of her eyes before she turned away. Her voice was heavy with emotion as she said, "You'd better go on back to Beth."

He regarded her taut features, his own emotions warring between desire and the reality of the situation. Reality won. He rose from the chair slowly. Season watched as he moved toward the back door. "Thanks for the haircut," he said just before the door closed quietly behind him.

Season's Sunday did not improve after Gard left. She picked up a romance novel, hoping to drive the image of his face from her mind, but the attempt failed miserably. The love scenes were unendurable—she became the heroine, Gard the hero. The caresses were felt as if they were being administered to her own fevered flesh. Disgusted, she tossed the steamy novel aside and set out to frenziedly clean already immaculate closets and drawers. Lunch was cottage cheese and fruit, most of which eventually fed the greedy garbage disposal. Then she tried to nap, but found herself tossing and turning as she had the night before. A water bed wasn't the place to try and forget the taste and feel of Gard's mouth, the sensuous brush of his mustache, or the sexual longings his kiss had intensified.

Midafternoon found her outside, puttering with her flowers. Often using the flower beds as a means of working off her frustrations, she weeded around the purple and gold irises and the lemon-yellow daffodils bordering the front of the house. She next pruned back a trailing, blood-red rosebush that roamed prettily over a trellis near the garage. The Spanish-style house, with its colorfully blooming flower beds, left its viewers with the curious feeling that they had stepped into some artist's rendition of a south-of-the-border, pastel fantasy.

After her stint in the garden, Season bolstered her flagging energies by trying one of Gard's brownies. It proved to be remarkably good. As she ate it, she congratulated herself that she'd kept him off her mind for a good hour and a half, more or less, and decided to reward her efforts with a cooling dip in the pool. She was just pulling her dripping body from the water when she saw Gard and Beth step onto the patio of the Galbraith home. Obviously they were going to swim.

Beth was attractive, there was no doubt about it. Her short, dark hair framed a still-youthful face, and her body was as slim and supple as that of a woman twenty years younger. And she was a wonderful person, Season allowed. Maybe it wasn't so farfetched that Gard was involved with her. Season picked up a towel and began to dry off.

Beth waved at her. Season waved back, wanting nothing more than to go back inside. She didn't want to see them together, didn't even want to look at the man next door. The sight of his muscular body in brief, black swim trunks did things to her. Beth was a neighbor and a friend, though admittedly not a close one. Gard Kincannon was hers. So why did he keep trying to get a response from Season? It wasn't right for him to make overtures behind Beth's back. And it certainly wasn't right for her to respond to them—as she had to the kiss earlier in the day. Even as the thoughts churned inside her troubled mind, she saw Gard smile at the woman he lived with. Season's heart turned over.

Gard forced the smile to his lips. He couldn't let Beth know that the sight of Season in a daringly cut white swimsuit knotted the core of desire within him. He and his sister had shared a good day, catching up on happenings in one another's lives through animated conversations that never grew dull. They were thoroughly enjoying each other's company and had decided to indulge their general laziness by following their huge Sunday dinner and after-dinner naps with a few wakeup laps in the pool.

"I see Season is enjoying a swim, too," Beth commented, setting her sunglasses, oil, and towel on a glass-topped table.

"Yeah."

Beth reached up and ran her hands lightly through her brother's hair. "She really did a good job with the haircut."

"Yeah, I thought so."

Beth's finger traced the fringe of brown hair on his upper lip. "She trimmed the mustache a little, too, didn't she?"

Gard's white teeth nipped at her fingers. "Yep."

Squealing, Beth snatched her hand away and pushed playfully at his chest. "Beast!"

"Beast, huh? Come here, Liz." He lunged at her, one arm catching her around the waist.

Beth succumbed to a bout of giggles, her arms and legs flailing the air. "Don't call me Liz!" she choked out as her elbow hit him in the ribs.

Air whooshed from Gard's lungs. *"Pax!"* he cried, releasing her and putting his hands on her shoulders. "I won't call you Liz if you won't call me beast. After all, would you let a beast, even though he is good-looking, squire you around town?"

Beth wrinkled her nose at him. "Not only are you a beast, Gardner Kincannon, you are a disgustingly conceited beast."

"But you love me," he said with a disarming smile.

His sister's eyes grew serious. She raised up on tiptoe and brushed her lips against his cheek. "Indeed I do," she said, returning his smile.

"Here, let me put that oil on your back," Gard said to Beth as she uncapped a bottle of suntan oil. Anything to get his mind off the woman next door, whose elegant, bronze body was playing havoc with his ability to laugh and talk naturally to his sister. Beth needed the fun they were sharing. She'd been desolate after Victor's death, but Gard hadn't been able to spend much time with her because of his job. Now, just as she was about to burst from her chrysalis of grief, this maniac had started his persecution. Why Beth? She certainly wasn't the murderer she was accused of being. Did it have anything to do with the campaign? Gard sighed softly. It didn't make any sense. None of it made any sense. There had to be something he was missing, some piece of the puzzle he hadn't found yet. God knew the boys downtown were doing all they could with what few leads they had. Riccitello was working overtime on the case. If only Beth wasn't in the limelight so much. But then, if she was an ordinary housewife, none of this would be happening anyway.

"What's the schedule for the week, sis?" he asked. Once he knew her plans he could provide extra security.

"I have a meeting with Fred on Monday, a speech to local businessmen on Thursday, and the art show on Saturday night. I'm supposed to speak to a women's group on my stand on the environmental protection bill Victor introduced, but they haven't let me know for certain when that will be," Beth told him.

Gard groaned mentally. Protecting Beth was a monumental task, and he was dreading, for reasons he didn't examine too closely, the art show in particular. In fact, he'd rather have a good case of the flu than go.

"Okay," he said, "I'll take care of extra personnel at all the functions."

"Ouch," Beth suddenly complained. "You're scrunching my shoulders."

Gard immediately relaxed his hands. "Sorry. I was thinking," he confessed with an apologetic smile.

"About the man?"

Neither had to specify who *the man* was. They knew.

"Yes."

Beth drew in a shaky breath. "I wish you hadn't mentioned that." She laughed, a strained mockery of the usual sound. "We were having such a good time." Her voice broke on the last word.

Gard pulled her up and into his arms. He cradled her head against his broad chest and rested his chin on the top of her head.

"Hey, don't fold on me now, Beth. You're doing just

fine. Just hang in there and keep that smile in place. Let me do the worrying.''

''I'm trying. And I know you're doing all you can, but . . . Gard, I'm scared.''

''I know you are, honey.'' *And I'm scared for you,* he thought, cursing his inability to do anything to give her peace of mind.

They stood there for several moments, Beth drawing strength from the protection of his arms. She was glad he was with her, but worried constantly that she was also putting his life in danger.

She pulled back to look up at him. ''You are careful, aren't you, Gard? When you go out and do''—she hesitated —''whatever it is you do?''

Gard captured her face in his palm and smiled tenderly down at her.

''Yes, worrywart,'' he said, bending to rub his nose against hers. ''I'm careful. Now, how about going inside and playing a heavy game of Monopoly? I think I know how I can beat you this time.''

Beth recognized the ploy for what it was and blessed him for it. He had the ability to take her mind from her worries. Laughing up at him, she determined to play her part in the game. She couldn't let him down. ''Oh, you think so, huh?''

''It's a cinch,'' he told her smugly.

''So how do you think you're going to do it?''

''I'm going to cheat,'' he told her, flinging an arm around her shoulders and heading them both in the direction of the house.

Beth's happy laughter splintered the silence and danced on the afternoon air . . . all the way to the house next door.

Season had watched him rub suntan lotion over Beth's back, had seen him pull the older woman up and into his arms. Smiling down at her, he spoke softly, intimately. He wasn't even aware that Season Ashford was in the same world, let alone the next yard.

A foreign emotion twisted Season's insides as she watched Gard draw Beth against him and walk toward the house. Her stomach coiled even tighter at the sound of Beth's tinkling laughter. There was no doubt in Season's mind what was next on the couple's afternoon agenda.

Season grabbed up her things and fled into the house. It wasn't until she stood beneath the stinging spray of a hot shower that she recognized the emotion for what it was. Jealousy. She was jealous of Beth Galbraith. Jealous of her relationship with Gard.

"I won't care for him! I won't!" she said out loud, pounding her fist against the apricot-colored tiles. She hoped that if she said it loud enough, often enough, her determination would make the statement true.

Chapter 5

"You're not reading," Beth's soft voice accused.

Gard dragged his gaze from the window back to the Monday-morning newspaper spread open on the kitchen table, but abandoned by him. His eyes then rose sheepishly to meet those of his half sister. He smiled. "I'm not, am I?"

"No, you're not," she concurred, adding, "nor have you been for a full five minutes." Occupying the seat across from him, she reached for her glass of freshly squeezed orange juice and brought it to her lips.

Gard reached for his own glass of juice and drained it, leaving the pulpy residue clinging to the sides of the glass like desperate survivors.

"Don't worry about it," she consoled, reaching across the table's short distance to touch his hand. "Something will turn up."

Gard knew she was referring to the fact that Rick had called nearly forty minutes before to tell them, in a voice charged with regret, that the lab had turned up nothing. The letter had been as clean as a sanitation workers' convention. Gard felt a pang of guilt at the realization that his sister had caught him with something else on his mind.

Giving her hand a loving pat, he agreed, "Yeah, something will turn up. It always does."

While it was true that the lab's failure to uncover anything had upset him, Beth's predicament had not been the prime focus of his thoughts at the moment she'd spoken. Perhaps it should have been, but it wasn't. His mind, instead, had been occupied with memories of the raven-haired woman next door. She was stealing his sleep—if one could be arrested for erotic dreams, he'd be in jail this morning. And his waking hours were no better. Thoughts of Season kidnapped his mind at unexpected moments throughout the day.

He knew where he'd made his mistake. He never should have kissed her yesterday morning. If he'd just left the kiss in the realm of fantasy, instead of giving it life, he would never have known for certain just how intoxicating her mouth was. He might have fantasized about its softness, might have imagined its fiery warmth, might have dreamed of its nectar sweetness. As it was, her kiss was more than he ever could have fantasized, imagined, or dreamed of, and it had left him weak with wanting more.

"Gard?"

Against his will, his eyes had strayed to Season once or twice the previous afternoon when he and Beth had been out by the pool. It had been a torture of nearly unbearable magnitude knowing she was that close, yet not being able to go to her because of Beth's problem. Besides, he reminded himself, for his own sense of self-preservation, he didn't want to get involved. Call it gut instinct, but something told him that any entanglement with Season Ashford could never be casual.

"Gard?"

He knew without a doubt that the biggest favor he could

do himself would be to stay away from Season, just as she'd told him to.

"Gard?" Beth's voice rose in intensity.

Gard's head jerked toward the sound. "Oh, I'm sorry," he said, still somewhat distractedly. He snatched the newspaper out of the way, making room for the eggs, sausage, and toast that the maid placed before him. He didn't see the curious and somewhat concerned look his sister gave him.

Talk during the meal returned to a normal range of subjects, mostly politics, and Gard was just finishing the last of two eggs that were as sunny-side up as the April morning outside when a thought occurred to him. "By the way, Rick said to tell you he'd pick you up about nine-thirty." At the look on his sister's face, he ordered, "Now don't give me that frown."

But she gave him precisely that. "Oh, Gard, I feel like such a pack of trouble. Do you really have to baby-sit me every waking moment? Can't I just get in the car and drive to the meeting?"

"First, you are not a pack of trouble; yes, you have to be baby-sat every waking moment and no, you cannot just get in the car and drive to the meeting."

When his sister had informed him that she had commitments at her campaign headquarters that morning, he had arranged for Rick Riccitello to escort her. Both men agreed that it was best to share the body-guarding responsibilities. It gave Gard a break; also, if whoever was issuing the threats was observing her, it cut down on the possibility that he would recognize any one person as her protector.

"But . . ."

"No buts." He smiled, trying to lighten the moment. 'I'll make a deal with you, Beth. I won't tell you how to be a politician if you don't tell me how to be a detective. Deal?"

Beth's frown turned slightly upward as her gray eyes viewed him with a hint of merriment. "Deal."

"That's better," Gard teased back. "Oh, by the way, you're getting another maid. Or at least that's what you're going to tell everyone."

Beth's face clouded up to a frown again.

Gard gave her a threatening look. "Don't start again, sis."

The situation clearly found disfavor with Beth, but, looking at the stubborn set of the jaw of the man sitting across from her, she wisely chose not to belabor the point.

Understanding at least a portion of what she must be feeling, Gard tried to explain. "What would happen if Rick and I both had to be out on a case? It will be easy to have one of the female officers brought into the house as a part-time maid so we won't arouse anyone's suspicions. We don't want this . . . person . . . to think you're being watched over."

Beth made no reply. For long moments she stared, thoughtfully and with total absorption, into the swirls of coffee in the cup at her fingertips. A deep sigh escaping her lips, she finally looked up. "I can't actually believe that anyone could seriously want to kill me." There was more than a hint of incredulity in her tone.

Gard's eyes scanned his sister's face, noting the finely etched wrinkles around her eyes that seemed to have appeared overnight, wrinkles that formed a saddening alliance with the dark, shadowy circles.

"We can't afford not to believe it," he replied in a soft voice that perhaps he unconsciously hoped would counterbalance the harshness of his statement. He thanked heaven for the sound of a car horn outside the house. "Run and get your things, sis. That's Rick and he hates waiting for his women." Gard gave a smile of encouragement.

Beth returned a faint smile and once again reached for his hand. "I'm going to tell you a secret, Robert Gardner Kincannon," she said, her gray eyes warm with emotion. "I'm awfully glad you're my brother."

"Me, too, Elizabeth Christina Galbraith," he said, squeezing her hand.

Beth, who had a suspicious haze in her eyes, laughed shakily and hastened upstairs for her notes and handbag, while Gard stepped outside to speak briefly to his partner. A few minutes later he found himself enjoying a second cup of coffee and reading the paper he'd neglected the first time around. He promised himself that he was going to shelve worries and thoughts of the woman next door, for at least the length of time it took to read the morning news.

He had just taken a generous swallow of the cooling coffee when he saw the article on page 5B. Wedged between a pithy and unflattering critique of a currently running movie and an article detailing the spring plans of the Tulsa Symphony were two columns of copy advertising Jim Nighthawk's upcoming exhibition. He scanned the promotional piece with interest. Three quarters of the way through he muttered an explosive curse into the kitchen's solitude that all but rattled the cabinets.

"How could she do this?" he ranted. He forced himself to reread the list of Tulsa aristocrats who were planning to attend the gala, but was no happier with the second reading.

"According to Season Ashford, chairperson of the event," the paper read, "many of Tulsa's leading citizens have already set that Saturday night aside, a Saturday night that promises champagne and glitter and an introduction to a young artist whose name will soon be a household word in the art world." Season Ashford had then proceeded to give a thorough listing of those people who had already pledged their attendance. Beth Galbraith's name stood out, at least to Gard's frustrated eyes, in print that was even bolder than the rest.

"Why doesn't Season just call the maniac and tell him where Beth is going to be?" he snarled. "If you're going to set her up like a helpless duck, Ms. Ashford, set her up good." Kincannon ordered himself to be fair; Season had no idea what she was doing. But it didn't lessen the impotence he felt.

Ten minutes later, as he left the house for a much needed jog, he was still vacillating between wanting to strangle Season and telling himself it wasn't her fault. And to add to his misery, the hands that wanted to throttle her neck also wanted to ease upward and cradle her face to await his warm kiss.

Season hung up the phone after her talk with Lisa Paden, padded barefoot across the cool tile floor of the kitchen, and grabbed up the suntan lotion and over-size beach towel she'd left on the countertop. She then sailed out the back door toward the swimming pool.

She felt no sense of guilt at not going into the salon this morning because she rarely scheduled appointments on Monday anyway. That day of the week was a slow one in the hair trade, a slowness that she made up for the rest of the week, and she often spent the day just going over the bookkeeping. Today she wouldn't even do that. Getting some early sun before the approaching summer got too hot to really enjoy it, lazing around, and finalizing everything for the art exhibition scheduled for the weekend were Season's sole objectives. She might even try to work in a nap. God only knew she hadn't slept last night.

At the thought of two successive sleepless nights, she deliberately refused to look in the direction of Beth's house. This preoccupation with the man next door had to stop. She had never experienced anything like it. Never had she been this aware of a man, sexually or otherwise, and she was at a loss to explain the mysterious hold he had over her. However, she did know what to do about it. She would ignore him. After all, who was better at ignoring things, and people, than she? Hadn't she spent her childhood ignoring the insensitivity of her father?

Setting the suntan lotion on the edge of the circular, redwood patio table whose yellow-flowered umbrella was doing little to block out the already warm sun, she moved to spread out the beach towel on the matching lounge chair. Spying the purple and white petunias that sprawled over the edge of a vast, granitelike pot as if in search of moisture, she uncoiled the water hose and doused them thoroughly. She then turned the hose on decorously placed urns of wandering jew that were placed along the low brick wall bordering her backyard. All this she did without one glance in the direction of the Galbraith house.

"What's this?" a masculine voice drawled. "Playing hooky?"

Season dropped the hose she'd been rewinding, her hand flying to her chest. At the same time, her eyes flew to the man who was just then presumptuously unlatching the gate to the fence.

She closed her eyes, gave a disgusted sigh, and a disbelieving shake of her head. "I'd give a hundred dollars to know why you don't stay at home." As she spoke, she made the mental note that Gard must have been jogging. The gray sweat shirt he wore, short at the sleeves and long on washes, clung in damp patches to his perspiring body. His slightly wavy hair was wet, too, especially around the edges, and his breathing, though far from showing wild exertion, caused his chest to heave.

He'd give a hundred dollars to know why he didn't stay at home, too, Gard thought. He hadn't expected her to be home on a Monday, but when he'd seen that she was, his feet had just jogged, of their own accord, in her direction . . . countermanding the message his brain was sending that less than three quarters of an hour before he had been furious with her for the indiscreet notice in the paper. He knew he shouldn't go near her, but then again, he told himself, life was dull as hell if you only did what you should.

"You playing hooky?" he repeated.

"In a way," she answered.

"I think I'll play with you," he said, peeling out of the

sweat shirt and tossing it to the cool deck. "Hooky, that is," he added with a slightly crooked grin.

The absence of a shirt revealed his broad, massive chest, glistening with beads of perspiration, and the dark hair matting it looked like lush vegetation growing in a rain forest.

Ignore, ignore! Season commanded herself.

Speaking to the figure now untying and removing tennis shoes, she asked with a puzzled frown, "What are you doing?"

"Dying of heat and sweat."

"Couldn't you do it next door?"

"Yeah, but I wouldn't have an audience."

"Where's Beth?"

Cutting his eyes up to her from his still bent position, he answered, "She's not home."

"While the cat's away, the *rat* will play?"

"I believe that's mouse," he corrected, straightening and moving to the edge of the pool. "And yes, I think I will play. And cool off." Without looking back, or seeking permission, he dove into the heated pool in his cutoff jeans and spent the next several minutes swimming laps in the clear, blue water.

Gliding toward her, his hands reaching out to catch the edge of the pool, Gard called to her, a smile on his face and an entreaty in the blue eyes that stared up at her through long lashes spiked with moisture. "Come on in. I'll share your pool with you."

"That's awfully decent of you," she replied in a voice that dripped sarcasm, "but I'm sunning, not swimming."

"Suit yourself. But I think you're dark enough, Pocahontas."

"Your prejudice is showing," she shot back.

A mischievous glint sparkled in his eyes seconds before he glanced down at the lower portion of his body, clearly visible in the translucent water. "Oh, my God, where?"

Season fought to smother the smidgen of a smile that

tugged at the corners of her lips, a smile that she was helpless to keep from twinkling in the depths of her dark eyes. In a voice that was gruff with suppressed laughter, she commanded, "Just go swim."

"That's one."

She frowned. "One what?"

"That's the first time I've ever seen you smile."

The smile that a moment before hovered on Gard's lips and in his eyes slowly faded. Season made no reply. He said nothing further. They stared at each other, he wondering what had happened in her life to make her so sober, she wondering what he would say if she responded that she hadn't had a lot to smile about. Seconds stretched to a long minute before Gard replied, "I think I'll go swim."

Season watched him push himself away from the pool's edge, his arms cutting through the water in deep, bold thrusts. She felt confused. Up until seconds ago her relationship with Gard Kincannon had been based solely on physical attraction, but somehow, in some way, he had just managed to involve even deeper emotions.

She forced herself to look away.

But time and again her eyes were drawn to the lean figure slicing through the water.

Ignore! she reminded herself, which was easier said than done.

She pretended to be totally unaware when he dragged himself from the pool to sit on its edge. She likewise pretended not to notice his hand wiping back the wet hair from his face and his fingers raking through the moist, water-beaded hair on his chest, and she definitely pretended not to follow his movements as he walked, with soaked jeans plastered to every masculine curve of him, toward the lounge chair where she'd laid out her towel.

Ignore him, and maybe he'll just go away. *Yeah, and maybe the sun won't rise tomorrow,* some part of her brain mocked.

Determined to disregard him, though she could hardly

discount the increased tempo of her heart beat, she leaned forward from the waist, the ebony wealth of her hair spilling to the cool deck. With quick, deft movements, she gathered the hair and twisted it into a heavy knot at the back of her head. From the lounging position on the chaise, his body resting in sublime indolence as he allowed the rays of the midmorning sun to dry his body, Gard watched her, fascinated by the skill and dexterity of her hands. The finished hairdo looked as if she'd worked at it for hours.

She reached for the plastic bottle of suntan oil on the table and started to uncap it.

"Let me."

"I can do it."

"Not all over," he pointed out logically.

Season turned to him. She regarded him warily, her feminine instincts warning her of possible danger. There was too much of Gard Kincannon's bare flesh exposed to suit her. The brief cutoffs hung low on his slim hips, drawing attention to the width of his naked, still moist chest and the hard leanness of his stomach. The dark cloud of hair matting his chest was repeated more sparsely, though not at all less noticeably, on his muscled legs. It would be stupid to let him touch her, she cautioned herself, yet wouldn't it be equally stupid to risk sunburn?

She moved toward him slowly, her long legs seeming to have a will of their own. Her eyes found his and clung to them—blue ice to Cimmerian blackness.

Gard watched her approach, the slenderness of her copper body carried with grace and dignity in the bright red swimsuit that did nothing to disguise her utter femininity. Cut indecently high at the tops of her thighs, the swimsuit accentuated her hipbones and the almost concave flatness of her stomach. Though of one piece, the suit was cut low in the back, sloping to the beginning swell of her tight derriere. The straps over her shapely shoulders veed to a point just above her navel and were held together, tenuously so it seemed, with white lacing.

Gard told himself he was a fool for coming here and an even greater one for staying.

When she stopped at the side of the lounge, he spread his muscular legs so that the bare soles of his feet rested on either side of the chair. Careful to avoid his fingers, Season handed him the oil and sat down between his thighs, her back to him.

"Scoot back," he ordered huskily.

Wordlessly, Season lifted both feet to the lounge chair and, using her heels, pushed backward to a point just short of contact with him.

The flawless expanse of her back invited his touch from rigidly held shoulders to the delicate sweep of waist and hip. Gard sucked in a lungful of air and uncapped the oil. He squeezed out a small pool into the hollow of his hand, quickly dumped it into his other hand, and, starting at the base of her neck, began to smooth it over her back.

At the first touch of his hands on her flesh, the tension she always felt in his presence ebbed from her like the waves of the ocean at low tide. His hands moved gently, yet firmly and insistently. There was not an indecisive bone in Gard Kincannon's body.

As his fingers moved lower, he delighted in the feel of her pliant flesh beneath his massaging hands—the way her waist melded into the curve of her hip—the malleability of her body to his sculpting strokes. The combined heat of the sun and her body intensified the coconut scent of the oil, heightening Gard's awareness. Without thinking, and because it seemed so natural, he slipped the straps from her shoulders with a smoothing, kneading movement. If he pressed his mouth to her glistening skin, would she taste like coconut? Action followed thought as his lips grazed her shoulder. Ah, hell! She tasted better than coconut; Season was ambrosia. He parted his lips and began to deliver miniature kisses and nibbles over her back.

Season, her eyes drifting closed, chastised herself; this was no way to ignore him. She was just thinking that she had forgotten how heavenly a man's touch was against her skin when her mind registered the tickle of his mustache as he kissed her back, followed by the rasping sensation of his tongue. No, she thought on a deep sigh, *nothing* had ever felt this heavenly.

Gard's hands began to move with a slow feverishness up and down her arms, each downward stroke dragging the straps lower and lower, revealing more and more of her breasts until at last they lay bare to the heat of the sun. Looping his left arm around her midriff, he pulled her back against his chest, furred muscle meeting oiled satin in a gentle collision. The hair of his forearm teased the undersides of her slightly flattened breasts as she reclined against him. She could feel the heat of his gaze touch her breasts, a warmth that far exceeded the sun's hot rays. She should protest the brash baring of her body. Instead her nipples peaked at the masculine attention.

He settled her more firmly against his moist body, her own body snug against his male hardness. Then, levering his feet from the deck to the chair, he wedged her tightly between his thighs. Reeling from the strange disorientation enveloping her, Season could hardly breathe. To steady herself, she reached out and curled tapered fingers around the fleshy part of his thigh above a knee. Her head was thrown back against his shoulder, her eyes still closed, when she felt something wet trickle in a warm stream across her chest. Her eyes flew open in startled curiosity to see a trail of suntan oil meandering slowly down the shadowy valley between her breasts. She watched as the calloused fingers of both his hands scooped up the excess oil and began to smear it softly over her breasts in a circular, caressing motion.

She could ignore him no longer. With a sigh born of intense longing, she relaxed against him, closing her eyes in surrender to the emotions engulfing her. She wanted this. If she was honest, she'd admit to wanting this from the first moment she'd seen him. The earthy, elemental part of her nature surfaced, and Season realized that nothing mattered beyond the moment and the feelings Gard created in her. Almost nothing, she thought as a shard of guilt pierced her conscience.

In a low, agonized voice, she managed one word. "Beth—" Her head angled backward, her eyes seeking his.

Gard heard the word, saw the torment in her passion-hazed eyes, and knew it was time for the truth—at least part of it. "Beth and I aren't lovers," he whispered tenderly.

Season's eyes widened. Not lovers? Oh, God, was he telling the truth? Or was he just saying it because he knew that was what she wanted to hear? Right this moment, she wanted to believe him. She *needed* to believe him. But only if it was the truth.

Gard saw the conflict in her face. He leaned forward, his lips barely brushing hers. "Trust me," he whispered against her mouth.

As he pulled back, Season saw the earnest entreaty in his eyes. And the honesty. She believed him. It was as simple as that. She believed he and Beth weren't lovers.

But then his magic hands were driving all coherent thoughts from her mind, leaving her with only one significant piece of knowledge: He was man; she was woman.

She was sensation.

She was the sound of masculine breathing, harsh and heavy as the synchronized beating of two hearts melted into one.

She was the clean smell of chlorine that was filtering from him to her. She was the tropical smell of coconut inhaled to the core of her existence with each shuddering drag of air into her nearly bursting lungs.

She was tingling nerve endings screaming for the release of the ever increasing longing that was building in the heart of her femininity as Gard's hands, slick with oil, squeezed, smoothed, molded, and stroked the heavy bronze fullness of her sensitive breasts. His thumbs demoted dusky rose nipples in full bloom to tight buds of desire. And then one hand slid with an ease and a rightness that neither questioned beneath the swimsuit, over her flat belly . . . and lower.

Season moaned. Moving without volition, she arched her hips against his seeking, pleasure-giving fingers, impatiently positioning her thighs to give him easier access to her eager, aching body.

"Look at me," he begged, his voice thick with desire.

She angled her head upward and back, forcing weighted eyelids open to stare into irises no longer pale blue, but now nearly silver. There she caught a momentary glimpse of her passion-glazed features, the image of his face blurring before her just seconds before his mouth, cool and minty, took hers. His lips parted hers in ravenous, uncontrolled hunger, devouring her while his fingers, gentle compared to his kiss, carried her ever upward in a spiraling crescendo of passion that all previous encounters of lovemaking had only hinted at.

And then it was happening. The release her body had craved for days was becoming a sweet reality. A sob of intense feeling rose in her throat as her breathing escalated along with the rapid pounding of her heart. She wanted to be closer . . . closer. Needed . . . she needed . . .

"Oh, Gard," she whimpered, "yes, yes, yes . . ."

"Hang on," he murmured.

The moment was an eternity. The moment was seconds. The moment was indelibly etched in her mind. Her body trembled in the aftermath, even as a sensual, sleepy lethargy claimed her. She was aware of nothing. Not the sun showering its warmth down on her semi-nude body, not the noisy whirring of the hummingbirds at the feeder, not Gard's gentle touch on her forehead as he brushed back the sweat-damp tendrils of hair. Nothing. Not even the sound of a car door slamming shut in the drive.

When the sound reached Gard's ears, he swore harshly. His hands reached down and immediately began to pull up the straps of Season's swimsuit.

She moaned in protest.

Combating her resisting movements, he arranged the straps over her shoulders. "Don't fight me, Season. We have company."

Without further explanation, he scooped her up into his arms and carried her to the pool where he carefully negotiated the steps to the shallow end and, wading out, released her to stand in the waist-high water.

Season raised confused, glazed eyes to his.

"I'm sorry, but there's somebody here." His blue eyes shone with an undeniable tenderness. He reached out and touched her bottom lip. "Let's take a few laps to cool off."

The words had no sooner left his lips when a male voice called out, "Season?"

Season's eyes flew to Gard's face. "Oh, my God, it's my ex-husband!"

Gard swore again. The last thing he wanted was to see Clayton Ashford. Not after what had just happened. Not with the feel and sight of Season's body still fresh in his mind. My God, how vulnerable she had been for those few magic moments. He had felt a protective urge so intense . . . From the depths of his mind, Gard heard Season's anguished words.

"Oh, my God, it's Clay! What am I going to do?"

In a decisive, low command, he said, "Swim, woman." She hesitated. "Now!" he barked, pushing her lower into the water.

When Clay came around the corner of the house, he saw his ex-wife swimming as if her life depended on it. He also saw Gard Kincannon scaling the brick wall. Clay frowned. He'd told the man to keep an eye on her, but he hadn't intended for them to socialize.

Before he could wonder at Gard's methods of surveillance any longer, Season reached the ladder and began to pull herself out of the water. When she spoke, she was surprised to hear that her voice sounded normal. "Hello, Clay." Well, almost normal. "How are you?"

"Fine," he said, dragging his eyes from Gard's retreating figure back to her. "I went by the salon to see you, but Lisa said that you were spending the day at home."

"I needed the time to clear up some last-minute details about the party Saturday." Padding to the chaise longue, and feeling peculiarly naked every step of the way, she reached for the towel that she and Gard had lain on only moments before and brought it to her face to wipe away the water. The smell of him filtered to her nose, and she felt the curious pairing of sensual arousal and acute embarrassment. Dear God! What must Clay be thinking? She assuaged her anxiety by telling herself that even with Clay's jealous streak, whatever he was thinking fell far short of what had actually happened. Never in her ex-husband's wildest dreams would he suspect what she and Gard had just done. No, she admitted miserably, what she'd allowed Gard to do to her.

Guiltily, Season glanced and saw Clay's eyes once again on Gard as he disappeared through the back door of the Galbraith house. Clay's eyes then zeroed in on her.

"That's Gard Kincannon," she explained nervously. "He's staying with Beth."

"I see," Clay responded.

Season draped the large towel about her waist and fastened it. Then she reached for the suntan oil. "What do you want, Clay?" she asked, her nervousness giving way to irritation. Why didn't he leave her alone? she thought. Why didn't he get out, and stay out, of her life?

"More to the point, what did *he* want?" Clayton Ashford asked.

"Gard?" Season returned with feigned naiveté. "Just to swim, I guess."

Clay was so intent on studying his ex-wife's face for a reaction that he missed seeing her hands tremble slightly as they turned the knob of the kitchen door.

Chapter 6

THE CLOVERDALE ART GALLERY HAD NOT BEEN DE-
signed by Frank Lloyd Wright, but it had been constructed,
sometime in the late thirties, in adherence to the man's
architectural principles. Built of brick in an earthy brown
color that blended with its hillside environment, the structure consisted of three main rooms flowing together in an
uninterrupted space that merged easily and naturally with a
narrow balcony running the length of the building and
overlooking a small, man-made lake. A wide, low roof,
long, narrow windows, and a front comprised of four
paneless sheets of glass serving as entry doors characterized
the structure. It was through these doors that Season found
herself gazing expectantly.

Any minute now guests would start arriving, pouring
through the doors in large numbers. That fact accounted for
the anticipatory excitement and natural nervousness that
were surging through her body. Up to a point. Beyond that
point, her nervousness could be blamed on the fact that she
would soon have to face Gard Kincannon. Almost a week

had passed, and she could still die of humiliation at the
thought of the scene that had been played out in her
backyard Monday morning. How it had happened she
would never be sure, but happen it had. Gard had brought
her to that always wondrous moment of release right there
on the chaise longue, right there under God's warm
morning sun, right there in the April air. Shame scorched
Season's cheeks at the thought of how she had aided and
abetted him every stroke of the way. Though never a shy
lover, her blatant, immediate response to him confused her,
bewildered her, and embarrassed her. If Clay hadn't interrupted them, would she and Gard have eventually ended up
in the house, this time each pleasuring the other in equal
degrees?

Season groaned inwardly. She was afraid she knew the
answer to that.

Forget Monday, she ordered herself, *and concentrate on
getting through tonight. Just ignore the man.* She almost
laughed aloud at that one. She'd have to do a better job of
ignoring him than she'd done Monday.

"Everything looks great," Jim Nighthawk said, quietly
slipping up behind her and draping his arm about her
shoulders.

Season jumped at the unexpected sound and touch.

"Hey, you all right?" he inquired, his dark eyes searching hers. "You're awfully jumpy tonight."

She forced herself to smile up into his handsome face and
half lied, "Just gala jitters."

"I'm the one who's supposed to be nervous," he teased.
"It's my career on the line, remember?"

"You've got nothing to worry about, Jim," she replied
earnestly. "They're going to love you."

"We'll see. One thing's for sure. They're going to love
the way you're dressed. You look absolutely sensational."

Season felt that inward pride a woman always feels when
a man compliments her looks. She had given a lot of
consideration to her dress for the evening, finally deciding

on a basic black, 100 percent silk crepe de chine shirtwaist. Its simplicity guaranteed its elegance, from the tiny shoulder gathers to the long, full sleeves to the self-fabric bow tied at her waist. Black heels, sleek in style and fashionably high, and pearls at her throat and ears completed the ensemble. Her raven-black hair was swept upward and coiled into a soft, uncomplicated knot on the top of her head, the sides draping loose and full about her face.

"You sure know how to ease a woman's jitters," she said with a smile, adding, "and you don't look too bad yourself." Her words of praise were meant for the black tux and golden-hued, ruffled shirt he wore. She had just slipped her hand beneath one slender lapel of his tux jacket when Clayton Ashford came through the door. Season immediately saw the spark of jealousy in his eyes. Why, why wouldn't he believe she had nothing going with Jim Nighthawk? If Clay wanted to worry, he should turn his attention to . . . She refused to complete the thought.

"Clay," she acknowledged, moving toward him with less than complete enthusiasm, "I wasn't sure you'd come."

"Didn't I say I would?" Clayton Ashford returned, his mouth brushing hers proprietarily and receiving a smudge of red lip gloss.

Season tried not to grimace as the faint smell of liquor and something else—a woman's perfume?—wafted to her. Some things, or rather some people, never change, she thought. "You remember Jim Nighthawk," she said conversationally as she looked toward the man who hovered nearby.

"Certainly," Clay responded as he extended his hand. "Good to see you. Congratulations on the exhibition."

"Thank you. I appreciate your attendance this evening," Jim returned politely.

The minutes passed, polished by a veneer of congeniality. She doubted seriously if Jim even sensed the slight strain she did, and she certainly knew he was unaware of Clay's suspicions. At least she'd never told him of them. More than once she found herself wishing Clay hadn't come. She most definitely wished he hadn't started drinking so early in the evening, then reminded herself that Clay was no longer her concern. Thank heaven.

After several minutes she excused herself, using the pretense of checking last-minute details that had already been checked a half dozen times. With a critical eye and a slight frown on her lips, she studied one of the room's three arrangements of cut flowers and decided that the fragrant grouping of carnations, roses, daisies, and baby's breath would look better at the other end of the room. She carried them there and placed them on a round column beside glass-fronted shelves permanently housing a collection of Indian pottery, basketry, and artifacts. At some point while tending to these final details, she saw Jim Nighthawk greeting other arrivals. Clay had begun a slow survey of the forty-two paintings, all Jim's, that adorned the walls of the room. Sighing, she crossed the brown and black marble floor and began to mingle.

Fifteen minutes later, the gallery buzzed with chatter and activity. People were now arriving in steady groups and with each new arrival the noise level rose an exciting decibel as guests touched and were touched in greeting, with kisses and well-wishes being generously tossed in. Black-and-white frocked servants, properly detached from the gaiety, passed among tuxedoed men and brightly and glamorously dressed women, tempting them with glasses of yellow-white champagne and delicious-looking canapés. The smell of food, perfume, and success blended in equal parts to form a pleasantly scented backdrop. The elite, many of whose meteoric rises from rags to riches were due to the wealth of oil that had lain for years beneath their holdings, had turned out for Jim Nighthawk with customary Tulsan enthusiasm.

Season moved fluidly and with assurance from group to group. The perfect hostess, she welcomed, fed, and personally introduced as many as she could to Jim. She even escorted many from painting to painting. It was during one such guided tour that she first saw Gard.

She was just explaining that Jim Nighthawk concentrated on no one theme in his art, that while some of his scenes captured elements of Indian life—daily activities, dance rituals, family life, relationships with nature, and peyote-induced visions—he also dealt with more general, multicultural themes, when she glanced up and across the room. A pair of blue eyes, pale but piercing, pulled her attention with as basic a force as the moon's tug on the ocean. In the span of an unguarded second, Season made the mental notation that if looks were worth money, a million bucks had just walked into the room. She quickly tore her eyes from Gard and turned her attention back to the group she was with. The noise in the room suddenly receded to accommodate the wild, loud beating of her heart as it pounded in a primitive, pulsating rhythm.

"What do you think, Ms. Ashford?" some anonymous voice asked.

Season glanced up guiltily. "I'm sorry. What did you say?"

She was going to avoid him, Gard thought. He was as sure of that as he'd ever been of anything. She was going to pretend that Monday had never happened. He wished to hell he could do the same. He hated abandoning her the way he had, but there was no way he could have faced Clay. How do you face a man when you've just seduced the ex-wife he wants back? Hell! Gard thought. He wished he could pretend as well as Season. He'd deliberately stayed away from her all week trying to forget, but every time he thought he was making headway, he remembered how gloriously beautiful her full, heavy breasts were.

"What do you think?" Rick Riccitello said.

Gard forced his gaze from the black-haired woman across the room to the dark-haired man who'd just spoken to him.

"What do I think about what?"

"Where the hell you been, Kincannon?" Rick chastised in mock irritation. "I've been talking to you for five minutes."

Gard eased his index finger around the starched collar of his laterally pleated white shirt as if the wearing of the garment constituted cruel and unusual punishment. "I've been standing here wondering if our 'friend' is in attendance," he lied. "After the publicity this thing got, he'd be a damned fool not to show."

"That's what I just asked you. Do you think there's a nut in the room?"

Gard scanned the ocean of laughing, talking faces. "My conservative estimate is that half of the people in the room are nuts, including you and me, Riccitello, but whether the one we want is here is another matter. I know one thing," he added, nodding toward his sister, who was talking to an elderly couple a few feet away. "We don't dare let her out of our sight. One of us has got to stick to her like glue every minute."

"Yeah," his partner agreed. "To tell you the truth, I don't think she should be here."

"I couldn't agree more, but she is and so are we. Just keep your little eyes open." Gard's right hand unconsciously slid inside his tux jacket and felt the outline of the Magnum .357 holstered to his side.

"And who are we going to tell people we are?" Rick asked, his eyes openly following the seductive movements of a young woman in a clinging white sheath. "We don't exactly look like we belong with this crowd."

Gard scooped a glass of champagne from an immaculately polished tray. His mouth crooked upward in a smile at the same time his eyebrows rose in mischief. "I don't know about you, but I'm going to tell them I'm James Bond."

"Cute, Kincannon. Real cute."

Season sipped at the tawny-tinted champagne, her attention supposedly on the older gentleman before her who was telling her of his recent purchase of an Alexander Calder piece. In reality, however, her attention kept straying, unobtrusively she hoped, to the trio across the way. Beth looked smashing, she thought, which only reinforced the conclusion she'd come to once before. The older woman still had plenty of looks and a lot of charm. Yes, she looked lovely and, ironically, she was wearing a black dress very much like her own.

Courtesy dictated that she go over and speak to Beth, and she would before the evening ended, she promised herself, but she'd wait until Gard moved away. Which might not happen, she admitted, the way Beth had clung to him all evening like smothering ivy. Gard had told Season that he and Beth weren't lovers, and she believed him, but there was obviously some sort of close relationship between them. Friends? No, there was more to it than that. There was more than friendship in Beth's eyes. Relatives? No, Clay had said she had no close relatives. What then? Since there was no man in Beth's life and obviously a lot of social obligations, was Beth paying Gard to be her companion, her escort? The idea seemed possible. If so, and remembering the flirtatious scene on the patio and how she was holding onto him now, she wouldn't be surprised if Beth hoped it might turn into more. But then, what woman wouldn't?

Season turned her thoughts back to safer ground, forcing her attention to the other man beside Beth. She decided he was probably someone involved in her campaign. Season was still sneaking peeks when she saw Gard, one hand in the pocket of his perfectly fitting pants, the other cradling a champagne glass, slip from Beth's side to casually survey the pictures on the far wall. She watched to see if he were likely to be away for any length of time. When he seemed genuinely caught up in the art before him, she excused herself from the gentleman who was still expounding the artistic virtues of Calder and wended her way toward the older woman.

At her approach, Beth's face lit up with a warm smile. "Season, what a wonderful turnout."

Returning her smile, Season answered, "Yes, it's been better than we'd hoped."

"Everything is perfect," Beth praised, "the food, the champagne, and most of all this Jim Nighthawk."

Season felt a warm glow at the woman's unrestrained plaudits, particularly those aimed at her friend. "I told you he was great."

"I believe you." Reshouldering the strap of her black satin evening bag Beth added, "Season, have you met my friend, Rick Riccitello?"

Season automatically extended her hand as her full, sensuous, and perfectly glossed lips turned upward. "No, I don't believe I have. Nice to meet you, Rick Riccitello. Are you involved in Beth's campaign?"

Meeting her hand with his own, Rick replied with only a minimum of hesitation, "You could say that I'm more than a little interested in seeing her elected." He congratulated himself on his fast thinking. He also knew that he'd seen this woman before, though exactly when and where eluded him. When realization dawned that she was the cold neighbor Gard had spoken of, he made the quick assessment that if this woman was cold, he could learn to love ice.

As they continued to talk, Season cast surreptitious glances in Gard's direction. She had no intention of facing him this evening . . . if it could be avoided. As she spoke she noted that he still seemed absorbed in the paintings. And then, out of the corner of her eye, she saw Clay approach him. That, she thought, ought to keep Gard tied up for a few minutes longer. Then her heart sank. Lord, was Clay going to question Gard about what he was doing at her pool Monday? Knowing Clay's jealous disposition and the liquor he'd already consumed, he was quite capable of creating a scene. But she reminded herself as she had once before that night that Clay was no longer her concern. And Gard Kincannon could take care of himself.

Gard's eyes roamed the paintings with a growing sense of annoyance. At a rough guess, he'd estimate that Season had posed for a quarter of the work here. She certainly had for the last three he had seen. There was no question that she was the model for the portrait of the Kiowa squaw in the buff-hued, buckskin dress decorated with flowing fringe and rainbow-colored beads. Nor could there be any doubt that she had posed for the painting of what Gard supposed was a brave and his woman. Standing in front of an Indian warrior who, Gard thought in irrational irritation, looked remarkably like Jim Nighthawk himself, was a woman draped only in a gray, black, brown, and ivory blanket. Her dark hair fell unfettered about her shoulders like shadowy tendrils of the blackest night, and her eyes, wide and clear and seeing life with no illusions, held a stoic pain and a primitive pride. The eyes of the warrior reflected a caring possessiveness.

Gard admitted that his untrained eye could find no fault from an artistic point of view. His eyes once again came to rest on the portrait directly in front of him. But, dammit, he could find plenty wrong from a personal point of view, especially with this piece of erotica. Okay, he reasoned fairly, so it didn't exactly qualify as erotica, but the sensuality captured by charcoal pencil and artist bordered on the obscene. Season wore the feathered halter he'd seen the night he'd borrowed the sugar, and while it scooped low, too low in his thinking, over the full roundness of her breasts, that wasn't what really annoyed him. It was her expression. Her eyes were glazed with arousal and her lips were parted, waiting, begging, for a man's kiss. It was the same look of need he'd seen on her face Monday. And curse it to a devil's hell, Jim Nighthawk had no right to that look, not even to commit it to canvas or paper. Gard felt a surge of possessiveness stronger than any he ever remembered feeling. But did *he* have a right to the look? he asked himself.

"He loves to use Season as a model," came Clay's piqued voice at Gard's shoulder.

Unaware that the man had moved to stand at his side, and wishing fervently that he hadn't, Gard cast a look in Clay's direction and replied in a tone only slightly removed from sarcasm, "So I've noticed."

"I suppose he's good," Clay commented, his attention focused on the charcoal sketching.

"I suppose," Gard answered, his eyes returning to it as well.

Long moments passed as the two men stared quietly at Season's likeness. Clay wondered why his ex-wife wouldn't see reason and come back to him, while Gard wondered, more than a trifle uncomfortably, just how many times the man at his side had seen the same look of need on Season's face. He then reminded himself, forcefully, that Clayton Ashford had once had every right to see it. He'd been married to her. Somehow that fact filled him with little consolation and a lot of disgust. Thoughts of the marriage led to thoughts of the divorce, and Gard wondered what had precipitated it. Men talked. He'd heard it whispered that Clayton Ashford liked his women pretty and in large numbers. Maybe marriage hadn't stopped his roving ways and maybe Season had been unwilling to compete. Yes, he thought, staring at the dark, compelling eyes of the portrait, this woman wouldn't share her man. But then, what man would be fool enough to ask her to?

Clay spoke. "She's beautiful, isn't she?"

It was a rhetorical question, and Gard's silence treated it as such. He had no intention of discussing Season's beauty with this man or any other. Tearing his eyes from her portrait, he asked in a conversational tone, "How are you, Clay?"

"Fine. And you?"

Gard shrugged his powerful shoulders at the same time as he again dragged his finger around the shirt collar's crisp edge. He grimaced. "In this outfit, I'd say somewhere between a grunt and a growl."

The other man's face, as well as his voice, revealed a subtle hint of condescension. "What's wrong, Kincannon? Not casual enough for you?"

"Not by a long shot," he admitted. "We crude, classless cops prefer faded jeans and worn-out tennis shoes." As Gard brought his glass to his lips for a slow but generous sip of champagne, he was aware that Clay had said something, but his mind had already fled to the woman across the room. He knew she had deliberately waited until he strolled away to approach his sister. She was still pretending. Still trying to forget Monday. The question was, he thought, shifting his weight evenly to both feet, was he going to let her? At the moment, he didn't know the answer. Keying back into Clay's voice, he caught the tail end of a sentence. "Sorry. What did you say?"

Substituting an empty champagne glass for a full one, Clay said again, "I was a little surprised to see you here tonight."

With a polite shake of his head to the waiter, Gard refused a second glass, thinking as he did so that Clay would have been better off to have declined the drink as well. While the man might not be drunk, he wasn't sober either. "Season asked Beth and she wanted to come," he offered as an explanation. "I just trailed along."

A few quiet moments passed in which Gard wondered if Clay would take this opportunity to remark that he'd been surprised to see him at Season's Monday morning. If Clay did, what would he say? Somehow he didn't think telling Clay that he'd been over there seducing his ex-wife was the wisest thing to do. Not unless he was heavily into physical pain.

"About Monday," Clay dropped into the silence.

Instinctively, Gard brought his glass to his lips in nothing more than a stall for time.

"What about Monday?" he asked.

"You left before we had a chance to speak." Clayton glanced in his companion's direction. "What in the hell were you doing there, anyway?"

"I have her under surveillance—remember?" Gard made no attempt to hide his sarcasm.

Two pairs of eyes locked stubbornly together, Gard wondering if Clay would pursue the issue and Clay asking himself the same question. Clay's eyes wavered first.

"Did she go out with him Saturday night?"

Gard knew to whom he referred. "Yeah," he answered, not liking this conversation either, but knowing it was inevitable.

Clay's attention shifted to his ex-wife, who was reaching for a rich canapé with red-tipped fingers and laughing at something a dark, Italian man had said. Taking a swallow of his drink as if garnering courage for his next question, he asked, without even looking in Gard's direction, "Did he spend the night?"

Gard didn't answer.

"Look, don't try to spare me," Clay growled. "Did Nighthawk spend the night?"

"No," Gard answered.

"Are you sure?"

"He didn't spend the night, Clay," Gard threw back gruffly. Holy heaven, how had he ever gotten into this spying mess?

Quiet, restless moments passed.

"Sorry," Clay apologized. "It's just that Season has me bent out of shape."

"Forget it," Gard said with a weary sigh. He guessed he could identify with that. She'd done a little of her bending magic on him, too. The hand that had rested off and on in his pants' pocket now perched, with fingers and thumb spread wide apart, at his waist. "Look, Clay, you don't have anything to worry about. She isn't sleeping with him." The moment he said it, he cursed his loose tongue and unthinking mind.

Clay's azure eyes instantly met Gard's, which were many shades lighter in color, but no less intense. "You sound as if you know that for a fact," Clay said, a puzzled look on his face.

Gard shrugged, wondering what Clay would say if he told him he did know it for a fact, that last Saturday night when he'd stood in Season's kitchen, asking her if she was sleeping with Jim Nighthawk had seemed the most important question in the world. "Just call it gut intuition," he answered finally.

"And just how reliable is your gut intuition?" Clay wanted to know.

"Reliable enough."

"And what does this gut intuition tell you about other men she may be seeing?" Clay asked.

"How the hell should I know?"

"Because it's what I'm paying you for," the other man shot back.

Gard studied the smug, confident expression on Clayton Ashford's face. It suddenly dawned on him what he hadn't liked about the man all these years. He thought he could buy and sell everything—and everybody. Gard swallowed the last of his drink with a slow deliberateness that forced the man beside him to wait for a reply. "A deal is a deal, Clay. And I'm going to see that you get surveillance equal to the amount of money I put in my bank account."

"Good," Clay replied with a pleased smile. "All I want is what I bought."

The older man's smile disappeared as quickly as it had come when he observed Jim Nighthawk, now nearly electric with the excitement and success of the evening, move to Season's side. Gard's eyes followed, and both men watched the artist's arm encircle Season's shoulders with a familiarity that annoyed both, but knotted the stomach of only one.

"I'll tell you what *my* gut intuition says," Clay muttered. "She may not be sleeping with him, but it isn't because he hasn't tried."

"I won't argue that," Gard replied. Though the words had been spoken slowly, quietly, they still carried a sting as sharp as a razor cut. Clay threw the man beside him a curious, lingering look.

The two men watched in stony silence as the foursome burst into laughter. Season tilted her chin upward to find Jim's eyes as he lowered his face to find hers. Their smiles broadened. The man's arm tightened about Season's shoulders. Clay's lips thinned in anger; Gard's stomach twisted into a knot. Seconds ticked away. Jim Nighthawk, now speaking with animation, slipped his arm from Season's shoulders to her waist where he hugged her casually yet possessively to him. Clay swore, while Gard's stomach coiled into an even tighter knot that threatened to hamper his breathing. Moments later, the tall, handsome man at Season's side slipped his hand—unconsciously, no doubt— to the high swell of her right hip.

"So help me, God," Gard muttered, totally unaware he was voicing his thoughts, "if he lowers his hand an inch . . ." He left the threat unfinished.

Clay's eyes, suddenly cold with suspicion, turned to the preoccupied profile of the man beside him. "You're being paid to watch her, Kincannon, not fall for her. Remember that."

Gard's head turned slowly, and his eyes met Clay's. Blue combated blue for warlike moments. In a voice that was even, steady, and gave not the slightest hint of any emotion, he said, "You're paranoid, Clay. To say nothing of drunk." With that, Gard turned and walked away.

Season stepped out onto the deserted, softly lit balcony and into the Tulsa night. She was tired, she thought, as her heels beat out a hollow sound on the wooden floor. She was tired of the noise, she was tired of the constant smiling, and she was tired of these expensive, beautifully styled shoes that were waging war on the arches of her feet. She braced herself on the redwood railing, slipped from the pumps, and settled her stockinged soles on the hard surface. She sighed deeply in contentment. She couldn't care less if the wood splintered a run in her pantyhose.

Raising her face to the starless, cloud-filled sky, she let the warm night breeze whisper across her coppery skin. Heaven, she thought. This was heaven. In a move she didn't dare analyze, this celestial pronouncement turned her thoughts to another topic: Gard Kincannon. She sighed again, this time in frustrated weariness. While it was true that she was tired of the noise, the smiling, and the shoes, she was mostly tired of avoiding Gard. The more she tried to ignore him, the harder she tried to stay at room's length from him, the more accurately her senses homed in on him. Now, after almost two hours of dodging and evading him, she was so sensitized that he might as well have been the only other person in the gallery. If only he'd leave, she thought. If only Monday hadn't happened. If only . . .

"Why do women wear those damned things?" A man's voice, soft and raspy, like molten gold oozing over sandpaper, halted her reverie.

Gard! Season experienced a momentary sense of startled surprise, even a mild panic. But then, from some deep place in her heart, she acknowledged what she had known all evening. He was going to force her to face him.

Staring straight ahead, her eye catching only a glimpse of him as he moved to stand beside her at the railing, she spoke. "I guess women are masochists at heart." She intended the answer to be in response to his question about the shoes, but realized the words held a double entendre. *A woman would have to be a masochist,* she thought, *to get tied up with you, Gard Kincannon.*

He made no reply. Elbows resting on the railing, he

peered into the dark evening for such a long time, that it appeared he had forgotten he wasn't alone. The topic of shoes and masochism seemed long since abandoned. Season eased her feet into her shoes in preparation for going back inside.

"You've been avoiding me all evening," he accused softly, suddenly.

"Yes," she answered without hesitation. She deliberately tried not to look at him.

For a sliver of a second her frankness surprised him. Any other woman would have denied the charge, but then he should have known that Season wasn't any other woman. "Why?" he asked.

"You know the answer to that."

"Yes," he admitted just as truthfully, then added, "But I want to hear you say it."

She still kept her gaze straight ahead. "All right. I'm embarrassed."

He turned his head, his eyes searching out the aristocratic outline of her face. "Embarrassed?" he repeated in a disbelieving tone. It had never crossed his mind that she would be embarrassed by what had happened Monday. That she regretted it he didn't doubt, maybe even hated herself and him for letting it happen, but that it had embarrassed her stunned him. It was obvious he had given her rejection of that morning a purely male interpretation.

"Embarrassed, mortified, ashamed—circle your choice," she said, fidgeting with the pearls at her neck.

"In God's name, why should it embarrass you, Season?"

"In God's name, why shouldn't it?" she retaliated, now more than ever unable to look his way. "I let a man who's practically a stranger come into my backyard and . . ." Here she hesitated, unable to even speak the words.

"And what? Give you pleasure?"

Season closed her eyes at his words . . . and at the memories.

"I know this is going to shatter your illusions," he said, "but what we did is hardly unique. It's been happening between consenting adults for a long time."

"I'm aware of that, Gard," she said in an irritated voice, "but we're the wrong consenting adults."

"It happened, Season. Live with it."

"I acted brazenly, wantonly—" she continued.

"It happened, Season. Live with it."

"—and while it may happen to people all the time, it doesn't happen to me." She groaned softly. "I didn't even try to stop you."

Gard's hand snaked out and captured her chin. Turning her face to meet his, he said gently, "Will you shut up? You were not brazen. You were not wanton. And why the devil should you have tried to stop me? What happened was normal between two people who are attracted to each other." His eyes searched the fathomless, midnight-blackness of hers. "And for better or worse, like it or not, that's what we are—attracted to each other." He let the impact of that statement sink in, into her mind and his. "Aren't we?"

Season studied the face of the man holding her attention, the blue eyes impaling hers, the cheeks and jaw tight with anticipation of her answer, the lips frozen. Even at this moment, the sight of him, the nearness of him, the touch of his hand on her chin were doing things to her body she could only marvel at. Attracted to him? Dear God, yes, she was attracted to him, elementally, physically, primitively . . . and had been from the first moment she'd seen him.

"Aren't we?" he pursued relentlessly, his voice a mere throaty whisper.

"Yes," she whispered back, her breath fanning warm against his hand. Words seemed wholly unnecessary, totally unreliable and inadequate, so neither attempted them. Slowly pulling her chin from his grasp, she turned back to stare out at some faraway point in the night. She felt him watching her, then he turned and leaned against the railing as well. The April evening grew older and warmer as each seemed lost in thought. Thunder rumbled ominously in the distance.

It was his voice that finally broke the silence. "I'm sorry I left you to face your ex-husband alone." He was careful to avoid Clay's name.

He could see her delicate shrug in the dark.

"That's all right. I'm used to handling Clay."

Another silence.

Season's next words surprised her. But why should they, she thought, when they'd been in her mind all evening? "What is your relationship with Beth?"

His eyes cut quickly to her. Now it was his turn to be surprised.

Her eyes just as quickly found his. "I believed you when you said you weren't lovers. So what are you two to each other?"

A thousand answers bombarded his mind. The simplest thing to do would be to tell her the truth, that he and Beth were brother and sister. But he backed away from that. He didn't want to blow his cover, even with Season. The fewer who knew of the death threats against Beth the better. *Liar!* he chided silently. *You know damned well that's not the real reason. If you tell her about Beth, you're afraid you'll have to tell her you're a cop.* And cops and women don't mix. Season Ashford was a woman he wanted to get to know better. He wanted to get to know her before he had to give her up. But none of this left him with an answer for her questioning eyes. He could feel his palms growing wet. What the hell was he going to tell her? Then, thankfully, he heard her voice giving the answer he sought.

"It even crossed my mind that you two may have a financial arrangement of some sort and that you act as her companion and escort. That certainly isn't unheard of. What with the obvious age difference . . ."

"Companions!" He seized on the word greedily. "You're right. I'm Beth's companion."

Season waited for him to elaborate but he didn't. She had to content herself with finally knowing the relationship, if not fully understanding it. She felt a measure of relief, but remembering the warmth in Beth's eyes and the possessiveness of her touch, she still wondered how long it would be before Beth tried to make him more than her companion. And what did Gard feel for Beth? Was he attracted to her? He had just spoken of their attraction, an attraction she couldn't deny, but like everything else, one she didn't understand.

"I don't understand," she said, giving her thoughts a voice.

"Understand what?"

"This attraction I feel toward you." Genuine perplexity laced her words.

Gard didn't look her way, but busied himself with tracing a meaningless pattern on the redwood railing. "If it makes you feel any better, I don't understand mine to you," he confessed. "I guess such things can't be analyzed. They just are—like sunshine, flowers, rain." Somewhere in his mind, Gard admitted to the charge Clay had leveled at him earlier. He was falling for Season, falling like some adolescent boy with his first crush. Hell, he'd already fallen for her!

Another few moments passed.

"You're the wrong man for me," she said. Even though he and Beth weren't lovers, they were still involved, and she didn't want to be the third corner of a triangle.

Gard knew what she meant. She was referring to Beth. He laughed cynically. Even if she knew the truth about the relationship, he'd still be the wrong man for her—even more so. Cops just didn't have futures with women.

"Aren't you?" she repeated curiously, and quite uncharacteristically seeking confirmation.

He swallowed back the knot in his throat. "Definitely."

"An affair with you would be messy," she said, as if trying to talk herself into believing it.

"Probably," he answered.

"We'd both regret it," she added.

"Quite possibly."

Another rumble of thunder filled the quiet void that had once again settled over them.

"So what do we do about this attraction, Season?" he asked.

A firefly streaked by as if seeking refuge from the approaching rain. Season idly wondered if fireflies actually felt a physical drawing to each other. And if they did, how wonderful it must be to just act on it.

"Nothing," she answered simply. "We ignore it."

He angled his head to look at her. "Can you do that?"

She turned her head, her eyes finding his. "Yes. And I'm going to start right now." With only a slight hesitation, she pushed from the railing and started for the door. She had taken only a few steps when he spoke again.

"Season?" His voice once again had a low, compelling, guttural sound.

She stopped but did not turn around.

"Do me a favor. Smile at me the way you've smiled at everyone else here tonight."

At the totally unexpected request, Season pivoted to face him. Her eyes instantly found his, even in the darkness.

A slow smile crooked Gard's mouth, sending his mustache tilting upward. "Come on, smile, Pocahontas. It'll only hurt a minute."

The smile that was teasing his lips suddenly erupted into one that filled his face . . . and Season's heart. Despite herself, she smiled back. Dear heaven, she thought in that moment but not for the first time, what kind of strange power did this man have over her?

"Come here," he commanded softly. She hesitated. "Come here. Let me tell you something."

No longer in control of her legs, she moved forward to stand before him. Despite her height, she still had to tilt her head upward to meet his eyes.

"You're beautiful when you smile, you know that?" he said. "Ah, hell, you're just beautiful period." His hand stretched forward to caress and fondle the long string of pearls encircling her neck. His fingers felt warm and gentle and tickly as they brushed her skin and dress. And then his hand splayed open to lay fully against the vee of her exposed neck. His smile began to fade, his head began to lower.

Season's hand grasped his at the wrist at the same time as she pleaded, "No." His head stopped its descent, and for endless seconds their eyes waged a lover's battle. She felt the pulse in his wrist surging. He felt the pulse in her neck throbbing erratically. There they stood, captives of the moment, until both were jostled to awareness by a louder, nearer rumble of thunder.

"It's going to rain," she whispered.

He nodded. "I don't think it's going to cool anything off, though, Pocahontas. I think things are just too hot to cool."

Season didn't trust herself to reply. Instead, she fled the balcony—and Gard's charm.

Umbrella! Season tried to focus her mind on the umbrella that was in her car in the parking lot across the street. She smiled mechanically to the guests she passed, even managed a distracted word or two as she headed toward the entrance of the Cloverdale Art Gallery. If she concentrated on getting her umbrella before the rain started, maybe, just maybe she could push thoughts of Gard and the scene on the balcony out of her mind.

The man was driving her crazy! she thought, pushing open the door and easing out onto the small brick porch, then down the three shallow steps that led to the sidewalk and the street. Giant raindrops were already splotching the concrete in a random pattern, and clouds streamed across the faint moon like long, filmy fingers attempting to strangle the light. Season was oblivious to all but her mission. She was oblivious to the absence of other people, oblivious to the gathering darkness, oblivious to the car parked parallel to the curb.

An unseen hand switched on the car's ignition. The engine purred softly, balefully in the quiet night. Adrenaline rushed quickly through the body of the driver, and he congratulated himself on his patience. All things did come to those who waited. Dragging the gear into drive, the man angled the wheel and eased the car from where it nestled inconspicuously among those of the guests. He'd have to hurry.

Season stepped from the curb. If only Gard would leave and she wouldn't have to face him again. He was playing havoc with every emotion she had.

The foot in the brown shoe in desperate need of polish pushed down heavily on the accelerator, and the car, its headlights as black as the night, lurched forward. A piece of paper slipped from the dash and onto the seat. The name *Elizabeth Galbraith* had been scribbled in an uneven hand on every inch of the white space.

Victor Galbraith had already paid for what he'd done, the man thought, his palms sweaty and his breathing irregular with anticipation of the next few seconds, and his wife would soon pay as well. They'd never hurt anyone else again.

Season heard the car only an instant before she saw it, and in that millisecond she knew the numbing coldness of fear, a coldness that far exceeded the chilling kiss of metal. She reeled from the force of the car, then felt herself falling, falling . . . until she was stopped by the hard impact of concrete slamming against shoulder. A burning pain seared her flesh just as she heard the sound of the sundering fabric. She heard someone scream . . . and would only later realize it was herself.

Chapter 7

THE SCREAM DIED. BEFORE THE SOUND OF SQUEALING brakes and running feet could do more than marginally register in Season's mind, Gard was kneeling before her.

"My God, Season, are you all right?" He choked the words out around an expulsion of air that testified to his concern for her safety and the speed employed to reach her side.

Season raised confused, bewildered eyes to him.

"Are you all right?" he repeated.

She nodded vaguely. "I think so," she said in a weak voice. She tried to raise herself to a sitting position but grimaced at the effort. "My shoulder," she groaned, her hand moving instinctively toward the streak of pain.

Gard slipped his hand to the small of her back and gently levered her upward. He pulled her hand away and examined the injured area. The sleeve of the black dress gaped open at the seam and hung, almost comically, down her arm to reveal abraded skin, raw and tender from the concrete's assault. He wiped at the oozing blood, then smeared the bright red stain across the leg of his elegantly tailored pants. Still kneeling, he straightened his spine and ran his hand into a hip pocket.

"Here, sweetheart, hold this over it," he commanded, producing a neatly folded white handkerchief. Season obeyed like a mindless automaton. She frowned slightly at the contact of cloth to flesh, though she made no sound.

"Can you move your shoulder?" he asked, grasping her upper arm and rotating it even as he spoke. Her teeth sank into her bottom lip, a testimony to her pain, but Gard was satisfied that no bones were broken.

He checked her head, pushing back a swath of hair torn from its orderly place, then ran his hand gingerly down her other arm. When he slid both hands under her skirt and slip and up the long length of her legs, over now shredded pantyhose, she did not protest. This intimate survey of her body felt so right that it registered only as normal and natural in her mind. As if he somehow had the right to be touching her this way.

"Can you get up?" he asked when he finished his examination and was relatively certain she had sustained no serious injuries. His voice was soft, gentle, nearly a croon.

He placed his hand on her uninjured arm and attempted to help her stand, but she stopped him by grasping, almost desperately, the lapel of his tux. His eyes instantly flew to hers. She was in a state of shock, he thought.

"I didn't see it," she whispered. "I didn't see the car until it was right on me. I don't think it had any lights. Why wouldn't it have any lights, Gard?" Her question had a childlike ring to it, as if begging him to make her understand.

Gard swallowed back the anger that instantly lodged itself in his throat. He knew why the car had no lights. He had known the moment he'd seen the blackened headlights, the moment he'd seen Season hurled to the ground, the moment the car had sped away. If he could get his hands on the driver's throat, he'd be tempted to forget his police principles for what the madman was doing to his sister and for what he had done to Season simply because she'd had the misfortune to be mistaken for Beth. Any dark hair, any black dress in the black night would appear the same. At the thought of the serious injury that Season could have sustained so easily, Gard's stomach roiled like a pit of angry vipers. Then the realization that she could have been more than injured turned the hot anger into a cold, desperate panic.

"Do you think the driver was drunk?" she asked, trying to make some sense out of what had just happened.

Gard forced the anger and the panic from his face and voice. Now wasn't the time for either. "Probably. Come on, Season, let's get up." This time, his arm slipped around her waist and he pulled her, and himself, to their feet. "Easy, sweetheart," he cautioned when her legs buckled. "Can you walk?"

Fitting snugly into the crook of his arm, she nodded. Then, as if the idea had just occurred to her, she asked, "Should we call the police?"

"I'll take care of everything," he promised.

The warmth of his words settled over her like a woolen blanket, making her feel safe and secure. He would take care of everything, she consoled herself. He would take care of her. There was nothing for her to worry about. Except how to put one foot in front of the other with legs that felt rubbery and unsure. With an instinctive feminine vanity, her thoughts turned to her appearance. She couldn't go back to the party looking like this. She really should try to readjust her hair and smooth out the wrinkles in the skirt of her dress. Maybe she could stop in the ladies room and make herself more presentable. Somewhere in her mind she told herself she wasn't thinking clearly, that there was no way she could stitch up her dress and remove the runs from her stockings. There was no way she could look as if she hadn't just been run down.

Run down. My God, how calmly she'd just acknowledged it!

At the sidewalk, Gard took an abrupt right turn and
headed toward the red Thunderbird several cars down at the
curb. His free hand fumbling in his pocket, he found the
key, inserted it, and pulled open the door. Gently, he
started to lower her onto the seat.

"What are you doing?" Season protested. "I've got to
go back inside. I'm the hostess."

"I don't care if you're the Queen of England, you're not
going back." His voice was gentle but undeniably firm. His
eyes were soft, but clearly unswerving in their intent. At
her hesitation, he added, "Don't fight me, Season. Let me
take care of you."

She stood, one hand holding the handkerchief in place,
the other bracing herself on the open car door. Neither she
nor Gard seemed to notice that it had started to drizzle.
Suddenly she felt tired, and her arm was a painful reminder
of what she'd just been through. Maybe she did need to be
taken care of. Just for now. Without a word, she eased
herself into the black leather seat.

Gard squatted on his haunches beside the open car door.
"I'll be back in a minute. You stay right here, okay?"

She nodded. His hand gently brushed the side of her
cheek before he pressed down the lock button, slammed the
door, and moved off into the darkness. She watched as he
ran the distance back into the Cloverdale Gallery. Once
he'd disappeared from view, she settled her head back
against the seat and closed her eyes. Gard would take care
of everything.

And he did. Within the span of a few short minutes, he'd
cornered Rick Riccitello and, with a succinct brevity, filled
him in completely. He also left a vague description of the
car and the first two numbers of the license plate for his
partner to phone into headquarters. The two men decided,
out of earshot of Beth, that Rick would accompany her

home as soon as possible and would stay the night with her. Gard gave no explanation as to how he intended to spend the evening. And Rick asked no questions, other than if Season was all right. Gard gave a brief explanation to Jim Nighthawk—Season had taken ill suddenly, probably with the flu—and no explanation at all to Clayton Ashford, who seemed to be putting the make on the woman in the white sheath.

Less than five minutes later, the Thunderbird was moving through the Saturday night traffic. The sight of alabaster skyscrapers rising majestically and almost arrogantly beside spiral-topped columns heralded downtown Tulsa, but Season stared straight ahead, totally unaware of them. Gard passed through the congested area quickly, past the fifty-two story Bank of Oklahoma Tower, the state's tallest building and part of the $200 million Williams Center, past all the new construction in the growing city. They sped past countless buildings aglow with thousands of lights shimmering like expensive, proud jewels in the wet Oklahoma night, lights whose sparkle began when the Lochapoka Indians, long ago forced from their home in Alabama, carried the sacred ashes for a new council fire from their old town, or *tulsey,* to this new location. Only when Gard turned onto Main Street did Season seem aware of their location.

"Where are we going?" she asked, angling her face to find his in the neon-streaked darkness of the car.

"My apartment," he answered, then added, as if knowing she was certain to object, "don't argue with me." His eyes sought hers, lingered in their obsidian depths, then moved back to stare out the windshield. The only sound in the car's close quarters was from the wipers swishing back and forth as they cleared the rain-splattered glass in fanlike arcs.

She ought to insist that he take her home, but right now she seemed incapable of insisting on anything. With her mind's confusion and this borderline feeling of unreality, it was easier to let Gard make the decisions. And he seemed so capable of doing so. She pulled the handkerchief from her shoulder to look at the scraped, lacerated skin. It was too dark to see anything, but not too dark to feel the dull, throbbing ache.

"Does it hurt much?" Gard asked, again snatching a look in her direction.

"A little," she answered. Turning her attention to the torn dress, she made a totally feminine comment. "The dress is ruined. And it was so pretty."

"Forget the"—he used a short, very expressive expletive—"dress! I'll buy you another one."

Gard maneuvered the Thunderbird through the multistoried downtown area and out into the sprawling Tulsa suburbs. Gone was the formality of the city, replaced by a livable informality, the casualness of all-night grocery stores, crowded fast-food restaurants, and people milling about in search of a good time on a Saturday night. Pulling into a small shopping mall, he whipped the car into a vacant slot and cut the engine. At Season's curious look, he explained, "I've got to get something to bandage your arm. Wait here." Before she could reply, he was out of the car. Bending to look in at her, he added, "I'll only be a minute." Once again he locked his door and sprinted off in the direction of a drugstore.

She watched as his long, strong, jogger's legs covered the distance. She smiled faintly. He made quite a picture dashing through the slow, slanting rain in a tuxedo. When he reached the protection of the mall, she saw him shake the rain from his hair, then disappear into the drugstore. She felt curiously alone in the night without him near her. *You shouldn't be here, Season*, her hazy brain reminded. *You shouldn't be here at all. He shouldn't be here at all. He should be with Beth*. But she was powerless to keep her eyes from watching for his return.

Only minutes passed before she saw him. Traveling the distance between building and car in record time, he pulled open the car door on the driver's side, which Season had only seconds before stretched across the seat to unlock, and slipped inside. His fast but even breathing filled the car with a comforting sound just as his presence emanated a warmth that almost radiated in tangible waves. He placed a small sack in her lap, then combed back a strand of moist hair from his forehead. Season noticed that he had undone the black bow tie, allowing it to dangle carelessly, and had unfastened the first two buttons of his shirt. She caught a brief glimpse of dark hair.

"Okay?" he questioned, his eyes, almost colorless in the car's interior, scanning her wan features.

"Okay," she answered. *Now that you're here,* she could have added.

Less than five minutes and three miles later, Gard turned into a modern housing complex, parked the car, and, after dashing through the rain, opened the door of a brown and beige, stucco-and-wrought-iron condominium. He nudged Season forward, ushering them both into the darkness. A musty smell, as if the apartment had been closed for a while, curled about her nose, and she was instantly reminded that Gard was not presently living here.

"I'll get a light," he said, moving from her side. With unerring familiarity, he stepped through the small living room and into the kitchen separated from it only by a countertop bar. When he flipped on the kitchen light, the darkness scurried to the outer perimeters, washing the living room with shadows. "Sit down," he commanded softly, indicating the sofa in front of her.

Season quietly obeyed him and eased her body—a body that was beginning to ache from the fall she'd taken—onto the sofa. She only idly noted that the room seemed to be done in earth tones with an attitude more toward the functional than the decorative. It was the home of a man who needed a place to stay, she would have reasoned had her mind been sharper, not the home of a man who loved where he lived.

"I'll be back in a minute," Gard said, disappearing up a short flight of stairs. In the bedroom, he shrugged out of the tux jacket, ripped the bow tie from around his neck, and unfastened another button of the shirt. The gun and holster, his real reason for detouring to the bedroom, he hid away safely and secretly on the top shelf of the closet.

When he came downstairs, he found Season lying on the sofa, her head propped on a pillow his mother had embroidered for him. She still held his handkerchief to her shoulder, and tiny lines of discomfort edged her mouth. Her eyes were closed. He felt the strong taste of bile in his throat at the close escape she'd had. Thank God he'd seen her leave the gallery! Thank God he'd followed her!

"Let me see your shoulder," he said. As soft as the words were spoken, they still startled her and she jumped slightly. Her eyes fluttered open to find his. Tugging at his pants' leg, he knelt before her and placed a hand over the one that was holding the handkerchief. He gently drew the bloody cloth away. His lips curved downward at the sight of the raw and bruised flesh. "It's not too bad," he said. "Just not very pretty."

"It hurts," she said simply.

"I know," he returned gently. "Sit up a minute."

When she levered herself to a sitting position, he took her hand, turned it over in his, and unmoored the tiny button on the sleeve that bound her wrist, then repeated the same procedure at the other wrist. His fingers moved to unfasten, one by one, the neat row of buttons running down the front of the silk shirtwaist. Untying the belt at her waist, he started to ease the dress from her shoulders.

"Gard . . ." she spoke softly and in confusion at what he was doing.

His hands stopped. His eyes traveled from her partially exposed shoulder to the vulnerable hollow of her throat, then up her neck and over sensuously shaped lips, lighting at last on her dark eyes. "I have to strip the dress to your waist so I can get to your shoulder," he explained, his voice huskier than he realized. He smiled slowly, teasingly at her sudden attack of modesty. "I never ravish maidens with hurt shoulders." The smile faded as slowly as it had appeared. "I've already seen what you're trying to protect," he reminded her. "Remember?"

Yes, she remembered. Graphically. And in sensual detail. After a few undecided seconds, she eased one shoulder, then the other, out of the dress. She sat before him, her bronze skin naked except for the string of pearls and the black satin slip that clung fondly to her full, braless breasts. She felt one thin strap betray her as it fell low on her arm. She raked it upward with a finger.

"Want to lie back down?" Gard asked.

"No," she answered, shaking her head. She'd sit, she told herself. Lying before him made her feel too vulnerable . . . and she was already feeling the tiniest flicker of some warm hunger.

Gard worked quickly and with sure movements. Dabbing a cleansing antiseptic on a ball of cotton, he blotted the already purpling skin around the wound. "This is going to sting," he warned as he started to care for the injury itself.

Season closed her eyes but made no sound other than her faint breathing.

"Sorry," he apologized. Reaching into the sack for a tube of ointment, he uncapped it and smeared the colorless salve lightly over the abrasion. It felt cool and soothing, almost as good as his hands on her skin. She watched as snips of the scissors produced strips of tape that plastered a sterile bandage in place.

"There," he announced in a warm voice, "I think you'll live."

She smiled faintly. "What do I owe you, doctor?"

He paused slightly, his eyes taking in the mature, sensuous woman before him. "You can make me some brownies," he said after a slight hesitation. His voice had once again grown low and gravelly, and she had the feeling he hadn't given the answer he'd wanted to.

"I don't know how to make brownies."

"I'll teach you." He stood and extended a hand to her. "I think you ought to rest now. Why don't you go upstairs and lie down?"

She automatically took the hand he offered, and he raised her to her feet. "I'm all right," she said, looking into his eyes. "I don't need to rest."

"You need to rest," he said, denying her statement. "Just stretch out on the bed for a minute." He took her silence for acquiescence and turned away, his steps headed toward the kitchen.

"Gard?"

Her voice was low, almost inaudible, but he heard the whispery sound of his name. He pivoted toward her. She stood where he had left her, directly in front of the sofa and only steps away from him. Her hair drooped in dishevelment on one side, while the bodice of her expensive dress still hung about her waist, leaving her shoulders bare except for the thin straps of the slip and the incongruous strand of pearls at her throat. Runs riddled both legs of her pantyhose. All this Gard barely noticed, for his attention was caught by the watery hazing of her eyes, the slight quaking of her bottom lip, and the hands at her sides that were beginning to tremble noticably. The blissful shock was wearing off, being replaced even as he watched with painful reality.

"Gard?" she called again, even lower than before and now little more than a mouthing of the word. "Hold me. Please, hold me."

Her plea struck something within him that spoke to every cell of his being. He could no more have denied her than he could have refused the next breath of air to his lungs. Crossing the distance to her side, he pulled her roughly, tenderly, into his arms, hugging her to him until her breasts flattened against the unyielding wall of his chest. He moaned softly as he buried his face in the curve of her shoulder.

He felt so good, she thought, so warm, so big, so safe. Her arms slipped around his waist, fiercely anchoring him to her. The tears that welled in her eyes overflowed, coursing down her cheeks in an ever increasing stream. She fought them at first, then gave way entirely to sobs that shook her whole body.

He held her, oblivious to the fact that he was witnessing something no man had ever seen. Season herself was totally unaware that this was the first time she'd ever cried before a man. She'd certainly never weakened before her father, who'd so often been the cause of her young tears . . . or Clay who wouldn't have understood her tears of disillusionment.

"Oh, Gard," she sobbed, "I was so scared."

His hand moved to the back of her head, splaying itself in the thickness of the inky-black hair, hair that was spilling from its knotted confines. "I know, sweetheart," he said gruffly. "I was scared, too."

"I didn't see the car," she said as if reliving the moment in her mind. "I didn't see it."

"Shhh, sweetheart," he consoled. "It's over. It's all over. You're all right." His lips gently kissed the scented side of her neck where his head nestled against her soft flesh. "It's over," he said again, his mouth inching to the delicate spot behind her ear. "Shhh, don't cry," he commanded softly, gently as his lips moved to kiss the salty wetness of one cheek. "Don't cry, sweetheart." His lips traveled lower to the corner of her mouth. ". . . Sweetheart." He mumbled something as his mouth edged the other corner of hers. ". . . Sweetheart," he breathed in sweet repetition seconds before his lips moved onto hers.

Season felt wonderfully smothered by the warm mouth moving over hers, wonderfully drugged by the taste of him, wonderfully alive. Her mouth began to stir beneath his, slowly, hesitantly at first, then greedily, almost savagely. Suddenly her tears were forsaken.

He groaned, moaned, spoke something into the wet hollow of her mouth even as his own shifted to take hers at another angle. His lips moved with the same desperation as hers, a desperation born of suppressed emotions. Parting his mouth, his tongue thrust forward searching for, needing a closer intimacy. Her tongue met his.

"Oh, Season," he whispered when his lips pulled from hers, "what are you doing to me?"

Her only response was to cradle his face with both hands and draw his mouth back to hers. Passion ruled. Desire curled in the core of her feminine body even as his male body responded with steel-hard appropriateness. His hand, restless and unsatisfied, pushed her slightly from him and moved between their bodies to find her full, still covered breast.

"Touch me," she begged. "Really touch me."

With unhurried but eager fingers, Gard dragged a slip strap down her arm. The black satin fabric cupping her breast draped low, then lower yet, to reveal the golden-skinned treasure he sought.

When his hand, big and calloused, closed over her warm, soft, willing flesh, she murmured raggedly, "Yes, oh, yes."

His mind answered no, oh, no. He should be worrying about Beth, shouldn't he? And if not about Beth, he should be worrying about himself. The feelings he had for this woman were not of the casual, fleeting type. He knew better than to get involved in a situation that called for an emotional investment. Dear God, hadn't his marriage to Lynn taught him that? His hand, in total denial of his reasoning, slipped the other strap from her shoulder, drawing it determinedly down the length of her arm. She eased her arms from the satin bondage, leaving both breasts entirely naked to his touch. His eyes ravished her before his hands moved to cup and claim her fevered skin. Both groaned at his conquest.

His lips fused hungrily with hers as his hands performed their magic of kneading and lifting, caressing and palming. His thumbs brushed across the pert, dusky, alert nipples, sending shivers of delightful sensations through her. And then his head dipped to capture one dark-tinted, swelling peak in his mouth. He kissed it, tongued it, sucked it. She moaned low in her throat, her hands grasping his shoulders to balance her swimming head.

"I shouldn't do this," Gard breathed around the now almost painful peak of her breast.

"I know," she whispered into the crown of his rain-moistened hair.

He raised his head, his mouth again taking hers. As the kiss deepened, his hands trailed up her arms, over her bare shoulders, then back down her arms. As Season's arms encircled his neck, his hands eased downward and began an investigation of the sweet curves of her body, the inward sweep of her waist, the gentle, womanly thrust of her hips. His fingers skimmed and shimmied over, up and down, down and up the smooth, silken surface of the dress fabric.

When his hand smoothed over the front of her dress and eased between her legs, molding that area of her now wild with wanting, Season sucked in her breath. "I shouldn't let you do this," she whimpered against his lips.

"I know," he answered huskily. "I know." He then added, "About that messy affair. I think we're going to have it after all."

"I know," she said, her breathing and her legs so unsteady she could hardly speak or stand. "In fact, I'm going to insist on it."

If Gard hadn't carried her, she never would have made it up the stairs. As it was, her legs betrayed her as she stood by the side of the bed in the dusky glow of the lamp. Gard felt her unsteadiness and gently eased her down and back onto the bed. He followed and, sitting on the edge of the mattress, quickly removed her shoes. As once before that night, he ran his hands under her dress, this time tugging away her pantyhose. At the sight of her naked to the waist and her dress and slip provocatively riding high up on her thighs, Gard's breath quickened. He moaned softly at the exquisite pain tormenting his body.

The fact that he so obviously wanted her aroused her as no man ever had. Her own breathing, labored and sharp, was painful in her chest; hot flames of desire licked the heart of her femininity. She was burning in the conflagration.

"Gard," she whispered as her hands twisted the spread beneath her in sheer agony, "for God's sake, make love to me."

His eyes always on her, he rose from the bed and practically ripped the clothes from his body—a button from his shirt sailed across the room and the zipper of his pants jammed for one excruciatingly long second. Stripped naked, he stood before her more boldly masculine than she could have ever imagined, more powerfully aroused. Without a word, he lowered himself to her, intent on removing the remainder of her clothing, but when she writhed beneath the touch of his hand on her inner thigh, his intentions altered. "Oh, God, Season," he groaned, moving his fingers to the enticing, warm moistness between her legs.

His gentle, probing, rubbing touch sent her beyond the realm of all control, all reason. All the days of subjugating her needs, stifling them, pretending they didn't exist had taken their toll. Her body knew only one thing: need. She needed him to ease this ache that was burning, flaming within her. She needed the weighty feel of his body on hers, the masculine scent of him filling her nostrils, the wondrous feel of him deep within her.

"Now, Gard," she begged. "Now."

Gard fought to rid her of her dress and slip.

She stayed his hands with a fierce urgency. "No! Now! This second!"

He studied her, his own passion wildly out of control. "Oh, God," he growled, a deep guttural sound that seemed to have its origin in his soul.

With fevered, near frenzied movements, he shoved her clothes upward and entered her waiting, wanting body, quickly, completely, and most satisfyingly. Gone was all subtlety, all finesse, all delicacy. The act they performed was basic, elemental, as primitive and as beautifully natural as time. Their movements, his deep and thrusting, but caring and tender, hers steady and arching, were choreographed by the ancient need of man and woman. He surged against her; she answered in sensual undulation. Neither heard the song of the rain above their ragged, jagged breathing. Neither heard the clock ticking away the night. Neither heard themselves falling in love.

Season did hear him calling her sweetheart. And she did feel his hands everywhere on her body as his mouth claimed her mouth again. She felt his breath warm at her ear, felt the wonderful weight of his body on hers, a heaviness that pressed her firmly into the bed. Slipping her hands to his tautened thighs and hips, she pulled him even tighter, even closer. She exchanged each masculine stroke with its feminine counterpart. And then she felt his sensual rhythm accelerate, heard his breath grow more wispy, felt her own emotions responding and beginning to build to match his.

"No," she whispered in denial. "Longer . . . make it last longer." She tried to halt her movements beneath him. She tried to still his movements above her.

Scooping her buttocks in his hands, he continued the plunging rhythm. "It's too late, sweetheart," he squeezed between gritted teeth.

And Season realized it was too late for her as well. It started as a tiny tingling, a quivering that swept across her like a flash fire. She clung to him and he to her as their passions ignited, smoldered, burned. At the crest of emotion she cried out loudly, a sound of uninhibited pleasure that sparked Gard's excitement, a sound that mixed and mingled with his own full-throated groan. And then the throb melted into a delicious glow.

How much time passed she didn't know. The delightful burden of his body still rested upon her, pinning her to the bed. She still felt him deep within her. Slowly he shifted and his weight eased, though it didn't disappear. Season opened her eyes and fought to focus them. When she did, she found him looking down at her. Wordlessly, they stared at one another. At last a slow smile curved her mouth, and she reached out a finger to lightly trace his love-swollen bottom lip.

"I thought you said you never ravished maidens with hurt shoulders."

A matching smile sauntered across his lips and settled in one corner of his mouth. "There's always the exception to the rule." The smile lingered for a moment, then suddenly faded, replaced by a look of perplexity. "I'm not sure what just happened here. I mean, I know what just happened here—I passed Biology one-oh-one—but I'm not sure what just happened here."

As strange as his words sounded, Season understood completely. "I'm not sure either," she admitted seriously.

"I've never been in such a white-hot heat that I couldn't at least get the woman's clothes off," he confessed.

"If I remember correctly," Season said with a total absence of embarrassment, "you were trying to, but I stopped you." At the unspoken question in his eyes, she added, "No, I've never been that brazen before. I've never wanted a man as much as I wanted you." Even as she said it, the admission amazed her. Clay and she had shared a satisfactory sex life, at least she'd thought so at the time, but he had never inspired in her the emotions, the fundamental need she'd just experienced with this man. Her lovemaking with Clay now seemed artificial, mechanical, somehow less than the real thing. And, though Clay had been considerate, the act had contained a degree of self-centeredness.

"I've never wanted a woman the way I wanted you," Gard said, as if the confession startled him equally.

Season shifted under the weight that had suddenly grown uncomfortable. Gard moved from her. As he did so, he tangled himself in the dress sleeve and swore softly. With resolute pulls and tugs, he glided her clothes over her hips and down her legs.

"Better late than never," he proclaimed, dropping them carelessly to the floor and stretching out on his side. She rolled on her side to face him, her eyes even with his.

Slowly, as if mesmerized by the woman before him, Gard stretched out a hand and worked the pins from Season's softly tumbled hair, allowing it to cascade freely about her shoulders. He threaded his fingers through the thick, black mass, then found the shoulder hidden beneath it. Gently, so as not to apply pressure to her injury, he trailed a hand down her arm, leaving it to explore the hollow of her waist and the jut of her hip. His hand next moved to fondle, almost in reverence, the perfect swell of a breast that lay heavy and full between them.

As impossible as it seemed, Season felt the tiniest prickling of desire as his hand investigated the deep cleavage. The desire deepened as he playfully fitted the pearls she still wore in a provocative circle around her breast. My God, she thought, how can I be feeling this after what we just did? To scatter her thoughts, though in the end it proved no help at all, Season settled her hand in the silky down of his chest.

"You're an incredibly beautiful man," she said, her fingers moving through the curly spirals in slow circles.

He raised an eyebrow. "Am I?"

She nodded. "Incredibly beautiful."

His hand moved to her hair again, and he combed it

forward to settle and drape about a breast. He parted the dark strands so the nipple could peer through. "I fantasized about making love to you in a thousand different ways," he admitted, "but it didn't turn out the way I planned in any of them."

Her eyes roved from his chest to his eyes. "What was your plan?"

"I was going to devastate you with my wonderfully slow technique."

She smiled. "I thought your technique was fine."

He was smiling now, too. "It was so quick, how could you tell?"

Her laughter echoed softly in the room. "I could just tell." As she spoke, her hand moved lightly over his shoulder in an acquainting search, even as his own hand continued to wander over her body. When her fingers brushed across the scar she'd seen on his shoulder that day at Beth's house, a frown settled on her face.

Gard saw it. "Vietnam," he offered in simple explanation.

Vietnam? she thought, feeling a sudden ache in her heart at the pain he'd lived through. Raising herself up, she pressed her lips to the imperfect spot. "I'm sorry," she whispered against his skin.

"It wasn't your fault," he murmured, lacing his fingers in her hair and gently drawing her lips down to his for a kiss. "But it was worth the pain just to have you kiss it." His lips melded with hers again. As they did so, he rolled her to her back and followed to hover above her. When their lips parted, their eyes did not. Long seconds passed before he said, "You don't seem right."

Tiny creases formed in Season's forehead.

"You don't seem right for Clayton Ashford," he explained.

She shrugged her shoulders in a delicate movement. "I wasn't."

"Why did you divorce him?"

"I wanted a husband. He wanted a harem." For so long it had hurt for her to admit that, but no longer. No longer did she view it as some inadequacy in herself, but rather as an aberration in Clay's personality.

"The man's a fool," Gard said as he kissed the side of her neck.

"Have you ever been married?" Season asked. Gard hesitated. She noted the slight tensing of his back muscles.

"Once," he answered, resuming his kissing of her neck. "We divorced. Irreconcilable differences."

Season found herself wondering about the circumstances of his divorce. And about the kind of woman he'd been married to. "Did you love her?"

His lips stopped delivering kisses, and he raised his eyes to hers. "Yes. Very much."

Why that news should hurt so badly, Season wasn't certain, but it did hurt . . . worse than anything Clay had ever done to her. "Clay says there's no such thing as love."

His eyes, blue and scrutinizing, imprisoned hers. "Do you believe that?"

"I don't know what I believe. Some days I think he must be right. Why else would I have gotten over him so easily? But then some days I think he's wrong. My mother loved my father even though he didn't deserve it."

Gard studied the woman lying half beneath him, the same woman he'd just made love to. "There is an emotion called love, Season. Maybe you got over Clay so easily because you never really loved him, not the way your mother loved your father." He longed to know more about this undeserving father but felt he had no right to ask. His relationship with Season was too fragile . . . and far too tenuous.

"Do you still love her?" She hadn't meant to ask the question, wished she hadn't the instant she did, but longed intently for the answer he'd give.

"No," he said simply and with no hesitation. And that

astounded him. He had carried the memory of his wife, Lynn, for so long that he had always assumed he was still in love with her. He had remained in the habit of loving her. Yet now, in the flash of a second, he realized he no longer did—and probably hadn't for a long while. He shook his head slightly, as if truly astonished at the revelation, and smiled. "No, I'm not in love with her."

Season smiled back for no reason she could explain, but because she was helpless to stop it.

His smile broadened. And so did hers.

"I like it when you smile," he said, the fingers of one hand outlining her upturned lips.

"I like it when you call me sweetheart," she answered back. "No one ever has."

His finger hesitated at the indentation of her upper lip. "No one? Ever?"

She shook her head. "I don't think so. My mother calls me baby, and my father called me nothing at all if I was lucky. Never any endearment."

Gard's frown had reappeared. "And your husband?"

Shrugging her shoulders lightly, she replied, "Just Season. Always just Season." Unconsciously, her fingers were playing in the dark wispy down of his chest, roving over muscle and bone, and distractedly and repeatedly raking across his male nipples.

He caught her hand, staying its movement by pressing it flat against his chest. "If you don't stop that, I'll . . ."

"You'll what?" she taunted.

He fought at the smile trying to appear. "I'll be forced to show you my slow technique."

"Yeah?"

"Yeah."

Sincerity immediately replaced teasing. The same pleasurable heaviness she'd experienced so short a time before was beginning its pulsating renaissance, and she felt Gard's maleness hard against the side of her thigh. Her hand eased from under his and trailed slowly, sensuously over his chest and down his stomach to touch his turgid, swollen body. She felt rather than heard his deep moan.

"I want you again," he said simply but unnecessarily.

She had already acted foolishly, she told herself. Letting him make love to her again was folly extraordinaire, stupidity of the highest order, a foolhardiness she'd never been guilty of before. And she didn't give a damn. For twice in her life, for twice in one night, Season Ashford was going to be foolish.

When he parted her legs, she didn't deny him. Nor did she protest the slow descent of his mouth. All she knew was a heaven on earth as his warm breath brushed across the most intimate part of her body. "Oh, Season . . ." his breath rasped. "Oh, sweetheart . . ."

She had no idea what awakened her. Gard, his arm thrown possessively about her waist, slept contentedly on his side. His breathing sounded even and steady in the dark room. Season smiled softly. Never had she desired more strongly; never had she been satisfied more completely. He had sated her with caresses and kisses, warm, intimate touches, and endearments that left her feeling pleased, playful, and pleasured. Her smile widened and flashed in the dark depths of her eyes. And if he could bottle his slow technique, she thought, he could sell it to every woman in the world.

A low rumble of thunder growled its ominous presence, and a bright flash of lightning tore across the sky. Season's smile waned. It must have been the weather that awakened her. In tandem with the thought, she heard the sound of rain as it flung itself, recklessly and mercilessly, against the house. As often happened, the rain made her feel restless.

Easing gently from the weight of Gard's arm, she slipped from the bed. He stirred slightly, and she glanced quickly toward him. In another streak of lightning, she saw that he lay flat on his back, his hair tousled with irresistible boyish charm, his mustache limp with peaceful languor. She fought the urge to reach out and touch him. On bare feet, she moved around the bed in search of the dress she knew must be on the floor somewhere. Before she could find it, Gard's shirt ensnared her foot. Reasoning that this would be better than her torn dress, she picked it up and eased her hurt shoulder into it. The other shoulder followed, and she quickly rolled up the sleeves and adjusted the buttons. The last button was missing, and she recalled with a tiny flush of embarrassment that in Gard's haste it had landed somewhere on the floor, probably never to be found again except by accident. The shirt on and covering her to midthigh, she walked from the room and down the stairs.

Once in the living room she didn't bother with a light. Gard's neighbor had left on a porch light, and it cast a muted incandescence through the large picture window in Gard's living room. Unhesitatingly, she went to stand before the window. A bright ribbon of lightning greeted her arrival. For long moments she watched and willed the wet weather away. But it paid no heed to her wishes. The capricious weather seemed intent on reminding the Tulsa residents of its extremes—the torrential downpours that provided the usual relief from the long, dry spells that plagued the area. Rain pummeled the glass, tunneling rivulets that ebbed and flowed, changed and rechanged their paths. Perhaps in an effort to thwart the inclement weather and her own restlessness, Season stretched out a hand and laid her palm against the cool windowpane.

At that exact moment, she felt a pair of arms slip around her waist. She jumped slightly.

"I didn't mean to scare you," Gard said as he snuggled close behind her, his hastily thrown-on jeans chafing her bare legs, her shirt abrading his nude chest.

"I didn't mean to wake you." She pulled her hand from the glass and rested it on the hands folded across her stomach.

"You didn't. It was the empty space you left that did." He propped his chin on the top of her head. It made no sense, but she could feel that he was going to smile. "What do you have on?"

"Your shirt."

"That's what I thought. Believe me, it does things for you it never did for me."

She answered his smile. "Yeah?"

"Yeah."

Both lapsed into a natural quietness.

"What are you doing down here staring out the window?" he asked at last.

"Watching the rain." She sighed heavily. "It makes me feel sad. And guilty."

Gard's forehead wrinkled in incomprehension. "Sad I can understand. But why guilty?"

Season said nothing for so long that he thought she wasn't going to answer him. "When I was growing up we lived in a small, run-down, white-frame house that was forever in need of repairs. My father was always going to get around to them, but somehow he never did. But then, it's hard to get around to anything when you're drunk most of the time."

She paused and Gard heard the bitterness in her silence. He wisely chose to say nothing.

"The summer I was twelve, a friend from school invited me to spend the night with her. It was the first time I'd ever stayed over with anyone. I remember now thinking that Jennie Treen's bedroom was the prettiest thing I'd ever seen. Looking back, it wasn't all that grand, but compared to mine, it was. When I went home it was all I talked about. That, and could I do this and could I do that to my own room."

She laughed softly, a bittersweet sound. "God bless Momma. I don't know where she found the material, but she made me a bedspread for my twin-size bed out of a blue and pink print. She even put a ruffle around it. And made a pillow sham," she added hastily as if the memory had just come back to her. "She also made a covering for the apple crate that I used as a stool in front of the vanity mirror. A bed, a small vanity with a cracked mirror, an apple crate, and a chest of drawers that not even the Salvation Army would have taken—that was my little world, and God, was I proud of the new look.''

Gard held her tighter, instinctively knowing the worst was yet to come. Still, he said nothing.

''My room had one window that always leaked when it rained. Since my bed was flush under the window, more often than not it got wet on the corner. Three days after Momma finished my 'new room,' it rained, and I asked my father if he'd fix the leak. He was drunk as usual and said he didn't have time. I told him he never had time. He told me that I was like my mother, always nagging. I told him he was always drunk.'' She hesitated only slightly. ''He slapped me, told me to go to my room and shut up.''

The muscles in Gard's arms tightened until they were like bands of steel. Season laid her head back against his shoulder and took a deep, cleansing breath. She raked her fingers through a strand of hair that had fallen too far forward.

''I did as I was told,'' she went on, ''and as I watched the rain spill onto my beautiful new bedspread, I wished he were dead.'' She said it so emotionlessly that Gard knew every emotion she had was involved. ''He died less than three months later, and the day we buried him, it rained. For a long time, I thought I caused his death. For a long time, rain reminded me of what a terrible thing I'd done.''

Neither spoke, she having said it all, he not quite knowing what to say. Slowly, Gard turned her in his arms. ''Surely you know you weren't to blame?''

''Of course I do, but even now when it rains I'm sometimes that twelve-year-old girl.''

Placing his finger under her chin, he tilted her head and brought his lips to hers. It was the only solace he could offer, the only comfort he could give. ''I'm sorry,'' he whispered against her lips. ''So sorry.''

Her own lips answered his kiss. "I didn't mean to make us sad," she said with a sudden attempt to break the somber mood. "Let's not be sad. Not tonight."

"What shall we be then?" he asked, his hands moving under his shirt to cup her rounded bottom.

"Let's just be together," she said on a soft sigh.

Chapter 8

GARD LED SEASON FROM THE WINDOW TO THE SOFA. There, he lowered her onto the inviting softness, his body following and blanketing hers. The starch of his freshly laundered jeans scratched the skin of her thighs as he insinuated one leg between hers.

"You're so very pretty," he murmured softly, nuzzling his face into the already gaping neck of the pleated dress shirt she wore. He pressed a moist kiss to her collarbone.

"Momma always said, 'pretty is as pretty does,'" Season quoted softly, a smile radiating from her eyes as well as curving her lips. As she spoke, she threaded her fingers through his dark hair.

Gard raised his head, his own lips arcing slowly, sexily. "I thought you did pretty well."

She giggled and drew his head down until their lips met in a gentle kiss. His mouth slanted against hers, warm and open, taking light nibbles and delicate sips of the sweetness she offered, asking for a response she was helpless to withhold.

She wouldn't have denied him if she could, Season thought. This man reached out to her in some mysterious way, seeking emotions she didn't even know were bottled up inside her, and finding them. He had taken away her fear after the accident with mere kisses, had filled her instead with a pagan yearning that sought and gained release in the most elemental of acts between the sexes. He had given her, for a few brief hours at least, a sense of fulfillment, a sense of worth, a sense of accomplishment. She knew she pleased him. Greatly. She could never remember feeling the total sense of peace within herself that she had in the few hours since she and Gard had first made love. The thought of his going back to Beth, even as only her companion and escort, was unbearable, unendurable . . . but reality.

"What's the matter?" he murmured gruffly, feeling that he'd lost her attention.

"Nothing."

Gard propped an elbow beside her head, his other hand lightly grasping her chin. A long index finger stroked the downward, frowning outline of her mouth. "Oh, Season, what am I going to do with you? You defeat me at every turn. You bait me, tease me, taunt me, even ridicule me, and still I can't stay away from you. You just told me you wanted us to be together, and now you're drawing away from me. Why?"

She said nothing. She couldn't tell him how she felt, for she had no way of knowing what their lovemaking had meant to him. Though he was hers for the moment, she knew that the moment, along with the last few hours, were stolen. Whatever his degree of involvement with Beth, it was still an involvement, an involvement she wanted no part of. She had shared Clay, and she'd promised never to share again.

At her lack of response, a sad smile crossed his mouth. "Do you want me to take you home?"

Did she? Did she want this brief and beautiful moment of her life to end? When, if ever, would there be another? If

Gard took her home, he would go back to Beth, and that would hurt. But having him take her home now would hurt, too. It would hurt not to be in his arms as long as she could. She looked up at the man whose face held a strange combination of pain, vulnerability, and the merest trace of anger. One slender, scarlet-tipped nail reached up, brushed the edge of his mustache, and traced the shape of his mouth. "No," she said, temporarily disregarding her promise to herself not to share, "I don't want to go home." She smiled softly. "I want you to love me again."

Gard's eyes dropped shut momentarily. She'd done it again. She had disarmed him with a single smile and a few well-chosen words. Without bothering to analyze why, he knew that Season Ashford was a dangerous woman. He opened his eyes to look down at her. The ebony mass of her hair sprawled untidily over the beige sofa cushion and spilled onto the floor. The pristine whiteness of his shirt and the creamy whiteness of the strand of pearls she still wore were a direct contrast to the copper of her silken skin. The light filtering through the windowpane gilded the slant of her high cheekbones. Shadows collected in pools at the hollow of her throat and the valley between her breasts.

Gard's gaze wandered lower and noted with satisfaction that the shirt had ridden up to expose a generous portion of her hip. His hand slid up her thigh in a light caress. His eyes met hers with a message as old as time, as potent as an aphrodisiac, as bold as a siren's song, yet somehow as subtle as a lover's smile.

She moistened her lips with a nervous flick of her pink tongue in anticipation of the kiss she knew was coming.

He shifted his weight until his body lay fully on hers, pressing her deeper into the cushions. She could feel how the masculine contour of him fit snugly against her. Their eyes still clung together.

"Am I too heavy?"

Season shook her head. "Make love to me, Gard."

His mouth hungrily fused with hers while his hands

fumbled for and found the buttons of the shirt she wore. The fastenings undone, he stripped the shirt aside and lowered his chest to her bare breasts, all the while delivering random kisses to her neck and shoulders. When his mouth accidentally grazed the bandage, he raised his head. The area around the protective pad was darkening to a sullen purple in a bruise that looked painful even to his untrained eye.

"No," she protested when his mouth stopped.

"Your shoulder . . . I don't want to hurt you."

"It isn't hurting," she whispered as her hands crept up to cradle his face. "I need you."

Without a word, he rose from the sofa. He unsnapped his jeans and was out of them in no time, lowering his naked body back down to cover hers. His hand splayed across the flatness of her belly. He wondered suddenly if she'd ever been pregnant with Clay's child. How would she look pregnant? How would she look pregnant with his child? Would she even want to have it? Lynn hadn't. Not his, anyway. She hadn't wanted to have the child of a man who might be killed in the line of duty at any moment. A painful memory strayed into Gard's mind, a memory of Lynn heavy with her new husband's baby.

"Gard . . ." Season's voice was a sweet entreaty to leave the memories of the past and concentrate on the present.

Responding to Season's gentle overture, he lowered his face to nuzzle her breasts, kissing their firm undersides, tickling sensitized tips with a flick of his tongue, then taking them into his mouth and drawing on them in a gentle suckling.

Season's breath caught in her throat as her hands held his head. "Please . . ." she whispered, begging him to complete the exquisite torture he was performing.

"Not yet," she heard his voice rumble. "I don't want either of us to ever forget this night."

He kissed her again. Softly, languidly, as if they had all

the time in the world. He didn't hurry as he caressed and petted, kissed and nibbled every delectable inch of her body. Eons, or perhaps seconds later—Season couldn't be certain—she felt him slide into the velvet warmth of her. Fully sheathed, he stopped and kissed her again, whispering, "Look at me, Season. I want to see your face while we make love."

Her eyes opened obediently to find his blue gaze. It was strangely tender. Neither spoke, and after a few seconds Gard began a slow, stroking rhythm that became, after a while, imperceptibly faster. He watched her, marveling at the emotions chasing across her face and the depth of her desire as her eyes widened and darkened to deepest, unfathomable black. Her passion, pure and unrestrained, drove him nearer, nearer to the brink of release. As the crescendo of emotion strained ever upward, ever higher, a sob was torn from her throat and it was echoed by Gard's rough voice.

"Dammit, Season! Damn you . . ." he groaned as they both fell into the dark void of desire.

Afterward he was unable to justify his choice of words at the moment his body had found release in hers. He knew that he wasn't ready to delve into the condemning words or their meaning. He wasn't ready to face the fact that Season Ashford was subtly changing the even tenor of his life. And that that fact scared him.

Season, boneless beneath him, pressed her mouth almost absently against his neck. She sighed, a sigh of repletion, a sigh of satiation, a sigh of weariness. In more than one way, this night had been packed to the brim with emotions of extreme highs and lows. Her mind was suddenly at ease, her body relaxed and ready for sleep.

"I'm sleepy," she murmured as her breath stirred the hair on his chest.

"You're out of character," Gard chuckled, warmly stroking a finger over her rib cage in lazy circles.

"What are you talking about?"

"That's the classic male statement after making love."

"Oh. Well, I am," she said with a smile.

"That's four . . . or is it five?"

She frowned. "Four or five what?"

"Smiles. You've been smiling so often I'm losing count. Could it be the company you're keeping?"

"Could be," she quipped.

He grinned as he rose and pulled her to her feet, snuggling her against his side.

"What are you doing?" she asked, falling into step beside him.

"Taking you to bed."

"Good." Season stifled a yawn that threatened to split her features.

When they reached Gard's room, he opened the French doors that led out onto the balcony.

"Won't it rain in?" she asked, climbing onto the rumpled bed.

"It's coming down straight. Besides, I want to give you a new memory of the rain . . . a good one." He stretched out beside her and pulled her over onto his chest, wrapping his arms loosely about her shoulders. Her breasts nestled in the hair of his chest, and she bent one slender leg up at the knee to lay familiarly across his.

A moist breeze danced through the room, carrying the scent of the wet earth and springtime flowers. Season drew the fragrance into her lungs slowly, savoring the moment. She clung more tightly to Gard and sighed contentedly as one of his hands covered her breast. It swelled in spite of her fatigue. "Sleep, Kincannon," she reminded.

"Nag, nag," he grumbled.

She felt him press a kiss to the top of her head and heard the soft pitter-pat of the raindrops that fell to shatter themselves against the still thirsty soil and puddled pavement. She knew then that he had succeeded. She would always remember this night. And from this time forward, rain would be synonymous with peace and contentment. "You did it," she said out loud.

"Did what?" When she didn't answer, he asked, "Season?"

The sound of her even breathing told Gard that she was asleep. He would have to wait until morning to ask her what she meant.

It was barely light when Season's eyes drifted open. She stretched, arching her back like a feline. She didn't know what had caused her to awaken, but her first thought was of Gard. As she rolled over, the sheet twisted around her. His side of the bed was empty. A movement out of the corner of her eye drew her gaze toward the foot of the bed, where he sat fully dressed in jeans and a knit shirt that exactly matched the blue of his eyes.

"Looking for something?" he asked, a slow smile tilting the corners of his mustache upward.

"You." Her eyes scanned him hungrily. He was so irresistibly masculine, and she knew every muscle that filled out the tight jeans and shirt.

"I made a terrible error in judgment last night, Season," he said in a suddenly serious tone.

"Oh?"

"I think I said that you were very pretty. That was a gross understatement. I've been awake for the past half hour just watching you sleep, and I think you are the most extraordinarily beautiful woman I've ever seen."

"Am I?" she asked, suddenly wondering if she would ever hear him say those words again. She wouldn't if she followed her no-share policy. But, remembering the night they'd just spent together, a night that had transcended the physical and embraced soulful emotions, wasn't it possible that he might leave Beth? As a woman, she had to believe in the possibility.

"Hey," he said, walking around the bed. "Why so solemn? I just said you were beautiful."

Season forced a smile to her lips. "My shoulder is hurting a little," she lied.

"Come here," he commanded, reaching down to help her to her feet.

Season tossed her hair back over her shoulder and stood very still while Gard examined her bared shoulder. She watched as his tanned fingers gently peeled the tape free and lifted the gauze pad. She watched, and remembered how gently they had stroked her cheek and traced the curve of her mouth.

"The abrasion looks pretty good," he said after a brief but careful scrutiny of the injury, "but the bruise is a real sweetheart."

Sweetheart. How she would love for him to call her that.

As he replaced the tape, she glanced up at him. His eyes met hers. He drew the shirtfront together, his fists holding it closed against the swell of her breasts. He saw the question in her dark eyes, a question he couldn't answer. He didn't know where they were going from here. His own emotions were as shaky as a condemned building; he felt as if he might fall apart at any moment. Too much had happened. Much, much more than he had intended. At first he'd wanted only to break through Season's veneer of coldness to see what lay beneath the hard, glossy exterior. Well, he had. And now he knew. Season Ashford was a woman who had overcome adversity, but she hadn't done it without acquiring a few scars along the way. She was a paradox of chic sophistication and fearful vulnerability, a blend of coolness and warmth, that reached out to him in a hundred different ways.

Season leaned against him and felt Gard's arms close around her. She wished she could ask if she'd see him again, but years of feminine tradition and pride kept her silent. Instead, she wrapped her arms tightly around his waist and buried her face against his chest. He smelled of soap and a musky, masculine cologne. Unable to explain why, she felt the prickling of tears beneath her eyelids. Cool, reserved Season Ashford felt like crying. "Gard . . ."

Gard, a captive of his own unstable emotions, dipped his head and brushed her mouth lightly with his. He could find no words of hope or comfort within himself to offer her. "Have a heart, Pocahontas. A man can only take so much, and I need to get you back."

Season searched his face and found tenderness in his sapphire gaze. Contenting herself with that look, she pulled away from him. If nothing else, she had last night. And its warm memory. "Yes," she said, moving toward the bathroom. "I'll get dressed."

It was seven-thirty when Gard slammed the front door of his sister's house.

"Gard?" Beth called from the vicinity of the kitchen. "Is that you?"

Gard, whose foot was on the bottom step, turned at the sound of her voice and called back, "Yeah, it's me."

He sighed and tucked in the back of his shirt in a gesture of irritability and unease. Why did he feel like a teenager who was about to be called on the carpet for coming in past his curfew? He was a grown man, for God's sake!

Beth looked at her brother carefully and thought that perhaps his night had been even less restful than hers. After Gard had covered Season's departure from the art show with the lie of sudden illness, everyone had settled down to enjoy the remainder of the evening, though many expressed their regrets that she had become ill after working so hard to make the show a success.

Elizabeth had been too keyed up to sleep after she and Rick had reached her house. They were both worried about Season's condition. Though no one had actually said as much, deep in her heart Beth knew that Season had suffered because she had been mistaken for her.

Both she and Rick were acutely aware that they hadn't heard from Gard; both knew that he had not brought Season home all night, yet neither would cross the line of good taste to broach the subject. Besides, their minds were already too weary with unanswered questions about the accident. Beth's shrewd assessment did not miss the stubborn set of her brother's chin or the belligerence in his eyes. She knew the man who stood before her as well as anyone, perhaps even better than he knew himself. She was no fool. She'd seen the way he looked out the window toward Season Ashford's house a dozen or more times a day. And looking at him now, she saw many things—guilt, an almost haunting loneliness, and defiance. She knew that he had spent the night with Season, and that the night hadn't been spent solely comforting her, but Beth hadn't been a politician's wife for sixteen years without learning a little about tact and diplomacy.

"Is Season all right?" she asked finally.

"Yeah. She's fine. I just dropped her off," he said, absently running his hand through his hair. His eyes begged his sister not to ask questions.

"Good," Beth replied. "You look exhausted. How about some breakfast?"

Gard smiled. "Thanks, I'd like that."

The sight of his partner, apron tied around his waist, expertly tossing pancakes into the air, coupled with the succulent smell of crisply fried bacon, dispelled thoughts of the night before. After eating a tower of the golden cakes, dripping maple syrup and oozing butter, Gard settled back to enjoy his third cup of coffee.

No longer able to hold back the question, Beth asked, "That accident was supposed to happen to me, wasn't it?"

Gard's head swung around sharply toward her. "What makes you think that?"

"Come on, Gard. Who would want to run down Season Ashford? No one. Level with me. I'm a big girl and I need to know."

Gard heard the brave words but also noted the quaver in his sister's voice and saw the fear lurking in her eyes. He looked askance at Rick. His partner's steady gaze was answer enough: They owed her the truth. Gard knew he was right, though all his brotherly instincts told him to protect her in whatever way he could. This last episode had been for real. The maniac was no longer playing games with words cut out from magazines and phone threats. The threats were now reality, ugly reality. Before, Beth had doubted the possibility that anyone could really mean to harm her. Now that doubt had been transposed from the realm of possibility to probability . . . and the only questions that remained were when and in what manner. Beth's life might very possibly hang on the fact that she knew this was no game.

"Gard?"

He sighed, the sound ripping harshly from his lungs into the silence of the kitchen. "Okay, sis, I'll level with you. You're right. I believe that whoever ran down Season thought she was you. You're about the same height and you both wore black dresses that were very similar in style. Your hair is short, but Season's was up on her head, very probably giving the same appearance. It was dark and beginning to rain, and it seems to me that the driver made a natural mistake."

"I agree," Rick said.

The room fell silent as Beth confronted the news she'd suspected and feared. Surprisingly, her appearance was one of calmness, as if she now knew the worst and felt stronger for it. "So where do we go from here?" she asked at last as she rose to warm her cold coffee.

"We try to trace the car," Gard replied. "I got a pretty good look at the make and color, plus two letters of the license plate.'' His eyes held a question as he glanced at Rick.

"Nothing yet," the other man answered. "We haven't traced anything yet."

At the negative response, Gard suggested to them, "There's always the possibility that it was a rental car, or one stolen just for this purpose." He sighed, turning his attention back to his sister. "It's hard to make a decent speculation, Beth, because we have no idea who we're dealing with."

"I understand."

"All we can do is take it a step at a time, Mrs. Galbraith," Rick told her, "and keep you as protected as we can."

A slight hesitation presaged her next words. "Gard . . .''

"Yes?"

"Is Season really all right?"

"She's fine. Her shoulder will be sore for a few days, but it's just a bad graze and a worse bruise. She was lucky."

"Yes, she was. I'm so sorry it had to happen to her."

At the look of guilt on the woman's face, Rick spoke up. "Now don't go blaming yourself. It isn't your fault."

"No, I guess not, but I'm still sorry it happened."

"We all are, Beth," Gard assured her, "but it's over, and she wasn't seriously hurt. The best thing for us to do is put last night behind us and go on from here." Even as he spoke the words, Gard thought that they were probably as appropriate for him as they were for Beth. He should forget the night he'd spent with Season. Forget the way she rubbed against him like a lost kitten . . . forget . . .

"Hey, Kincannon, wake up!" Rick growled. "I'm trying to talk to you."

"Sorry." Gard met his friend's knowing eyes. Riccitello was sharp. And so was Beth. A second-grader could figure out that he hadn't brought Season home the night before, so there was no hiding the fact from these two. As for their speculation as to what happened throughout the night, it would have to remain just that—speculation. But somehow Gard knew they would have that all figured out, too. "What did you say?" he asked.

"I asked your sister about her schedule for the week. There's the debate Monday night on Channel Two with her opponent, the EPA speech for the Business and Professional Women Tuesday noon, and the fund-raiser on Thursday night. That doesn't count shopping, the hairdresser, and any impromptu gathering she might be asked to attend. We need to work out a schedule that will work for both of us."

"You take what's convenient for you, Rick," Gard offered. "It doesn't matter to me."

"Okay. Sally and I have a date tomorrow night, so I'll let you drive her to the television station. Is that all right with you, Mrs. Galbraith?"

"Sure," Beth agreed.

"I'll also take the EPA thing Tuesday," Gard reasoned. He frowned suddenly. "What in hell is that?"

"You're so unpolitical," Beth chastised gently. "Haven't you ever heard of the Environmental Protection Agency?"

"Oh, yeah. But that's a national organization. What's that got to do with you?"

"Victor introduced a bill into the state senate for even tighter control of pollution in the state. He was particularly interested in chemical waste. There was quite a bit of flack when it was voted in, and a lot of businesses didn't like the more stringent controls it called for. I'll be speaking to a group of local businesswomen who don't have much to do with that type of business, but have a great interest in preserving the natural resources of the state. Oklahoma has some big factories, and Victor didn't want, and neither do I, to have any areas pop up here as they have in other parts of the country where people are exposed to chemical pollutants that do harm over a period of years."

"Good Lord! I didn't expect the whole speech, sis!" Gard groaned.

Beth smiled sweetly. "If you didn't want to know, you shouldn't have asked."

"It sounds like needed legislation," Rick chimed in. "But I can see how big business might fight it."

"Yeah," Gard agreed, "I can see why the big boys holler when it hits them in the old pocketbook."

"Surprisingly, it isn't the big companies that holler," Beth explained. "Oh, they do, but not as much as you might think. It's the little ones that it really hurts. There were more than a dozen that closed down throughout the state, some even here in Tulsa, because they didn't have the capital to revamp their waste-disposal systems. It's sad, but we have to take a stand at some point on this. At least Victor thought we did . . . and I'd like to continue to champion his cause."

Gard could see Beth's eyes mist over at the mention of her late husband. "So okay," he said, changing the subject, "I'll also volunteer for the fund-raiser Thursday—provided you take the hairdresser and the shopping." This he said to Rick.

Rick glared at Gard, who was now smiling broadly and triumphantly. "Okay, Kincannon. I can handle a little shopping."

Gard rose and stretched, arching his back and yawning mightily. He tucked his shirt in with an automatic gesture. "Good. Just think of it as another free night to take out . . . Sophie, wasn't it?"

"Sally," Rick corrected.

"Close," Gard said with a shrug, adding, "I think I'm going upstairs for a nap. Last night was a little rough." Even as the words left his mouth, he knew they were the wrong ones.

Rick's face broke into a grin. "Yeah. I'll bet."

Without giving his friend the satisfaction of a reply, Gard left the room.

Gard suddenly raised himself up from his stretched-out position on the bed, jabbed the pillow with his fist, and lay back down. The precious sleep he wanted was playing hard to get, and he was left with haunting memories of the night he'd just spent with Season. His mind overflowed with thoughts of the feel of her against him, the satiny softness of her flesh beneath his fingertips, the way her mouth opened to receive his kisses. He groaned in an agony of frustration and rolled to his side. He'd never intended for it to turn out like this—never intended for it to reach this level. He was in grave danger of falling in love with Season Ashford, if he hadn't already.

Fool! he chided himself. *Falling in love isn't in the blueprint of your life. It didn't work with Lynn, and it won't work this time. The career you've chosen simply will not mesh with having a wife and family. Lynn proved that, and Riccitello only reinforced it. Hell, look at Grady Harper. Wasn't his twelve-year-old in therapy because he couldn't handle it when Grady got all shot up a few months back? There is no room for a serious relationship in your life. No room for a wife. No room for a woman, period. She'd only get hurt or wind up hating you like Lynn did.* No, he corrected himself, Lynn didn't hate him. She'd just stopped loving him. And that had hurt. Hurt so much that he didn't think he could survive that sort of rejection again.

Gard rolled to his back once more. He gave a long, weary sigh. *So leave Season Ashford alone, Kincannon. Let it lay before you get in so deep you can't get out. It was nice while it lasted, but put an end to it now. Right now.*

Season waited all day for Gard to call. She knew it was stupid and went against everything she told herself was best for her, but still, after the night they'd shared, she'd expected him to get in touch. She knew he was still at

Beth's. At least his car was still parked in front of the house. Noon came and went, the afternoon shadows lengthened, and the day grew old with still no word from the house next door. Season paced the empty rooms of her own house—back and forth from the kitchen, where she could see the Galbraith yard, then to the front, where she pulled back the drapes to peer out at the driveway next door.

Gard's car hadn't been moved all day. No one stirred from the house except Rick Riccitello, the friend of Beth's who was working on her campaign. No one even came outside to wave him off.

She couldn't eat, she couldn't rest. Every time she shut her eyes, an image of Gard flashed onto the darkened screen of her mind. Gard, bare-chested, the Levi's riding low on his hips, pressing her down into the softness of the sofa. Gard, passion chiseled in every line of his handsome face, as he unbuttoned the white dress shirt and pulled it from the dark pants of his tux. Gard, holding her as if she were a precious heirloom, telling her she was beautiful, special, calling her sweetheart. Gard laughing, Gard teasing, Gard serious, Gard . . .

Tears stung her eyes. God, what bittersweet memories he'd left her with!

Nighttime came, and Season found herself at the pool, sitting at the edge and dangling her feet in the water. Moonlight lay in molten slabs of gold on the mirrorlike surface of the water, and crickets and tree frogs sang soothing spring ballads. She sat there for a long time before facing the fact that he wasn't going to call. She'd been a fool to ever think he was. At ten minutes past midnight, more than an hour after the lights in the Galbraith house had gone out, she went inside. Not to sleep, but to cry disappointed tears. Damn him! she thought. He hadn't even given her the opportunity to tell him she didn't want to get involved.

Monday found her at the salon. She spent a hellish day—the books wouldn't balance, all the girls were slow,

Lisa had messed up the scheduling for the following afternoon and had forgotten to order their pickiest client's favorite perm, which didn't do much for said client's frame of mind either. All in all, it was the kind of day she'd like to forget.

"Look, Season, why don't you go home?" Lisa proposed early in the afternoon. "You're obviously upset, and I really can handle things here."

"So now I'm not needed in my own salon, right, Lisa?" Season snapped. At the stricken look on the younger woman's face, Season's irritability faded. "Look," she said, putting her hand on Lisa's shoulder, "I'm sorry. I'm in a lousy mood and I'm taking it out on you."

Lisa was silent.

Season attempted a laugh that fell far short of mirth. "I think I will go home." She pressed her fingertips to her throbbing temples.

"Season, why don't you—you know—go out and try to find a man to get involved with—not seriously, but you do stay in too much. The only man you see is Jim, and I know there's nothing there for you."

Season smiled at Lisa's concern. She wondered what her salon manager would say if she knew about Gard. "Thanks, Lisa, but I'm not ready for another man just yet."

"Okay, boss lady," the other woman said with a smile, "but you look like the wrath of God. Go home and try to get some rest, huh?"

And Season truly tried, but when sleep eluded her, she put on shorts and wandered out into her front yard to pull weeds from the azalea bushes. The air was pleasantly pure and crystalline, though there was already a hint of the dryness that would quickly fade to a hot sultriness as the summer made its appearance. The now warm sun would heat up more and more until it would blaze with an almost demonic fervor.

She was on her hands and knees on the sidewalk when a movement from the Galbraith house caught her eye. The garage door was gliding upward. Beth's yellow Cadillac backed out and swung onto the circular drive. Beth herself came out the front door as the car halted. The driver's door opened, and Gard got out and walked to meet the woman without so much as a glance in the direction of Season's house.

Her heart lurched at the sight of him in gray dress slacks and a short-sleeve shirt in a gray, lavender, and pale yellow plaid. She saw Beth smile and saw him put an arm around her shoulders as they walked down the cement drive. He opened the car door for her. When he straightened, he looked across the yellow vinyl top of the car—directly at Season. Their eyes met and clung. Season's heart stopped, then beat in heavy staccato beats that reverberated throughout her entire body. Her mouth felt dry, and before she could stop the action or even think of what she was doing, her hand lifted in a casual wave. Gard's eyes still pinned hers, but he made no move to reciprocate. With a deliberateness that was apparent to Season, even from the distance of the two yards, he slammed the door shut and rounded the hood of the car. He never looked her way again as he lowered his body into the driver's seat and closed the door.

A numbness crept over Season. She watched as the car rolled on down the drive and pulled onto the street. With movements as stiff and jerky as those of an old woman, she pushed herself to her feet and walked into the house. Her mind reeled at the scene that had just been played out in her yard. Gard had seen her. He had! And he had ignored her with a deliberateness that even the most dense person couldn't fail to recognize. He had looked at her as if she hadn't been there. He had ignored her as she had tried to do him, but hadn't been able to.

Strangely, she felt no irritation, no anger, only an all-consuming numbness that held the pain and shame at bay. She went into the kitchen and made a pot of coffee. It was going to be a long night. She hoped the torpid feeling would last forever, but deep in her wounded heart she knew she would never be that lucky.

Chapter 9

ON TUESDAY MORNING THE *TULSA WORLD* STATED THAT Elizabeth Galbraith would speak at the Business and Professional Women's noon luncheon and that her topic would be environmental control legislation. KJRH and KOTV, channels Two and Six respectively, covered the event, and ran selective excerpts from her speech on the six o'clock news. The *Tulsa Tribune* splashed it across page three of the evening paper under the heading WIFE CONTINUES CLEAN LEGACY, and for those Tulsa citizens who missed all this, the ten o'clock news repeated it. It was the kind of publicity that makes vote-seeking politicians happy and their campaign managers ecstatic.

By 10:40 the evening news lay forgotten, and both Beth and Gard had retired to their bedrooms. Beth had fallen into an instant sleep, while Gard, his hands folded beneath his head, stared toward the ceiling with the intention of staying awake as long as possible. Every time he closed his eyes, every time sleep threatened to overcome him, he saw Season's face as it had been the afternoon before. It was always the same. Her eyes brightened at the sight of him, only to grow dull with pain when he purposefully did not return her wave. Keeping his hand still at his side had taken every ounce of strength he had, a strength he hadn't known he possessed.

He groaned softly, the sound filling the silence like the cry of a wounded animal. He had been right to do what he had, he thought. He was no good for her. He had nothing to offer her. It was better to hurt her a little now than a lot later. Rolling to his side, the sheet slipping low on his naked body, he tried to push her from his mind. He concentrated on the car lights that crawled down the street and flashed fleetingly into the bedroom's darkness. He wondered momentarily if it were the squad car making its rounds. Then, because the day had been so long and his body and mind were so tired, he drifted off into the sleep he'd tried so hard to avoid.

The car slowly made its way past the Galbraith house, pulled into the drive of a house, vacant and for sale, five doors down, backed out, and began a slow, creeping glide back up the street. At the entrance to the circular drive arcing around the Galbraith residence, it hesitated. The man at the wheel made a hasty reconnaissance of first the downstairs windows, then the upstairs. All the lights were out. The man smiled. The time was right for the next phase of his attack.

Cutting the headlights, he eased the car forward, stopping it directly in front of the doorway. He shoved the gearshift into park, swung open the car door, and reached across the seat for the potted daisies. Their soft, innocent, white petals and golden-eyed centers were a sharp contrast to the virulent note pinned to the green foil molding the pot. At the faint but pleasant fragrance wafting to him from the flowers resting in his arms, the man felt a pang of guilt. He wished he knew the name of the woman he had mistakenly run down. If he did, he'd send her flowers. He hoped she wasn't hurt. It wasn't right when innocent people were hurt. He had meant to hurt Beth Galbraith. He had meant to kill Beth Galbraith. But when he hadn't read anything in the papers or heard anything on the news, he had begun to doubt his success. Then he'd called her home and she'd answered the phone. That was when he had known he'd run down the wrong person. Guilt flooded through him again. He hoped the woman wasn't hurt. It wasn't right when innocent people were hurt.

Forcing his thoughts back to the present, he slipped from the car, allowing the door to close behind him, but not latch. With a quick and determined gait, he walked up the steps and over the portico. Bending down, he set the flowers before the door. As he straightened and turned around, the bright headlights of a passing car briefly illuminated him, then moved on. The man, his heart racing painfully, bolted down the steps and threw himself behind the wheel. Gritting the gears, he coasted out of the driveway and sped into the night. He was at the end of the block before he realized he hadn't turned on his headlights.

Season bent forward and, dividing her attention between the windshield and the tape deck, ejected the tape and turned off the unit. Though she usually found music soothing, tonight it was nothing more than an irritant. In fact, everything had made her irritable all day long, but she reasoned it was better to be irritated than to succumb to the gargantuan feeling of depression hanging over her like the sword of Damocles. She had deliberately worked late, adding last-minute call-ins to her appointment book that she would have declined normally. And then, instead of going home when her overloaded schedule had ended, she had called Jim Nighthawk and asked—no, begged was more like it—him to meet her for a drink. Though she was certain he suspected something had run afoul of her usual good

mood, he respected her privacy and said nothing . . . until
the moment he closed the car door after her and, resting an
elbow on the door, bent to look in the window.

"I doubt things are as bad as they appear tonight," Jim
said, sensitive to her mood. "Go home and sleep on them."

That was the problem. She didn't want to go home. Not
to the house next door to the one where Gard was staying
with Beth Galbraith. "I don't think sleep is going to help
this time," Season said, looking into her friend's eyes and
attempting a smile.

"It's that Kincannon guy, isn't it?" At the startled look
that flashed across her face, he added, "Come on, Season.
I'm not blind."

She sighed sadly. "Yeah, it's that Kincannon guy. I'm
discovering I'm not heavy into rejection." She tried another
smile, but it was slaughtered by the memory of how Gard
had so callously, so deliberately, avoided her. "For the first
time I know how Clay must have felt when I walked out. It
doesn't do great things for your ego."

Jim was silent for long seconds before he added, "No, it
doesn't, but we all learn to live with rejection." It was
obvious from the tone of his voice and the wistful look in
his eye that he was living with the rejection of the woman
before him.

"Jim . . ."

"Don't," he pleaded, his finger moving to silence her
lips. "Don't even say it." A smile had then stolen softly to
his mouth. "Go home and sleep on things. I promise they'll
be better tomorrow."

Okay, she thought as she turned the car left onto her
familiar street, that's what I'm doing. I'm going home to
get a good night's sleep. If possible.

The yellow Corvette sprinted past the house that had
been empty of occupants for nearly two months. The huge
wood, rock, and brick English Tudor had drawn many
lookers, but because of its exorbitant price, no buyers. She
then passed on by the other neighborhood houses. She

intended to avoid looking at the Galbraith house, but her intention fell short of its mark. For brief seconds the bright headlights of her car beamed across the front of the house, where they illuminated the figure of a man. Season thought she saw a fleeting glimpse of a flower arrangement set close to the door.

She frowned. It was an odd time to deliver flowers, but maybe the man was working late, as she had done. She probably would have given the matter more thought, may even have arrived at the conclusion that delivering flowers in the middle of the night was suspicious at best, but it suddenly occurred to her that maybe Gard was sending flowers to Beth. Maybe she hadn't appreciated the night he'd spent away from her, and the flowers were his way of apologizing. The fact that he felt the need to apologize made Season wonder if he regretted the night they'd shared.

Suddenly the thought of Gard regretting the night he had spent making love to her was almost more than Season could bear. As she pulled into her drive, she felt tears begging for release, but she refused to grant them freedom.

"No," Gard said flatly and in a voice that invited no argument.

"But, Gard, be reasonable," Beth pleaded.

"No."

"But . . ."

"You're not getting your hair done." He shoved aside the pad filled with his scrawling notes and leveled his full attention on the distraught woman before him. "Don't you remember what you found on the doorstep two hours ago?"

"Of course I remember!" Beth cried. "How could I forget?" At her waspish tone, she closed her eyes and took a steadying breath. She could never remember a time she had raised her voice to her brother. "I'm sorry. Truly sorry. I feel as if my whole nervous system is overloaded."

Gard scraped back his chair from the table and, walking to his sister, pulled her into his arms. He felt as if he was

nearing overload, too, he thought. And he didn't know
what to do about it. When he had seen her face, as pale as
the white daisies she carried and as scared as any hunted
creature, he had felt his own composure slip a notch or two.
The threatening note, handwritten and clear in its intent,
had slipped his self-control a peg or two more.

"Beth, listen to reason," he spoke softly, still holding
her close to him. "The man has already tried to run you
down, and last night he was reckless enough to risk coming
to your very doorstep. He's bordering on desperation.
There's no telling what he'll try next. There's no telling
what chances he'll take. You're going to have to cancel
everything that isn't of the most extreme importance."

Beth pulled back to stare at him, her face glowing with a
new concern. "But you said I could go to the fund-raiser
tomorrow night. Gard, I've got to go. People have already
paid money . . ."

"You can go," he interrupted. "I know you can't cancel
everything." Though, God, how he wished she would!

"Then don't you see," Beth argued, "that I have to get
my hair done? I can't go looking like this." She reached up
and tugged at one side of her brownish-black hair. "I may
raise money, but I'd sure lower appetites."

"Can't you do it yourself?" Gard proposed logically.
What was the big deal? he thought. A little water here, a
little shampoo there, and a few curlers thrown around the
head.

"You've got to be kidding," Beth replied as she drew
away from him and moved to the island in the middle of the
room. She absently poured herself a cup of coffee and just
as absently sipped it. "I've had my hair done every
Wednesday at the same salon for so many years I wouldn't
disclose the number even if I remembered it."

"That's my point," Gard said, pouring coffee into a mug
with the same absentmindedness his sister was guilty of.
"The worst thing you can do is stick to a predictable
routine."

Beth took another sip of coffee. Gard swigged a mouthful and grimaced.

Suddenly Beth turned on him. "If I went to another salon, could I get my hair done?"

Gard lowered his head in an I-don't-believe-this attitude. He gave a deep sigh. Women! Their priorities were mind-boggling. Someone wanted to kill her, and she wanted to get her hair done!

"Can I?" she pressed.

He raised his head slowly and studied the woman before him. Though fifty-four years old, she awaited his answer with childlike anticipation. How could he deny her anything she wanted? "Okay," he consented grudgingly. "But I'm going along."

Beth smiled in triumph. "I thought Rick had hairdresser duty."

"He did, but he's checking every florist and nursery in town."

Beth's smile faded, and a seriousness settled over her features. "Is it possible to catch him that way?"

"Don't get your hopes up," Gard cautioned. "He may have bought them at a grocery store or a dozen other different types of stores. With so few leads, though, we have to check everything."

When Beth smiled again, her face looked tired, her spirits weary, but there was a sincerity to the tilt of her lips. "I have faith in you, Gard." With that she turned and walked from the room, headed in the direction of the phone directory.

Gard watched until she disappeared, then he groaned deep in his soul. Dear God, maybe her faith was misplaced. He'd done little to earn it. He'd promised her he would catch whoever was threatening her life, but so far whoever it was was still doing precisely that. Gard walked toward the table and slumped down in a chair. With the hand that wasn't holding the coffee mug, he picked up a copy of the note that had been pinned to the flowers. The original was already in the police lab, and the daisies were decorating the trash can.

He read through the note again, hoping that this time the words would scream out some message he'd missed before. "You'll soon be pushing up daisies," it read. "You speak of the sin of waste, and yet you're the biggest waster of all—the waster of human life. The little people will win." Waste. Little people. Waste. Little people. It all went round and round in Gard's head. Nothing. It meant nothing. Yet there were shadowy moments when some idea started to take shape, but the thought was always short-circuited, dispersed into meaningless pieces before he could grasp it. He had to grasp it. And soon. He . . .

"I have an appointment, but we'll have to hurry," Beth announced as she strode quickly into the room. She unplugged the coffeemaker and snatched up her purse.

"That was quick," he grumbled as he tucked the red and navy plaid shirt into sleek-fitting navy slacks and checked his pocket for the car keys. "Let's take the Thunderbird," he said, moving in step behind his sister. Minutes later, as the car pulled from the subdivision and onto the main thoroughfare, he cast his eyes toward the passenger side. "Where to?"

"South Peoria," Beth replied as she freshened her lip gloss.

Gard drove for several minutes before the impact of her words hit him, but when they did, he jerked his head back in her direction, his eyes blanching to the color of ice. "South Peoria? Isn't that . . ."

"Yes," Beth confirmed, then added, "Thank heaven Season had a last-minute cancellation!"

With her one o'clock appointment under the dryer and her 1:30 not in the salon yet, Season allowed herself the biggest luxury of the day. She sat down in the chair at her station and eased her foot from one black, high-heeled shoe. She sighed as her toes reveled in their liberation.

"I think I'm in love," she heard Lisa Paden whisper in a breathless and secretive tone as she approached from behind. Season didn't bother to swivel the chair around, nor did she bother to hide a smile of amusement. That was the fourth time this week that her salon manager had announced that amorous fact, and it was only Wednesday afternoon. Early Wednesday afternoon.

"Who is it this time?" Season asked.

"You would not believe the hunk that just walked in," Lisa practically panted as she moved to stand in front of her boss, her hand splayed across her chest. "Honest, Season, I'm going to have to revise my GMB scale. This great male bod zooms right off the top. His face alone is a ten, and his tush . . . Lord, his tush is unchartable!" She gave a deep, dramatic sigh. "All I can say is this man is a f-i-n-e example of the male mammal."

Despite Season's depression, her smile broadened. "And what does this fine example of the male mammal with a tush that is unchartable want? Or did you remember to ask?"

"Oh, I don't think *he* wants anything, though I can assure you I'd give him anything he did." It never occurred to Lisa Paden to blush at her admission. "It's the woman he's with. She's your 1:30." Then, returning to a business-like pose, she added, "You had a cancellation, and I worked in a Mrs. Galbraith. Wonder if she's the one running for office?" Lisa added rhetorically, her lips pursed in sudden speculation.

Season would have felt calmer if World War III had been announced. Her chair swiveled sharply, and her eyes collided not with Beth Galbraith, who was walking toward her, but with the tall man following behind. "Gard . . ." she said, calling out his name in her surprise.

He attempted a smile that reached neither his eyes nor his lips. "Hi," he answered, thinking that right that moment he'd rather be doing five-to-ten in San Quentin than standing there. Make that five-to-ten in solitary confinement at San Quentin.

Season instantly forced her attention to Beth. "Nice to see you, Beth. I didn't know you were on the books for this afternoon." God, what was he doing here? she thought as her foot awkwardly groped for her abandoned shoe. Jamming her stockinged foot into the black leather, she stood.

"I made a frantic call," Beth explained, "and was told you'd just had a cancellation. For which I'm eternally grateful to some Tulsan."

A polite though unconscious smile found its way to Season's lips. "What can I do for you?" She deliberately made her eyes stay on the woman.

"Just a simple shampoo and set."

"Fine," Season answered. "I'll have Jeannie shampoo you." Indicating the direction Beth was to go, she noted out of the corner of her eye that Lisa Paden was taking great pleasure in showing Gard to the small waiting area situated almost directly across from her station. Lisa not only showed him where to sit, but also the magazines he could read and the coffee urn he could raid. Damn! Season thought. If any other station was vacant, she'd move to it. How could she concentrate on styling Beth's hair with Gard only feet away?

But she did manage, perhaps not well but at least competently. And she did her best to act normally. She'd die before she allowed Gard to see how very much she'd been hurt by his rejection. Once the wet lengths of Beth's hair had been coiled around plastic curlers, Season ushered her to a dryer at the back of the salon. She then busied herself with combing out her one o'clock appointment. It was only as she tried a delicate maneuver with the client's upswept style that she noticed her hands trembling slightly.

Time and again Season's eyes were drawn to the man outlined in the mirror, and time and again she forced her eyes elsewhere. The women's magazine looked more than a little incongruous in his masculine, rugged hands, and she idly wondered what he could be finding to read in the female-oriented pages. She didn't notice he was holding the magazine upside down.

He looked tired, she thought, unable to keep her gaze from his image. Strain had etched lines around his eyes she'd never noticed before. Did he regret their evening together so much it was preying on his mind? Or was it possible he regretted the way he'd avoided her afterward? No, she was certain the latter was not the case. Whatever the cause, she had the sudden urge to smooth the worry wrinkles away with her fingers and comfort him with her soft words. Instead she threaded her fingers through her client's hair and made some inane comment she wasn't even sure was an appropriate response to what the woman had just said.

She looked tired, he thought, his eyes peeking above the edge of the magazine. And there was a black weariness in her even blacker eyes he'd never seen before. She was trying so hard to act normally, and that fact slashed at his gut. He knew she would go miles out of her way not to show her emotions, but he could see them on her beautiful but drawn face. He had hurt her. Dammit to hell, he'd hurt her! Why did someone always seem destined to get hurt in any relationship? He was hurting. Why wasn't that enough to appease the selfish gods? Why must she hurt, too? But if he did what he wanted to—cross the distance to her, take her in his arms, and kiss her until they were both senseless —he'd only be hurting her worse. He had nothing permanent to offer her. He lowered his eyes to the picture of a woman wearing the swimwear predicted to be the fashion rage for the coming summer. The woman stood on her head, while her feet towered upward.

With a restless motion, Gard tossed the magazine aside as Season sprayed the woman's finished hairdo. His brooding gaze followed her every move. This was stupid! They had to say something to each other!

After a friendly good-bye, the woman moved away.

Season busied her hands by performing an unnecessary, nervous shifting of articles on the counter of her station. Once her eyes met his in the mirror, but looked quickly away as if fleeing a pursuer.

"This is ridiculous," he said, speaking to her from across the short distance.

She turned at the sound of his voice. "What's ridiculous?"

"Don't you think we ought to speak? After all, we do live in the same world."

Suddenly her good intentions fled and her resolve to conceal her hurt followed close behind. "I wasn't sure you were aware of that—that we lived in the same world, that is." Her voice was cold, sarcastic, and laced with the anger of wounded pride.

He said nothing. He just watched her for long, uncomfortable seconds. His face looked as if some sort of battle were being waged inside him. "Season, believe me," he said at last, his voice low and thick with his own pain, "it's best this way."

"I'm not accustomed to making love with a man three times in one night then having him refuse to make the civil gesture of returning my wave two days later." She deliberately focused on the wave, making it sound as though his impolite behavior was the source of her anger, but she knew she was lying to herself and him. She was upset because he had brushed her off as if she'd never existed. She was upset because he had tactlessly pranced into her salon with Beth on his arm, in essence telling her, Season, that he had no intention of altering his relationship with Beth, to forget Saturday night had ever happened.

"Forget that night, Season," Gard said, giving voice to her thoughts. "It never should have happened. You said yourself an affair would be messy."

Her chin lifted to a prideful angle. "You're right. That night never should have happened, and you can bet every dime in your bank account that I'm going to forget it. In fact, it's already forgotten. And you can take your messy affair and go straight to hell!'' She turned away, intent on moving to the back of the salon, where Beth was still under the dryer.

She'd barely taken two steps when harsh fingers tightened around her upper arm and swung her around. His eyes immediately captured hers and held them. He opened his mouth to speak, then closed it, the words still trapped inside. Gard felt his quickly flaring anger seeping away to be replaced by the overpowering need to just hold her—and be held by her. Season felt her anger dissolving into the familiar pain of his rejection.

Her eyes moved from his to the fingers still gripping her arm, then slowly back to his eyes. ''You're hurting me,'' she said at last. Her voice was low and devoid of emotion. Both knew the words went beyond the hand manacling her arm.

Slowly, he uncoiled his fingers. ''I'm sorry,'' he said. Both knew those words also had a deeper meaning. Then, without another word, she turned from him and walked away.

As Season put the final touches to Beth's hair, the latter spoke. ''I don't know when it's looked better. And thank you so much for finding the time.''

A genuine smile curved Season's lips. She liked Beth Galbraith, despite this ungodly triangle. ''You're welcome. It was my pleasure.''

A sudden light shone in the older woman's gray eyes. ''Do you have plans for Friday evening?''

''What?'' Season returned, a bit startled by the question. Her mind had been wandering again to Gard, who was now standing, both hands shoved into his pockets, a look of impatience scoring his features. He was ready to go.

''Do you have plans for Friday evening?''

''No,'' Season said, shaking her head.

"Good. Would you come to the house for dinner? I'd like to repay your kindness."

"No!" Season hastily replied, her eyes flying to Gard. His expression was one of similar negation. "I mean," she added, trying to soften her tactless reply, "that isn't necessary. I had a cancellation. You actually did me the favor."

"Since you have no plans, I won't take no for an answer," Beth said, coming to her feet and picking up her purse. "Would seven o'clock be all right?"

"I uh . . . I . . ." Season stammered, her eyes begging Gard to come to her rescue.

"Don't you have a political commitment that evening?" he ventured, hoping to hell Beth would take the cue. From the appraising look she turned in his direction, he was certain she had gotten his message. A feeling of relief swept over him. The last thing he wanted was to spend an evening in close proximity to Season.

"Actually, the fund-raiser tomorrow night is the last thing this week," Beth said, dashing two sets of hope. "Seven o'clock," she reiterated to Season, adding, "I'll look forward to it." With that she took off toward the front of the salon, leaving both Season and Gard staring at each other. Both seemed at a loss for words.

"Why did you do that?" Gard asked moments later as he slammed the car door and turned toward his sister. His posture and voice weren't one of anger, but of undeniable irritation.

"It's called older-sister perogative."

"And exactly what does that mean?"

"I have a right to interfere in your life because I'm older and wiser. And because I love you. And besides, Season Ashford's good for you."

Gard raised hurt eyes to his sister's. "It won't work, Beth."

"Give it a chance." Then she brought up the name she had often used during the five years Gard had been married, but had seldom mentioned in the five years he'd been divorced. "She isn't Lynn."

His eyes turned a shade paler with pain. "No, she isn't, but she is a woman." He reached over, started the Thunderbird's engine, then glanced back at his sister. "And I'm a cop."

"*Pax*," Gard said. He sat across from Season in the Galbraith living room, his left ankle squared and settled on his right knee. The right hand that rested on the ankle, almost in a clutching posture, had crinkly dark hair sprinkled across its back and all along its knuckles. "Do you think we could call a truce for the remainder of the evening? Oh, nothing real friendly, just something in the civil department." He knew his voice hardly held the civility he was asking for, but the evening was getting to him. The tension was so thick it could be packaged and sold.

Season dragged her eyes from the hand resting on his ankle—God, what a beautiful hand—to his eyes. She then glanced at the doorway through which Beth had disappeared only seconds before on her way to the kitchen to get coffee and dessert. Season's eyes found Gard's once again. She shrugged. "Do you think we can handle it?"

Gard checked his leather-banded watch. "It's eight-thirty. It'll take fifteen, twenty minutes to have dessert and coffee, another ten minutes for chit-chat—you can't just eat and run—then say another five minutes or so to make a polite exit. With any luck, you could be out of here by five past nine." His eyes glued to hers, he added, "Yeah, I think we could handle it."

"Why don't I just ask Beth to sack my pie and coffee? That way, I could be out of here by eight forty-five, eight-fifty tops," Season suggested derisively. Actually, she couldn't wait to leave. It was uncomfortable sitting in the Galbraith living room pretending she and Gard had never spent the night together.

"Great idea," he answered with the same sarcasm. He

threw himself out of the chair, rammed his hands into the pockets of his camel-colored slacks, and moved to peer out the window.

Dammit! Season thought, the evening had been a first-rate disaster. One minute Gard had been surly, the next pensively quiet. One minute he faked a tolerance, the next all pretense was gone. One minute he avoided looking at her, the next he couldn't keep his eyes from her. He was moody, cheerless, and snappy. But most of all, she admitted, he was just Gard, his face and body jarringly handsome and his every move incredibly sensual. She was achingly aware of everything he did and said. So much so that she was moody, cheerless, and snappy. Beth must be as blind as a bat and as deaf as a punk-rock audience if she couldn't pick up on the vibes sparking between them.

Season looked over at Gard, who still stood before the window. His broad shoulders seemed to strain the fabric of the tan-and-white striped shirt. She sighed. He had made a peaceful overture. Shouldn't she consider it? Wouldn't it make the remainder of the evening a little easier to get through?

Gard turned just as she opened her mouth. "I'm sorry," they said simultaneously. After a hesitation, tiny smiles appeared at the corners of both mouths.

"*Pax?*" he offered again.

"*Pax,*" she repeated softly.

On the immediate heels of the cease-fire, Beth entered the room.

"Here, let me get that," Gard said, moving to take the tray from his sister.

"No, you get the coffee server on the kitchen cabinet." The woman placed the tray, laden with three slices of pecan pie, empty cups and saucers, and blue linen napkins, on the coffee table. She smiled sheepishly up at Gard. "I overestimated what I could carry."

He returned her smile with a sweet one of his own and quickly disappeared to do her bidding.

Jealousy knifed its way through Season's heart. It was so obvious Beth cared for him, and, she swallowed low in her throat, just as obvious he cared for her. Season tried to push the hurt away. The truth was she liked Beth Galbraith. The woman had been so gracious, so sincere all evening.

"I want to thank you for having me over," Season said, coaxing her lips into a smile.

"Oh, it was my pleasure," Beth returned, passing her guest a napkin.

As Season stretched for the linen cloth, she felt the tie of her halter top, riding midway on her back, slip slightly. She had worn her favorite outfit, the peach-colored deerskin skirt and halter, the latter edged with the beige-brown feathers she knew to be so flattering to her face. As usual, the soft hide refused to stay tied tightly. She'd already had to excuse herself once in order to reinforce it. Easing back into the corner of the sofa, praying the bow would hold, she accepted the pie offered her.

Gard returned, coffee was poured and passed around, and conversation, for the first time that evening, Season thought, seemed less strained and more relaxed. The truce, though shaky, seemed to be holding.

"I had so many compliments on my hair last night," Beth volunteered.

The glow of pride warmed Season's heart. "I'm glad. You look very good with your hair pulled back from your face. It's not a style everyone can wear well."

"When did you first become interested in hair?" the older woman asked, taking a delicate sip of coffee. Genuine interest shone from her eyes.

Season thought a minute. "You know, I'm not really sure. I never gave it any thought. I guess," she added, now immersed in considering the question, "from the time I was a very young girl. I remember sitting for hours at a time in front of my vanity mirror experimenting with new styles. My family was poor, and I never had a lot of new clothes, but changing my hair was a way to have a new look." The mention of her poverty was made in such a way that it didn't even hint that she might be soliciting pity. She simply mentioned it as the fact it was.

"Did your mother encourage you? I mean, with the hair thing?" It was Gard's voice, and Season transferred her eyes from Beth to him.

His eyes could be so soft and warm, she thought, when devoid of animosity, but she felt peculiarly naked sitting before them. She had told this man things about her past, her father, that she'd never shared with another living soul.

"Yes, Momma was very good about encouraging me," Season admitted. "She even let me practice on her hair." A fleeting look of pleasure skittered across Gard's face as if it delighted him to hear that the young Season had had at least one champion in her corner. Season saw it and felt warmed by his concern. She also felt confused as to why it should matter to him. She forced her eyes from him and back to Beth, who was speaking again.

"I hope it's better."

"I'm sorry." Season apologized for her distracted attention.

"Your shoulder. I hope it's better," Beth repeated. At the words, her eyes traveled to the bandage still taped conspicuously to her guest's upper arm. "I can't tell you, Season, how I regret its having happened."

Season heard the passionate ring of sincerity in the older woman's voice—and wondered at it. For one short-lived second, it almost seemed as if Beth was apologizing. Season immediately tossed the ridiculous notion aside.

"It's almost healed," Season said.

"Then Gard isn't too bad a doctor?" Beth added on a lighter note.

Season refused to look into Beth's eyes or in Gard's direction, but she could feel his eyes on her. A thousand memories came rushing at her in an avalanche. His kiss. His embrace. His mustache. His masculinity plunging deep to satisfy the primeval ache torturing her. "No," she answered breathlessly, "he isn't a bad doctor."

The phone rang, sharp, shrill, intrusive. Season was so busy being grateful for the interruption that she missed the sudden fright that leapt to Beth's eyes. Neither did she see Gard's gaze immediately fasten on his sister.

"You want to get that, Beth?" he prodded at her hesitation and the phone's insistence. It had been decided he would no longer answer the phone. They were doing everything they could to invite the man to call and to speak once he had.

With a forced nonchalance, Beth rose from the sofa and approached the ringing phone. She eased the receiver from its cradle.

"Hello?" she said tentatively. A nearly imperceptible look of relief washed over her face. "It's Fred," she indicated to Gard, her palm across the receiver, while to Season, she offered, "My campaign manager."

Season encouraged her to take the call. With her hostess no longer there to carry the conversation, Season looked at the empty dessert dishes. She looked about the room. She looked anywhere but at Gard. Finally she looked at her watch: 9:21. The armistice had been more successful than planned.

"I really must go," she announced suddenly. Still without looking at Gard, she began to stack the dishes on the tray.

"Don't bother," he said. "I'll get it."

"No bother. I'll just slip this into the kitchen." Before he could object further, Season lifted the tray and started from the room.

The kitchen was just as she'd remembered it from the one other time she'd been in it—all sunny yellow and cornflower blue. She placed the tray on the countertop by the sink. As she did so, one of the napkins piled on the tray tumbled to the floor. When Season bent to retrieve it, she felt the tie of her top give way as it had threatened to all evening. Her hand instantly rushed to hold the halter in place. "Damn!"

"What's wrong?"

She whirled to find Gard standing near, too near, with the coffee server in his hand. She watched abstractedly as he set it down. Slipping her hands behind her, she began to tie the bow. At least, she tried to tie the bow. Fingers clumsy with Gard's proximity and the embarrassment of the situation kept her from achieving her goal.

"Turn around," he commanded, accurately assessing her problem.

Season hesitated.

"Do you want the thing tied or not?"

"I can do it."

"So far you're doing a great job."

Season opened her mouth, but Gard halted her with his words. "Turn around."

Slowly she did as ordered and presented her bare back to him. Holding the halter to her body in front, she held her breath and steeled herself in anticipation of his touch. She waited for the brush of his fingers. And waited. Finally, she felt his fingers graze her naked skin—warm fingers against her warmer skin. At last, as if acting entirely against his will, his hands settled, palms down, on her back. Season's held breath escaped in a low hiss. She heard a quick rush of air from Gard's lungs as if he, too, had been holding his breath. He made no effort to retie the bow. Long, long moments passed. And then his hands began to move slightly, kneading tiny circles on her back, blazing a lazy trail up and down her spine. Season's breathing accelerated. His hands then slid to span her rib cage. She closed her eyes and fought the feelings screaming to life.

"You have the most beautiful skin," he whispered as if the words were torture for him. "Like sun-loved silk."

By now the bow was completely untied, and the ends dangled to either side, leaving her back totally exposed except for the thin strip encircling her neck. Gard's hands stirred softly, restlessly in the new freedom, slowly inching around her midriff, then forward still until they met the resistance of her fingers holding the garment so protectively to her. He stopped. Then nudged at her hands. At the slight insistence, hers eased from their sheltering pose. The garment fell away, too, leaving him to touch her where he chose. For heart-stopping moments, his hands lay splayed across her midriff, his thumbs almost, but not quite touching the undersides of her breasts.

"God, why did you have to wear this?" he asked in an agonized groan.

She said nothing. She couldn't. Her thoughts were too fragmented between wanting him to touch her and silently begging him not to. And then his hands inched upward until his thumbs skimmed the deep, full undersides of her breasts. She sighed and unconsciously laid her head back against his shoulder. At her relaxed encouragement, his hands settled over her breasts. Their roundness filled his cupped palms completely.

It crossed her mind that Beth could easily walk in and find them in this more-than-compromising stance. The thought fled at the gentle kneading of his hands.

"Oh, Season, I . . ." His words trailed off as if it was an impossibility to put his thoughts into words. His fingers gently squeezed the flesh they held. Suddenly, and with a total unexpectedness, he tore his hands away from her already responding breasts. "Go home, Season," he begged hoarsely. "Please go home."

His words blew like a frigid wind over her heated emotions. Passion receded in the wake of embarrassment. My God, would she never learn not to let this man touch her? She felt his fingers, now as clumsy as hers once had been, trying to retie the bow.

"I can do it!" she cried, wrenching herself from him and somehow managing to secure the trailing strings into a facsimile of a bow. "And I can certainly take myself home . . . which is precisely where I should have stayed!"

She headed for the kitchen door, her intention only to put distance between herself and Gard.

"Season!" he called out raggedly. "You don't understand."

She whirled, her eyes finding his. The breasts that only moments before had rested in the warmth of his hands now threatened to spill out of the halter with the angry heaving of her chest. "Oh, you bet I understand! I understand your typical male attitude. You want to have your cake and eat it, too. You want to stay with Beth, then sleep with me, then run back to Beth. Fine! Dandy! Send her flowers! Send her a whole damn shop full of flowers! But don't try feeling me up in the kitchen the minute her back is turned. I don't like playing games."

Gard's features suddenly froze at Season's mention of flowers.

"Will you send her more flowers?" Season taunted. "An apology for what just happened? What's one grope worth? Surely not a whole arrangement like before. What about a single rose? Yes, I think that's appropriate, don't you?"

The pain in her heart and the anger with which she'd chosen to mask it kept her from seeing Gard's face pale.

"Season . . ."

"I'm sure you'll convey my regrets to Beth at having to leave so suddenly," she interrupted. With that, she spun around and practically ran from the kitchen. She had covered the distance to the hallway and her hand was reaching for the knob of the front door when Gard caught up to her.

Jerking her around, he asked, "What do you know about those flowers?"

There was a look on his face, an intensity in his eyes, that confused Season. It wasn't a look of anger, despite the words she'd just spoken, but the look of some other deep emotion. Something in the way he stared at her, something in the tone of his voice, compelled her to answer. "Nothing. Except I thought you sent them to her."

"Why would you think that?"

She shrugged. "It just crossed my mind that you sent them when I saw them being delivered Tuesday night."

Gard released his hold. "You saw who put them there?" There was an entreaty in his eyes she was hard pressed to understand.

Swallowing first, she answered, "Yes and no."

"What do you mean, 'yes and no'? You either did or you didn't." His voice mirrored his growing impatience.

Season reacted to that impatience. "I did see him," she replied, her voice rising, "but I obviously didn't see him well since it was so late at night."

"For God's sake, tell me what you can," Gard pleaded. "This is important."

"I don't know, Gard. It was dark and I saw him for only a second in the car's headlights."

Gard's impatience was back. "Was he tall, short, thin, fat? Surely you remember something?"

Season had no idea why it should matter so much, but it was more than apparent that it did. "Ahh . . . about average, I'd say, maybe on the shorter side. Definitely not fat, but not really thin either . . . oh, Gard, I don't know— it was late."

"What was he wearing?"

She shook her head. "I don't know."

"What kind of car was he driving?"

She shook her head again. "I don't know." Season felt stirrings of anger at his high-handed inquisition. Why was this man so important? Then it hit her. Maybe Gard didn't send the flowers. And maybe he was jealous of whoever did.

"Damn, you make a lousy witness!" he said, dragging his fingers through his hair.

"Well, I'm sorry," she said, her voice riddled with the irritation her unsettling thoughts had triggered. "If I'd known I was going to be tested, I'd have taken notes."

At the hurt expression on her face, Gard stretched out a

hand and started to touch her cheek. Instead, he drew it back without making contact with her skin. "Go home, Season," he said wearily, almost as if he were tired of her, of Beth . . . of everything. "Just go home."

The television set in the den came to life, and Gard turned his head in the direction of the sudden noise. When he glanced back at Season, she was opening the front door.

"Tell Beth I said good night," she said.

"Yeah." She was already through the door when Gard called after her. "Season?"

She turned, her face such a mixture of emotions—pain, embarrassment, confusion, sadness—that not even Jim Nighthawk would have attempted to paint her as she stood.

"I'm sorry."

"Sure. Aren't we all, Kincannon?"

Gard closed the door to the sound of his sister's voice. "Is Season gone?"

"Yeah," he answered, opting not to tell Beth what Season had witnessed. What purpose could it serve? He had learned nothing. Or very little. It would only upset Beth all over again.

"Interesting evening," Beth prompted, aware of the undercurrents but not discouraged by them.

"Yeah, interesting." *Especially if you like combat*, he added to himself. He looped his arm about her shoulders and headed them toward the den and the noisy television.

"Fred called to tell me that Channel Two is running footage on the environmental speech I gave Tuesday." Beth looked up at her brother coyly. "Want to hear it again?" At almost that precise moment, Beth's cultured voice came from the television. "There I am now," she said, pointing toward the twenty-one-inch colored screen.

"The Environmental Protection Agency," the voice on the television said, "is asking that penalties be raised to $10,000 a day against companies violating federal permits limiting waste discharge into the Arkansas River. That," the Beth Galbraith of the television set explained to her audience, "is powerful incentive for the companies in our area, large and small, to keep a tight control on their waste products."

For the second time that evening, for the second time in minutes, the features of Gard's face froze. His arm slipped from his sister's shoulders as he listened to the words coming from the television set. Waste—small companies—waste—little people—waste . . .

"My God," he said softly. "Is it possible?"

"Gard?" Beth said. "What's wrong? Gard?" she said again to the man rushing toward the room's telephone.

Punching in a series of numbers, he cradled the phone between his ear and shoulder.

"Gard?" Beth repeated. "What are you doing?"

Blue eyes met hers. "I'm finding out the hours of the public library."

Chapter 10

TIME DID NOT HEAL ALL WOUNDS, SEASON DEDUCED AS she stared into the amber liquid of the half-filled wineglass she held. It had been exactly one week since Gard had lacerated her heart by ignoring her wave . . . and only three days since he'd compounded the injury with his actions in Beth's kitchen.

One week. A lifetime. Three days. A fraction of a lifetime. Nothing eased the pain—not the physical work she'd expended at the shop and the house, not the sleeping pill she'd taken the night before, and neither would the wine she'd been sipping all evening.

What she ought to do was go to bed, but that meant tossing and turning and remembering the taste and feel of Gard. Still, as painful as the memories were, they were better than this empty feeling that seemed a permanent mark of her waking hours. She sighed and lifted her feet from the coffee table, curling her toes into the soft pile of the thick, red and black rug it rested on. She reached for the remote control and plunged the television screen into darkness. The inane Monday-night comedies she'd tried to watch bored her, and the news only deepened her depression.

She padded to the kitchen and refilled the wineglass from a bottle of Chablis in the refrigerator before making her way to the bedroom. A leisurely soak in a bubble bath of imported French bath crystals and her fourth glass of wine went a long way toward relaxing the tension tugging the muscles in her shoulders and neck. She shaved her legs, creamed her face, and brushed her hair until her arm grew tired before slipping a long, deep rose-colored gown of pure silk over her head. The soft fabric slithered sensuously over her body. Season glanced at her image in the bathroom's large, lighted mirror. The silver surface reflected back a beautiful woman. A woman whose dark eyes held a soul-deep sadness. She drained the wineglass and set it on the vanity.

She turned and went into her bedroom, flipping back the spread with a practiced hand. Succumbing to the lure of the purple satin sheets, she stretched out on the beckoning surface. The bed rocked gently. She stared up at the ceiling and wondered where Gard was. His car hadn't been at Beth's for three days. Maybe he had left the older woman. Maybe he would come back to her. She instantly hated herself for even entertaining this last idea. Even if he did come back, what did that mean? His hot-and-cold treatment of her, cruelly rejecting her one moment, the next unable to keep his hands off her, was driving her crazy. And yet, she admitted truthfully and with a certain self-disgust, she would like nothing better than to have him here with her at this moment. She closed her eyes. The image of Gard making tender love to her rose before her, but somehow, instead of the pain she expected at that memory, she felt a measure of peace. A slight smile curved her lips and stayed there as she drifted off to sleep.

A persistent buzzing assailed her ears. Season's hand flailed automatically for the alarm. Even as her hand found the button and one part of her mind told her the clock was already off, the noise sounded again. On the third ring, she realized that the buzzing was not the clock whose lit red numerals read 12:48, but the doorbell. Who could possibly be here at this time of night?

Too sleepy to even grumble, she turned on a bedside lamp and groped her way down the dark hallway to the front door. Another long ring shattered the silence of the house as her hand reached for the doorknob. Looking through the newly installed peephole, she saw Gard's face etched against the illumination from the light near her driveway. Her first reaction was elation, her second, anger. He had a lot of gall showing up on her doorstep at almost one in the morning! And especially after what he'd put her through!

Without stopping to think, she unlocked the door and flung it open, harsh words and accusations hovering on her lips. The words never materialized as her eyes took in the picture Gard made standing in the doorway, his hands thrust palm outward in the back pockets of his jeans. Exhaustion was her overall impression. His shoulders slumped, even as they strained against the fabric of his oxford cloth shirt. Usually neat brown hair was mussed and looked as if he'd been running his fingers through it. Dark circles were smudged beneath the lackluster blue of his red-rimmed eyes. The silence stretched to deafening proportions as they stared at one another.

"I need you," he said at last.

The words were spoken slowly, almost hesitantly. At first Season was afraid she hadn't heard him correctly. Then her eyes blazed and her mouth opened to tell him to go straight to Hades. Instead, as their gazes held, his obvious fatigue tugged at her heart. She ached for him. She was forced to finally face the truth of her feelings. It didn't matter that he was involved with Beth. It didn't matter how he'd treated her. All she cared about was that he made her feel alive as no man ever had, and that she wanted to erase the pain and weariness from his face. She didn't analyze how she could have allowed it to happen but she knew that she loved him.

Wordlessly, she moved aside, allowing him entrance to her home and heart. As he stepped into the hall, she closed the door and backed against it, staring up at him with wide, expectant eyes.

Gard tried to smile, but the effort looked more like a grimace. His hands slowly came out of his pockets as his eyes roamed over her face. A scant foot of space separated them. God, she was gorgeous! he thought. He reached out and slid one hand beneath her heavy hair, resting it on the side of her neck. Silently, he caressed the high sweep of her cheekbone with a calloused thumb. He delighted in the softness of her skin.

Season thought she detected a tremor in his hand. Without conscious thought, she turned her cheek into his palm and raised her shoulder a fraction, letting her mouth graze the ball of flesh beneath his thumb.

A strangled sound came from Gard's throat as he suddenly closed the gap between them, imprisoning Season between the hard wall of oak and the equally hard wall of his body. Both of his hands cupped her head as he tilted it upward for his kiss. His mouth was hard and hurting, and his hands crushed the delicate bone structure of her face while his open lips forced hers apart to receive the demanding thrusts of his tongue.

He was angry. He was hungry. It seemed as if he was trying to exorcise some demon that drove him, but all he managed to do was fuel the fire he had ignited in them both.

After several long moments of ravenous, hungering kisses, Gard's mouth began a slow reconnaissance of her face. "Oh, God, sweetheart," he murmured into her ear, "I'm sorry." His lips touched her jaw. "So sorry . . . for everything . . ." He kissed her again, his mouth gentle on hers, his breath warm upon her face as he whispered achingly, "Season . . . Season . . ."

Season's hands gripped the belt loops of his jeans. She

smiled against his lips. "You're tired." She pushed him away gently and, taking his hand in hers, led him down the hallway to her bedroom.

Gard stood silently before her as Season's fingers worked swiftly at the task of unbuttoning his shirt. He was here. He was here tonight, never mind tomorrow. She buried her nose in the cloud of dark hair covering his chest and inhaled the combined smell of his cologne and his maleness, which blended into an erotic scent entirely his own. Her hands tugged the shirt from the waistband of his jeans, while her lips sought and found the flat brown nubs of his masculine nipples. Her tongue flicked them lightly while her fingers walked around the lean hardness of his waist, pulling the shirt free, inch by tantalizing inch.

Gard's hands were in her hair as he held her head to his body. He tensed when she unbuckled his belt and drew it slowly, sensuously through the loops while her tongue circled and teased. Was there another woman like her anywhere? Her fingers were cool against the muscled plane of his abdomen as they slipped inside the waistband to unsnap his pants. The slow downward grind of the zipper matched the soft hiss of air that escaped his lips. He bent and pressed his mouth to the top of her shining head before lifting her face to look into her eyes, eyes now glowing with sleepy seduction.

A hint of devilry lit their depths, and a slow smile tilted the corners of her full, inviting lips. White teeth caught her bottom lip as her hands slid inside the starched denim. She ignored the growl of pleasure that escaped him and plunged her hands midway down his jean-encased thighs. Her nails raked slowly up the hair-roughened firmness and sought entrance at the openings of his shorts, her fingers spreading wide over his firmly muscled buttocks. She squeezed gently.

She threw back her head in a provocative pose, her black hair cascading down her back. In a movement that was as deliberate as all her previous actions had been, she raised herself up on tiptoe and fit her body against his throbbing maleness. At the same time, she crushed her mouth to his. Open mouths fused in rising passion as Season ground her body closer and closer against him in an invitation as old as time.

Gard captured her rounded bottom and pressed her even harder against him, but when he moved to take the lead in their lovemaking, she murmured a soft, "No."

Instead, she peeled the shirt from his tanned torso. Kneeling down, she stripped the tight Levi's from his long legs. She ran her hands lightly up his strong calves, hard from his jogging, her mouth following the trail her fingers blazed. When her hands grazed and her breath tickled the crisp hair on his thighs, Gard caught her by the shoulders and hauled her to her feet. He bruised her mouth with his.

Season gripped his bare shoulders, and her nails bit into his brown flesh as the flood tides of passion crashed over her. She groaned his name, pushing at his shoulders and then his chest, toppling him onto the water bed. The surface pitched sharply with his weight. She followed him, sprawling across his almost-naked body in wild abandon. Her hair fell over her shoulders and onto his chest. Season lowered her head and captured his mouth almost roughly with hers. She wanted him to remember her and this night so freely given, wanted desperately to deluge his mind with thoughts of only her. Her parted lips savored the taste of his while his hands stroked her shoulders and back with increasing urgency. When he started to lower the bodice of her gown, she pulled away. "Let me."

She straddled his supine body, her bottom resting on the very proof of his arousal. Crossing her arms in front of her, Season grasped the hem of her gown, now riding high on her thighs. She slowly pulled the silken garment up and off, tossing it to the white rug on the hardwood floor. The gown settled into a puddle of deep rose colored material. She arched her neck and shook the inky blackness of her hair so that it spilled down the sleek satin of her back. Its length tickled Gard's upper thighs.

"Temptress," he muttered, his voice harsh with need as she reached for his hands and carried them to her breasts. His fingers tightened briefly over the ripe fullness.

Season sighed deeply and pressed her knees against his sides in an involuntary gesture. Her eyes drifted closed, and her lips parted as his hands continued to caress her. His thumbs drew lazy circles on her nipples, and when they contracted at his touch, he raised up on one elbow and guided one brownish button to his mouth.

Season whimpered deep in her throat and clutched his head to her aching breast. Gard caught the point between his teeth and ran the tip of his tongue over the sensitized peak. He forsook one for the other, then lowered his head back to the pillow and began another slow circling of his thumbs against her wet nipples.

When his hands skimmed over her rib cage and across her belly, she opened luminous dark eyes to stare into his. She saw there in his blue irises the same passion sculpting her features. She slid down his body, kissing his chest and the hard musculature of his abdomen. She probed his navel with her tongue. He was so beautiful, she thought. Every inch vibrant, healthy, and male. Her hands slid inside his briefs, drawing them down over slim hips. A wicked grin curved Gard's lips as he kicked the unwanted apparel to the foot of the bed. He drew Season up and, shifting beneath her, slipped easily into her warm wetness.

She sighed, a sound of deep satisfaction, and twined her fingers in the curling hair on his chest. Moving and pushing so the water-filled mattress rocked gently, she provided the undulating rhythm that moved apart and brought their bodies together in slow, unhurried strokes. Sometimes she leaned forward to kiss him, occasionally he reached to fondle a breast, but mostly they were content to probe the secrets and emotions found in each other's eyes as he filled her wanting femininity with the willing tumescence of his manhood. Together they rocked and swayed, pleased and were pleased.

Unable to stand her gentle punishment any longer, Gard eased from Season and rolled her onto her back, lowering his head to her breasts once more, teasing, nibbling, savoring the taste of her sweet skin.

"Please," she whispered, attempting to draw him back into her willing warmth.

"Now?"

"Yes."

He probed with his manhood. "Sure?" he teased softly, moving a fraction deeper.

"Yes."

He thrust fully into her, eliciting a small moan of pleasure. "Like this?"

"Oh, yes," she breathed. "Exactly like that."

Gard had never felt anything so sensual as the feel of his body moving in perfect choreography with Season as she writhed beneath him—movement that set the bed into an erotic surging that brought them together again and again, faster and harder. He lowered his head and pressed a kiss to her closed eyes. Her breathing sounded ragged in his ear. She turned her head, searching blindly for his mouth as they met in one final thrust that sent them both whirling into a shattering, mindless ecstasy. Tears rolled down Season's temples and into her hair at the sheer emotion of it. Clay had never loved her so sweetly, so wildly, so thoroughly, had never filled her as this man did.

Gard's softly muttered, "Sweetheart, sweetheart," was a tickle against her ear, a sweet balm to her heart. She didn't know how it had happened, but she loved him.

I love her, Gard thought. *It shouldn't have happened, but it has. There's no turning back. Face it, Kincannon. At this moment you could do without air better than you could without this woman's touch.*

He lay on top of her slender body as the bed settled to a

gentle rocking, content to be near her now that their hunger had been appeased for the moment. "You're one hell of a woman, Season Ashford."

"You're not half bad yourself, Mr. Kincannon," she murmured softly, determined that self-recriminations and doubts would not mar the moment. She would worry about the folly of loving him later. For now she just wanted to be with him, to love him as best she could, until he walked out of her life once more. She didn't even wonder where her pride had gone. She didn't care.

When Season woke, Gard was gone. Her heart sank in her breast. Already he had gone back to Beth. She rolled onto her stomach, breathing in the scent of him still clinging to the satin pillow. Tears stung her eyes. She hadn't thought he'd leave without at least telling her. Not after last night.

A loud metallic clatter jolted her upright in the bed. Someone was in the house! The sound was repeated in a more muted tone, and an unintelligible masculine mumble followed. A surge of happiness flooded through her. It had to be Gard. A burglar wouldn't be making such an ungodly noise.

She leaped from the bed and pulled on the rose gown. Without bothering with shoes, she almost ran down the hall to the kitchen. She pushed through the swinging door in time to see Gard place a pan back in the cabinet.

He straightened and turned at the squeak of the door. Season stopped, her eyes drinking in the sight of him clad only in his now crumpled jeans.

"Hi." He smiled.

"Hi."

"Sleep well?" he asked, sauntering closer.

She nodded. "You?"

"Great." He stood inches from her, his blue eyes warm as they searched hers. Without touching her with his hands, he took her lips in a series of sweet kisses, turning and slanting his head from side to side. "Mmmm, good," he whispered huskily.

Season smiled. "I think you have me confused with Campbell's soup."

"What?" he asked, a blank look on his handsome features.

"Mmmm, good. Campbell's soup. Get it?"

Gard rolled his eyes toward the ceiling. "Yeah. But I wish I hadn't. It doesn't say much for my technique if it makes you think of soup."

"That was a slow kiss . . . slow technique, right?" Her hands moved down his arms to his hands. He laced his fingers with hers and shrugged, obviously not certain where this conversation was going.

"Why, Gard, surely you remember that's the one you need to work on. Your slow technique. The one we can't manage to get the kinks worked out of," she said with a coy smile.

He grinned. "Kinks, huh. You want to hear about kinks, lady? I'll tell you about kinks. I know this broad who tried to seduce me last night. Seduce? Hell, if I hadn't decided to give in without a fight, it would have been rape. And you talk about kinky!"

Laughter spewed from Season's lips. She tried unsuccessfully to free her hands. "Don't be crude!"

"But I am crude," he said, gathering her into the circle of his arms and swaying from side to side. "At least that's what you once told me. And I told you that it was a pity you couldn't get into crude . . . and here we are. What happened? Change your mind about me?" His tone and expression were suddenly serious.

"No, I didn't change my mind," she confessed with a half smile. "I just couldn't help myself."

"Me either, Pocahontas," he said gruffly. His mouth lowered to take hers in another kiss. Season stood on tiptoe and strained against him. As she raised her arms to encircle his neck, the phone rang.

"Don't answer it," Gard said against her lips.

"It might be important," she said, gently disengaging herself as the intrusion pealed once more. Season spoke into the mouthpiece of the almond-colored wall phone. Her heart fell to her feet when she heard a familiar feminine voice.

"Season, is Gard there?"

Beth! Beth knew Gard was here! Did she suspect that he'd spent the night? Was she calling to create a scene? Questions roiled inside Season's head. Nothing had changed. Nothing. A coldness crept through her body. She raised limpid eyes to Gard and said, "It's for you." She held the receiver out toward him.

Gard took the instrument in one hand and caught Season around the waist with the other. "Hello?" he said into the phone.

She jerked free of his hold and almost ran from the room, ignoring his softly called, "Season!"

Gard watched her go, a frown drawing his dark brows together. He knew what was going on in her mind. He knew she resented Beth and the time he spent with her. Sometimes he could see the worry—maybe even jealousy—in her eyes. The time had come to set her straight and make her believe him when he told her that he was really Beth's brother. Things had gone far past the point where his identity mattered.

Now he answered his sister's questions almost automatically. His mind was on the woman who had fled to some other part of the house.

"I'm all right, sis," he said, rubbing the flat of his hand in a circular motion across his bare chest. "Just beat. Three days and nights at the public library looking through newspaper microfilm doesn't do much for your eyes, shoulders, or disposition."

"You didn't find anything, then?" Beth asked.

Gard sighed. "No."

"Do you think it's a dead end?"

"No. At least I'm not ready to give up on it yet." He still had faith in the hunch that had first formed in his mind Friday night as he'd listened to the rerun of Beth's speech. He was as certain as he could be without proof that his sister's death threats were somehow tied in with Victor's environmental control bill. It had to be someone whose company had been affected by the initial cleanup. Determined to check out his suspicion, he had spent the last sixty-plus hours in the library, searching through innumerable newspaper accounts concerning the bill and everyone it affected, companies big and small, but particularly the small ones.

By midnight last night he'd had it. He had found nothing, but he still believed the answer was there. Like everything else in this case, it looked as if it would be slow going. Last night all he could think about had been getting to Beth's and getting some rest in a real bed. He didn't remember actually going to Season's. He was just suddenly on her doorstep, his finger pressing the doorbell. He'd been filled with an aching need to see her, to hold her, to forget his exhaustion. He didn't remember what he'd said to her, but she was suddenly in his arms, her hunger matching his.

"Gard, can you come home?"

It wasn't so much the words as the tone of Beth's voice that shattered his reverie. He was instantly alert. "What's the matter? Has something happened?"

A brief pause preceded her answer. "I'm not sure."

"What does that mean?" he asked, his voice laced with a slight irritation that was the result of too much worry and too many sleepless nights.

"The phone has rung twice this morning, but there hasn't been anybody there." Another pause. "Do you think it's him?"

"I don't know, Beth," he answered truthfully. "Rick's there, isn't he?"

"Yes, but . . ."

"I'll be home in a minute," he promised.

Cradling the receiver, he walked slowly toward Season's bedroom. Beth wanted him. Needed him. He could hear the desperation in her voice.

Season heard the door close behind him and turned her unseeing eyes from the scene outside the window. Her arms were wrapped around her waist as if to ward off a chill.

"That was Beth," Gard explained unnecessarily.

"I know." Season's tone was carefully casual. Her heart was breaking, yet her chin lifted a fraction. "Are you going back over there?"

"Yes. In just a few minutes. Beth needs . . ."

"Needs?" Season cried. "Dammit, Gard, what about my needs and yours? Don't they count for anything?"

"Of course, they do, Season, but Beth . . ." He shook his head. He didn't want to tell Season about the threats on Beth's life, but he did want to tell her the truth about their relationship. "Beth and I . . ."

"Beth! Beth! Beth! I'm sick of Beth. You come here and tell me you need me, and I fall for it. I welcomed you into my bed. Now you're going to leave me and go back to her. You are going back to her, aren't you?"

"Yes."

For a moment she said nothing. When she spoke, her voice was calm, a calmness born of desperation. "Will you leave her and move in here with me?"

Pain flashed across Gard's taut features. God, he didn't need this! Beth was next door, almost beside herself with fear and worry, and Season . . . hell, Season was acting as any woman would in the same situation. Gard felt an underlying sadness growing within him. He raised anguished eyes to hers.

His voice shook as he spoke the words. "I can't."

Season held out both hands, entreating him to come into her life. *Don't beg, Season*, she commanded herself, then countermanded her own order. "Please."

I love you, Season, but don't ask this of me. "I can't," he said quietly, urgently.

Primitive fury replaced the soft pleading in her eyes. Suddenly she wanted to hurt him just as he was hurting her. Rage tautened her slender frame as she whirled and stormed to the dresser, her gown flying out behind her as her long legs crossed the room. "All right!" she cried angrily. "Your services can be bought, right? She's paying you to be her companion, but from the look in her eyes she'd like you to be more."

Without waiting for an answer, she grabbed her purse and began rummaging around in it. She held up her billfold. "I have money! Not as much as she has, but I can surely afford you for a while. I can surely afford to keep you out of her bed and in mine for a while."

He was silent.

"Say something!" she screamed.

"Season, don't do this."

"How about a check?" she taunted, ignoring his plea. "Clay's alimony is more than generous."

"Season . . ."

"No! I know. Credit cards. How about this one? Visa? Do you take Visa?" She thrust the card at him.

Gard glanced at it automatically, the ache inside him growing, and at the same time he felt an almost uncontrollable urge to laugh. The strain and pressure of the last few weeks were catching up with him, he thought. In the beginning it hadn't mattered what she'd believed. Now it did. The whole situation was so pitiful, so unnecessary, so funny suddenly. He felt his lips twitch in a small, bitter smile. "It's expired," he said in a voice beginning to reveal the first notes of a laugh.

"I'm *so* sorry. But don't worry. I have others. How about Master Card? American Express?"

Gard began to laugh, gut-deep, rolling laughter that had its roots in pain. It was either laugh or cry at the mess he always managed to make of everything in his personal life.

"Damn you!" Season screeched. "Don't laugh at me!" She hurled herself at him, pummeling him with her fists while Gard continued to laugh and ward off her blows.

At some point in her attack, his laughter switched from an agonized release to the real thing. She was beautiful! Feisty. Magnificent. A well-aimed blow caught him on the mouth, splitting his bottom lip. Both of his arms came up tightly around her, and he flung both of their bodies to the water bed.

"Let me up, you bastard!" she hissed.

"Season," he laughed down into her face as a thin trail of blood trickled from his bottom lip, "I love you."

Her writhing, struggling body stilled. Her eyes, dark and seemingly depthless, stared up at him. Her mouth parted as if she intended to speak, but no words passed her lips.

Gard's own eyes caressed her perfect features. "I love you," he repeated seconds before his mouth took hers in a kiss so poignantly tender that tears welled in Season's closed eyes.

Had she heard him correctly? His kiss echoed the words. He sounded sincere. Oh, God, did he mean it? All these thoughts swirled in Season's mind.

Drawing back to look at her, he awaited her response.

"Don't tease," she begged. "Not about loving me."

"I'm not teasing," he said with a smile.

"And Beth?"

"Beth Galbraith and I have lived together off and on for"—his brows knit in contemplation—"about thirty-six years now."

At Season's puzzled frown, he smiled again, "Sweetheart, Beth and I really are brother and sister. We share the same father, different mothers."

For long moments Season said nothing. "You mean . . . I don't believe . . . you mean you really are . . ." Suddenly Season's eyes closed. "Please don't let him be lying," she pleaded out loud.

Gard's mustache crawled upward at the corners. "I'm not lying."

She opened her eyes and looked up at him. "Promise?"

"You're not very trusting, are you?" he teased. "Want me to bring over our birth certificates?"

"No. I believe you." And suddenly she did. The relief flooding her body was sweet and heady. "But why didn't you tell me?"

"I did, if you'll remember," he said, taking great delight in reminding her.

"But I thought . . . you could have told me later . . . why didn't you . . ." She rambled, but suddenly stopped. "And you really are writing a book?"

Gard's smile wavered momentarily, but he verified her answer. "Yes. I really am writing a book." *Tell her the rest, Kincannon. Tell her you're a cop. Tell her you're never sure when you leave for work if you'll be coming home that night.*

"It's unbelievable!" she cried, breaking into his jumbled thoughts. Then, as if it suddenly occurred to her, she asked, "Why did you let me believe you were Beth's companion?"

"Because it was the truth. I am her companion. She's been through a bad time lately, and I've been staying with her." *Tell her now that you're a cop.* "Season . . ."

She smiled at him, love shining from her eyes. Her heart was feeling lighter and lighter by the moment. "Now I know why you were always so loving to Beth."

"Season, I should tell you . . ."

"Tell me that you love me again," she begged. "I like the way it sounds."

Gard gave an inward moan. He couldn't tell her now. Not now while the reality of his love was still a sweet heaviness on his heart. He wanted to hold his love to him for a while. He needed its soothing comfort for the moment. He would tell her later about his job. He would explain to her that a woman could have no permanent place in his life. He would tell her about Lynn and how his work had destroyed their marriage. He would make her understand that he loved her, but he couldn't, wouldn't, put them through the same hell he'd already barely survived once before. He'd tell her, he promised himself, but not now. Not this morning. For now, all he wanted to do was lose himself in the dark pools of desire that were her eyes and tunnel into the warmth and security of her body that granted him fulfillment and contentment.

"Oh God, Season, I do love you . . ."

Season's hand slid up to touch the side of his face. "And I love you."

The week that followed held moments of magic that only revealed themselves to lovers as Gard and Season learned about each other. Every minute not spent working—Gard still devoted endless hours to the library—was spent together. He still spent a part of each day with Beth and even portions of the evenings and nights on the pretext of working on his book. He and Season swapped nights cooking, helped each other clean up the kitchen, and shared quiet times playing cards or watching television together.

Sometimes the depth of his feelings for Season frightened him. He loved her, and she loved him. It was simple. Yet it wasn't. She'd asked for nothing, content with what they shared. But how long, he wondered, would it last? How long before Season demanded more? He knew he could never offer her marriage. He couldn't bear to watch the pressures of his work eat at their relationship. He wouldn't. Yet every time her body responded to his, he knew that in all honesty he couldn't let her go until he was forced to.

To Season, Gard was fantastic, wonderful. And she loved him so much. She wanted to be with him every moment. She wanted to be there for him to come home to. She wanted to share the joys of her work with him. She ached to hear him ask her to marry him, to imagine a houseful of dark-haired, blue-eyed babies. She wanted to grow old exploring the new world he had opened up to her with him beside her. But she realized the relationship was still new, still fragile, still a learning experience. So, instead, she took him to the Gilcrease Institute, they ate Nellie Burgers at Nelson's Buffeteria, and on Saturday Gard introduced her to baseball.

Tulsa's AA baseball team, the Drillers, was ahead at the top of the ninth, and Season was glad when Gard suggested they leave early.

"Well, how did you like it?" he asked as they made their way through the throng of spectators, his arm possessively about her shoulders.

Season struggled to find an answer that wouldn't hurt his feelings. "It certainly is a fast game, isn't it?"

"You hated it!"

"Gard, no! Not really. I just don't understand it. I couldn't tell you the difference between a line drive and a bunt. And I wouldn't know a double play if I saw it on Broadway."

So Gard explained it all in great detail, ending with all the nuances of teamwork that make up a double play. Season was so engrossed in the man that most of what he said went over her head. All she really understood was that something happened twice.

Sensing that her mind wasn't on what he was saying, he said, "It's sort of like making love. Everything has to be perfectly synchronized to make it happen." His eyes held a strange combination of excitement and humor.

Season slanted him a dark look. "Oooh! There isn't one ounce of romance in you if you can compare a darned old double play to making love."

Gard laughed. He dropped a kiss to the top of her shining head. "Well, Pocahontas, I'm going to prove you wrong. Just as soon as we get home."

Once home, Season changed into a lounging gown and Gard put on a tape of soft, sexy music. He piled pillows on the floor and gathered every candle he could find, grouping them on the cocktail table. Then he poured them each a glass of wine.

When Season entered the living room, it was dark except for the illumination of the candles. Gard lay on his side, propped up on one elbow, swirling a glass of white wine while his eyes searched the liquid's golden depths as if seeking to unravel a secret. He had unbuttoned the top buttons of his shirt.

Season was only a few feet from him when he noticed her. His perusal began at the tips of her toes, peeking out from under the heavy lace edging of her gown, past the silky length of her body to her lace-encased breasts and on up to the clean lines of her face and the soft fall of hair over her shoulders. Her eyes glowed softly with love and happiness. A tightness constricted Gard's throat. He couldn't speak. Instead, he held up a hand in an invitation for her to join him.

Season knelt at his side, tucking her feet beneath her. Gard ran a hand caressingly from her knee up over her thigh and back down, delighting in the sensual feel of the cool, smooth fabric. The candlelight softened the hard masculinity of his face and kindled a flame in the depths of his blue eyes.

"You're beautiful." The sound of his voice was like the slide of satin against flesh.

"So are you."

Their eyes devoured each other, yet neither spoke. Gard's hand continued its slow rubbing up and down, down and up, her leg. Season's hand reached out and curled around the brown fingers holding his wineglass. The hand stroking her thigh moved upward to smooth down the length of hair from the top of her head to her lap where the ends lay dark against the ivory satin of her gown. The rough flesh of his fingers skimmed her bare arm to her shoulder. His hand closed over the soft curve. He tugged her slightly toward him until she, too, lay propped on her elbow facing him.

The sweet strains of violins wafted through the candle-scented air, weaving through the almost tangible emotions springing up between the couple on the floor.

Gard reached out one finger and looped a strand of inky-black hair back over her shoulder. Season's eyes closed dreamily, and a sigh fluttered from her lips.

Gard set aside his wine and took both of her hands between his. Blue eyes silvered with love met the darkness of hers. His voice held the merest tremor as he began to quote softly, " 'How do I love thee? Let me count the ways . . .' "

Chapter 11

WAS IT HER IMAGINATION, SEASON WONDERED, OR DID the sun actually shine more brightly this Sunday morning than on any other Sunday morning she could ever remember? And was that robin singing a spring song more melodic than any she'd ever heard before?

Season rolled her head to the side, her cheek delighting in the cool, smooth feel of the satin pillowcase. Her eyes instantly caught the pair studying her. For an endless span of time neither she nor Gard spoke, and the only contact their bodies made was the gentle, relaxed touching of toes against toes at the far end of the bed.

"You make me happy," she said at last. Her voice sounded sincere.

"You make me happy, too." He grinned lewdly at her. "You made me *real* happy last night."

Season started to laugh, but the gurgling sound was trapped inside her mouth by his. He slowly, thoroughly kissed her good morning. Her arms instinctively wound around his neck, holding him to her. His warm lips had just abandoned her mouth for the hollow of her pulsing throat when the doorbell pealed. Gard halted and pulled back to look at her.

At the questioning look in her eyes, he said, "Probably the paramedics come to jump-start my heart."

Slipping her arms from his neck, she wriggled her body from beneath his and stood. Snatching up a robe to cover her nakedness, she padded across the floor. She stepped over the gown she had so readily dropped hours before. "You don't need your heart, or anything else, jump-started, Kincannon," she threw back over her shoulder.

"Season?" he called out just as she reached the bedroom door.

She turned, raking her fingers through her long, disheveled hair. He lay flat on his back, the sheet provocatively falling low on his abdomen, his hands folded behind his head. A mischievous smile played around his mouth.

"Get rid of whoever it is. I want to make love."

"Don't you ever rest, Kincannon?" she asked in feigned disgust. The doorbell pealed again, and Season disappeared through the doorway.

Season hurried toward the third, restless ringing of the doorbell with mixed feelings. On the one hand, she felt a rush of warmth at what awaited her back in the bedroom, while on the other, she felt a wave of cool annoyance at whoever was so tactless as to interrupt her beautiful Sunday morning. Tightening the belt of the robe, she peered through the peephole. No one. She saw no one. She smiled. Whoever it was had given up. She had just turned her attention, and her steps, back toward Gard when the bell pealed with another loud, impatient intrusion.

Season swore softly and, not even bothering to check the peephole this time, yanked open the door.

Her first impulse was to swear again, this time more boldly, but she managed to keep the words confined, though she couldn't say the same for her look of surprise and displeasure.

"Clay!" Unknowingly, she tucked the folds of the robe's V neck more closely in an attempt to cover any sign of cleavage. She was suddenly more than conscious of her naked body beneath the thin fabric.

"Did I get you out of bed?" Clayton Ashford asked. His voice sounded as though he didn't particularly care if he had.

Bed! Oh, my God! Season thought. She had an ex-husband at the front door and a lover in the bedroom.

"Yes, as a matter of fact, I was in bed," she returned. The confident tone of her voice implied that his reason had better be good for dragging her out.

Clay ignored her attitude and, offering nothing that even resembled an apology, pushed past her and into the house. "I wanna talk to you," he said.

It was then that Season first noticed the slight slur of his words.

"Can't this wait, Clay? At least until you're sober?" A wave of disgust washed over her, leaving her annoyed and a little sad.

"I'm not drunk," Clay denied instantly.

"Whatever you say."

"I just had a little vodka with my orange juice," he confessed.

"Most people have orange juice straight in the mornings, Clay."

"I would, too, if you'd come back to me," he tossed back in a pathetic, illogical volley. "If you'd start acting like my wife, I wouldn't need to drink."

Season smiled wearily. "You drank vodka in your orange juice when I lived with you. And," she added, "I am no longer your wife."

The eyes that roamed from her mussed hair to her naked feet might just as well have been fingers stroking her skin, so strongly did Season feel their intimate, violating glare. A shiver passed over and through her, and she hugged her arms tightly about her.

"You're still my wife in every way that counts," Clay insisted in a low, seductive voice. "I still need you, and you still need me. C'mon, Season, let's be nice to each other—just for this morning."

His words, his tone, his indecent proposition angered her sufficiently, but the step he took in her direction instantly mobilized her fury. Stepping back and out of his way, she said, "I am not your wife. Get that through your head. I neither want nor need you."

"Season . . ." he began, as if speaking to a willful child.

"I'm in love with someone else, Clay."

The silence that followed was deafening. Shock, stunned disbelief, and anger all vied for an equal place on Clay's face. "But you said . . ." he trailed off, finally adding in a harsh tone, "You liar! There was always another man!"

"I never lied to you," she denied. "When I left you, there was no one else."

"You're lying again," he accused her. "It's Nighthawk, isn't it?"

"No!" she screamed. "A thousand times no!"

"Then who?" Clay begged. A strand of his usually perfectly styled white hair fell onto his forehead, giving him a look of desperation Season had never seen before. "I can make you forget him," he promised. "Whoever he is, I can make you forget him. I can make you want me again."

As he spoke, he moved toward her. Instinctively, Season stepped back.

"Clay, don't . . ."

"I'm willing to admit," he went on, "that maybe I even love you a little."

She took another step backward. "Clay, don't . . ."

"Let me love you, Season," he pleaded. His hands reached out and grasped her shoulders, pulling her against him. She flinched at the pain of his harsh touch. For a frightening moment she felt his warm, alcoholic breath fan across her cheek. She struggled. He strengthened his hold. Doomed to the taste of his kiss, she steeled herself.

A deep, low, deceptively controlled voice filled the room and halted Clay's actions. "I'd hate to have to break your neck before breakfast, Ashford, but so help me God I will if you don't turn her loose." Clay raised his head and saw Gard lounging in the doorway with a calculated negligence that made his presence seem all the more menacing. A shoulder was braced against the doorframe, while his arms were folded across his bare chest. He wore jeans and a night's dark growth of beard. It was obvious he'd just gotten out of bed; it was equally obvious which bed he'd just gotten out of. "Let her go, Clay," he commanded again. "Now."

For one second, when Clayton Ashford's eyes darted toward the sound of Gard's voice, the surprise he'd felt had shattered the usual composure of his face, but then the mask slipped back into place. With movements as deliberately slow as Gard's, Clay eased his hands from Season's shoulders. He stepped from her and casually, arrogantly adjusted the cuffs of one sleeve, then the other, as if the fact of his rumpled appearance far outweighed anything else that was happening in importance.

"Well, well," Clay said, elongating the words into an accusation, "I should have known."

Season, exhaling a sigh of relief, moved to the edge of the coffee table, where she sat down. Another cleansing sigh slowed her heartbeat to an almost normal rate. With slightly trembling hands, she rubbed her upper arms, attempting to massage away the feel of Clay's hands on her. She noted two things: Clay seemed a lot more sober than he had when he'd first entered the house and Gard was pushing away from the doorframe and moving toward her.

Stopping directly in front of her, he stroked a single finger across her cheekbone. "Are you all right?" he asked softly.

She tilted her head so she could meet his eyes and nodded. She fought the urge to encircle his bare waist with her arms.

Clay gave a harsh, angry laugh. "For God's sake, Gard, you act as if I'd actually hurt my wife!"

Gard whirled as if a strong, destructive wind had whipped him around. His insouciant posture fled, giving the impression that Clay at last had managed to break the threads binding his self-control. "Ex!" he hissed through gritted teeth. "Season's your ex-wife!"

A slow, sneering smile curled Clay's lip. "My, my, the man does have a temper. You know what I've always found hard to take about you, Kincannon? The fact that you were always in control. You were always one notch above the rest of us mere mortals. Nothing ever got to you, not Vietnam, not even your wife dumping on you." His smile broadened in width but not in sincerity. "Pardon me. Your *ex*-wife."

Season's eyes quickly cut toward Clay at the personal references he was making to Gard's life.

Gard ignored these same references. "Well, there are so many things I dislike about you, Ashford, that it would take a calculator to give us a total. But right now what I dislike most is your standing here."

"Speaking of standing here, why aren't *you* with your sister?"

Season's eyes once again darted to Clay. A frown creased her brow. How had he known about Gard being Beth's brother? Hadn't he told her that Beth had no family? And the two men spoke as if they knew each other. Season gave a mental shake of her head. Something wasn't adding up.

"Gard . . ." she broke in.

"Or for that matter," Clay continued, both men not paying Season the slightest attention, "why aren't you out spending all that money I paid you?"

Gard's head jerked in the direction of Season. He hazily noted the growing confusion on her face before turning back to the man before him. "Shut up, Clay!" he growled. "Just shut up!"

"Ah," Clay said with a malignant twist to his mouth, "I see you haven't told her."

"Told me what?" Season asked vacantly.

"What else haven't you told her, Gard?" Clay asked, viciously warming to the attack now that he had the scent of blood. Suddenly, he shifted his frosty gaze to Season. "Has he told you about being Beth's brother?"

"Yes," Season said, automatically rising from the coffee table as she sensed the approach of some unwanted piece of knowledge, "I know he's Beth's brother."

"That's enough, Clay," Gard said in quiet warning.

The older man's dark blue eyes sought out Gard's, and for one brief moment, Gard saw the purest streak of malicious pleasure he'd ever seen. Clay was enjoying himself—immensely. If Clay couldn't have Season, he was going to do his best to see that Gard didn't either.

"No," Clay drawled, "I don't think that is enough, *Detective* Kincannon."

Season's attention jumped from one man to the other. Clay looked like a mighty conqueror, while Gard looked . . . She wasn't exactly certain how Gard looked.

"Did he tell you he was a cop, Season? A detective?"

Confused, Season's eyes found Gard's. Even as she defended him with the words "He's a writer," she saw the truth in Gard's eyes.

"You're a policeman? A detective?" she asked dumbly.

"One of Tulsa's finest," Clay threw in sarcastically.

"Shut up!" Gard warned again, then turned back to Season. Both hands resting on his hips, he tried to explain. "I didn't lie when I said I was a writer. I'm writing a book on criminology."

"But you're a policeman, too? A detective?" she asked again as if her mind could not conceive of the idea.

"Yes," Gard answered on a long sigh, "I'm a cop."

They were the three hardest words he'd ever spoken because their very utterance forced his relationship with Season onto a new plane . . . perhaps one it couldn't survive.

"But why didn't you tell me?" she demanded, more surprised than angry. "Why keep it a secret?"

"Because I . . ." Gard began, then trailed off. How could he tell her, in the presence of Clay, that in the beginning he'd wanted to keep the investigation a secret— the fewer people who knew he was a cop, the better. But more importantly, how could he tell her that after he'd fallen in love with her he'd postponed telling her of his profession as long as he could because he was afraid of the consequences?

Clay laughed with deep satisfaction. "Because then you might have somehow suspected he was spying on you for me."

Gard threw Clay a look that could have killed.

Clay returned a look of triumph.

Season simply made herself dizzy vacillating between the two men.

"Spying?" She suddenly found her voice, at the same time as she felt the first stirrings of anger.

"Season, it isn't what it looks like," Gard began.

"It's exactly what it looks like," Clay countered. "I approached him about the job of spying on you, he accepted it, and took good money for his services. My mistake, though, was in asking the fox to watch the hen house."

Season swallowed convulsively, combing her fingers through her sleep-tangled hair. Her attention rested completely on Gard.

"Did Clay ask you to spy on me?"

"Yes, but . . ."

"And did you say you would?"

Gard hesitated.

"Did you?" she asked in a raised, impatient voice.

"Yes!" he answered in the same snapping tone.

She closed her eyes and muttered something that sounded like a mournful "Oh, God!"

"Season . . ." Gard began, but found his words interrupted.

"Why would you want to spy on me?" she asked, her attention now on her ex-husband. She stood behind the sofa, bracing herself against its back as if she needed the support.

"I wanted to know who you were seeing and how serious you were about the relationship." For the first time, Clay's face softened. "I wanted you back, Season. I still do."

Season heard the words, yet they made little impression on her mind. Her thoughts were all occupied with the realization that Gard had betrayed her. Spying on her! He had been spying on her! Her heart pounded so rapidly against her rib cage that she was certain it was audible, and her head spun so wickedly she felt as if the room were spinning, wildly and out of control. She eased herself around the sofa and sank into its soft depths. She suddenly felt sick. And tired. Crazily, she wondered where the beautiful Sunday morning had gone.

"Just leave, Clay," she said quietly. "Please."

"So you can go back to bed with him?" Clay snarled. "Can't you see he used you, Season? You were nothing but an assignment, a job."

Against her will, her eyes once again sought Gard's. Suddenly all they'd shared seemed so tawdry and, like an old photograph, a little dirty around the edges.

"But maybe," Clay continued, "you can overlook that fact when the two of you are in bed . . ."

Clay never got a chance to finish. With lightning speed, Gard descended on him and, with a low growl of barely contained fury, jerked Clay's arm painfully behind his back and marched him forward.

"I don't want to hurt you, Clay," he growled through gritted teeth, then amended the statement, "Yes, I do want to hurt you, but I'm going to show you some of that control you so despise." His hold tightened until the older man gasped. "I'm also going to show you the door. If you're smart, you'll stay on the other side of it. And if you're real smart, you'll always see there's a door between us." Wrestling open the front door, he shoved a stunned Clay out into the lovely spring morning. Then, with all of his strength, Gard slammed the door until the windows rattled and the pictures on the wall threatened to plunge to the floor.

He stood, both palms flattened against the door, head hung in dejection, for long moments, even after the roar of Clay's car was but a memory.

He knew what Season was thinking. He knew she thought he had betrayed her. Maybe that he didn't even love her. Ironically, he thought, the revelation that he'd been hired to keep her under watch meant nothing . . . not in comparison to the fact that he was a policeman. That was the fact jeopardizing their future. He lowered his hands slowly and turned toward her.

She still sat on the sofa, her head bowed at an angle that caused her hair to spill about her like a silky black veil. She absently played with the front closing of her robe. Slowly, as if sensing he was looking at her, her fingers stopped their nervous toying. Her eyes raised to his.

Neither spoke.

"Season . . ." he began after a span of silent seconds.

"Is it true?" she cut through his words. "Was I only a job to you?"

Gard crossed the room quickly and squatted down before her. His knee brushed briefly against hers, and Season shied away as if a stranger's skin had made uncomfortable contact with her own. Gard saw her reaction and grimaced. Deliberately, he threaded his fingers through her unwilling, resisting ones. "Give me ten minutes to straighten all this out, and then I'll answer any question you ask." There was a pleading quality to his voice. "Okay?" he asked when she didn't respond. When she still hadn't answered, he said, "For God's sake, Season, you owe me that much. At least let me give you my version of everything."

Season heard the heartfelt entreaty. She also saw it in the blue eyes watching her so intently. She supposed she did owe him that much, she thought. And herself. And, besides, even now, she seemed unable to deny anything he asked. "What is your version?" she asked softly, raggedly.

Gard breathed a relieved sigh and, disentangling his fingers from hers, he rose and moved away. "Oh, Season, everything got so out of hand." He stood looking out of the window, both of his hands rammed into the hip pockets of his jeans. Once again, he turned. "I am Beth's brother, half brother, just as I told you. And I am a writer, just as I told you."

"And a policeman," she added with a trace of bitterness, "just as Clay told me."

"Yes, I'm a policeman." But he didn't want to go into his job just yet. "My family and the Ashfords have known each other a long time. It was never anywhere near a close relationship. We just knew each other. Several weeks ago Clay came to my office and said he wanted me to do a surveillance job for him."

"On me," Season said in a toneless voice.

Gard nodded. "On you. I asked him the same thing you just did. Why? He told me the same thing he just told you. I told him no."

"But I thought you said . . . he said . . ."

"At first I told him no, that the whole idea was disgusting. He then implied, no, he more than implied, that he wouldn't support Beth's campaign—and that he'd see that others under his influence didn't as well."

Season frowned. "But Clay doesn't have that kind of political clout. Does he?"

Gard shrugged. "I doubt it, but I didn't want to take the chance, not when he was asking so little."

"So little?" Season's voice shook with the revival of anger.

"So little," Gard repeated. "All I ever intended was the most cursory of surveillances. Just a little bit, to appease him. For heaven's sake, Season, I'm a policeman—a damn good one. I'm not some sleazy divorce detective."

"But you did take his money." She made it sound like the accusation of the year.

"He wrote me a check," Gard admitted.

Season laughed unpleasantly, bowing her head and closing her eyes at the same time. "That's taking money, Gard."

"Not when you don't cash it."

Her head instantly jerked upward. Her eyes found his.

"I tore it into shreds and lined the wastebasket with it."

Season allowed his words to rake through the dying embers of hope.

"I couldn't even take the money when I didn't know you," he explained. "And I certainly couldn't have after I did."

"But Clay thinks you cashed it."

For the first time since she'd left their warm bed, Gard gave a genuine smile, though a small one. "Clay's got an accountant who's going crazy."

She couldn't keep a ghostlike smile from her own lips, but it drifted away as quickly as it had appeared. "Were you spying on me that night you came to borrow sugar?"

Gard raked a hand through his uncombed hair. "Yes . . . but not for Clay. I told myself it was for Clay, at least in the beginning of the evening, but by the time I came here for that stupid cup of sugar, I was spying for someone else."

Season's face registered her confusion.

"I was spying for me," Gard said. "I wanted to make damned sure Nighthawk didn't spend the night. Even then, I thought of you as mine."

At the words of possession, the embers of Season's hope

ignited to a smoldering glow. But she had little time to savor it, for Gard was speaking again.

"I want everything out in the open. I don't want any more secrets between us." He had once again moved to her and, just as minutes before, he crouched before her. This time she didn't flinch from the gentle touch of his body grazing hers. "What I'm telling you now I don't want to go out of this room. Do you understand what I'm saying?"

She nodded that she did.

Gard then proceeded to tell her that, although most people, including Clay, believed he had taken a leave of absence to comfort Beth after Senator Galbraith's death, the real reason was the frightening threats against his sister's life. He explained that he and Rick Riccitello—here Season's eyes widened again in disbelief—had been specially assigned the case and that, while leads had been slim and few, Gard thought they might at last be on to something.

Season's reaction was one of shock and concern. "My God, how awful for Beth!" Then, in a display of sensitivity, she added, "And how awful for you!"

"It's been rough," Gard agreed. He reached out a hand and absently tucked long, sleek strands of her hair behind an ear. "And it's been rough on you, though you didn't even know it."

"What do you mean?"

Looking evenly into her eyes, he said, "We think the man who ran you down thought you were Beth."

"Me, Beth?" she asked, her face once again a canvas on which shock had been painted.

"You were both dressed in black, and your hair was up. We think he just made a mistake, a natural mistake under the circumstances."

"My God!" she breathed again as the words sank in. "He meant to kill me?"

Gard nodded, his features set in a grim pattern. "Now I have two reasons for getting the bastard." His hand reached out to cradle her cheek, and instinctively she nuzzled the soft skin of her face against his coarser palm.

"Oh, no," she suddenly whispered, her eyes flying to his as her face pulled from his warm touch, "you think the man delivering the flowers was him."

"Yes," Gard supplied simply.

"Oh, Gard, I'm so sorry I didn't see him any better. I'm so sorry . . ."

"It's not your fault," he said, stopping her. "And I blamed you unfairly that night. I'm afraid I was still reacting from what had just happened in the kitchen."

The thought skipped through Season's mind that on that night, as he had on several other occasions, Gard had implied that she'd be better off without him, but she had been so busy just being in love, she had never questioned that hurtful sentiment. Why had Gard thought he was such poison to her life?

"Gard?" She hesitated. Her hands fidgeted uncharacteristically and her eyes lowered from his to watch the inane play of her fingers. "You still haven't answered the most important question."

He smiled softly, his hands stilling hers. "Ask it. I'll answer it."

"You weren't teasing when you said . . . I mean, it was the truth when . . ."

His finger gently raised her chin so that their eyes met again. "I love you, Season. That was always the truth. It always will be the truth."

The happiness flooding through her blinded her to the momentary look of pain in Gard's eyes. He loved her! Gard loved her! Everything was all right!

"Oh, Gard, I love you," she whispered as she slipped from the sofa and joined him on the floor. On their knees, neither mindful of the hard surface beneath them, each went willingly into the arms of the other. Wrapped in his tight embrace, Season laid her head on his bare shoulder, her face nestled in the curve of his neck. Her own arms hugged him to her, their strength telling him that she would like to fold him into the very essence of her. Words were exchanged for the even sound of each other's breath; touch was bartered for touch.

"Season," Gard spoke at last into the delicate shell of her ear, "always remember I love you. No matter what happens, remember I love you." His voice was thick with feeling, a feeling that had increased in its fervor even beyond the soulfully passionate embrace of moments before. For an instant his arms tightened to a painful grasp.

Pulling back, though still remaining in the shelter of his arms, she laid her palm against his whisker-stubbled cheek. "Nothing's going to happen," she consoled with a tender smile. "We're always going to be together. We'll always have each other." She laid her own cheek back against his chest. The crisp hair tickled the end of her nose. "Oh, Gard, we're going to be so happy." She giggled slightly, girlishly. "I'll even learn to bake brownies." Her hands unconsciously traveled his spine in comforting trails. "And I'll have your baby," she said softly, her voice suddenly serious. "I'll have all your babies."

The back muscles beneath her hands tightened, but she didn't notice.

A tiny tinkle of laughter spilled from her. "I think I've just proposed to you. In fact, I'm certain I've just proposed to you." Pulling back, she stared into his face, her own more beautiful than it had ever been. "What do you say, detective? Want to frisk me for life?"

Gard's arms released her, falling to his sides like weighted anchors. "Don't. Please, don't," he pleaded, his words so soft and ragged she barely heard him.

But heard him she had, and his words, coupled with the fact that he was getting to his feet and moving away from her, caused her to experience the first pangs of alarm. Oh, God, she thought, she'd been too brazen!

She smiled softly, and with embarrassment, but with his

back to her he saw nothing and heard only the rustle of her robe as she, too, rose.

"I'm sorry, Gard. I guess I've been listening to too much women's lib. To be honest, I surprised myself. I should have realized you'd want to do your own asking." She raked her hand through her hair and gave a half laugh. "I feel a little foolish."

He turned, his face a portrait in pain. "Don't feel foolish. Your proposal was the"—he swallowed—"it was the nicest thing that's ever happened to me. It's just . . ." He turned back to the window, unable to complete the thought.

Season's heart fell to her feet. "It's just what?" When he didn't answer, she asked again, "It's just what, Gard?"

"I can't marry you." The words sounded torn from him, ripped from his very soul.

Season thought she was going to stop breathing. "But . . ." she stammered. "But I thought you just said you love me."

Still staring out the window, Gard spoke softly, "I do love you, Season. More than I could ever say."

"Then I don't understand." Confusion, bewilderment, and a tiny note of hysteria sounded in her voice. "You love me. I love you. For thousands of years that combination has led to marriage."

"Please believe me when I say I can't marry you . . . or anyone."

"Why?" Season demanded.

Gard said nothing.

"Damn you!" Season threw at him. "Turn around and look me in the eye and tell me why."

Gard whirled toward her. "Because I'm a cop!" he shouted.

His reason effectively silenced her for a moment, but only for a moment. "And I'm a hair stylist. What has that got to do with anything?"

"I have a high-risk job. A dangerous job. When I leave in

the morning, I never know if I'm coming back. I can't ask a woman to live with that uncertainty.''

''I can handle it,'' she said, looking him straight in the eye.

''My first wife said that, too. Only she couldn't. Every time I was five minutes late, I found her hysterical. And at night, I'd wake up to her muffled sobs. She begged me to find a 'normal' job, but I couldn't. I'm a cop, Season. Plain and simple. I was a cop yesterday, I'm a cop today, and I'm going to be a cop for whatever tomorrows I have. I don't know how to be anything else. I don't want to be anything else.''

''I don't want you to be anything else,'' she said.

''You say that now, but in time you'd grow to hate it. And me. I thought I'd die when Lynn walked out on me, but I *know* I would if you did.''

Season considered what he had said. She had read of the high divorce rate among policemen; she knew his fears had validity. Not only that, he had lived through the nightmare of divorce once before. She told him she could handle it. Could she? Could she live with his being late? Could she live with not knowing where he was and if he was safe? Could she live with the always present doubt of whether someone less moral was quicker on the trigger? A certainty took seed in her heart and quickly blossomed. She could live with anything as long as she could live with him.

''I want to marry you, Gard.''

He groaned. ''Don't do this to me, Season.''

''Don't do this to us.''

''Season, I can't . . .''

''What do you propose for our future then?''

Gard looked about helplessly as if the answer might be hiding somewhere in the room. ''Can't we just go on the way we are for now?''

Season shook her head. ''No. For the first time in my life I know what love is, and I won't settle for less than a whole commitment. I'll give you all of me, Gard, but I won't give you part.''

Their words had warred, and their eyes were locked together in the fiercest combat known to the sexes. Gard had just opened his mouth to speak when the phone trilled an untimely interference.

Chapter 12

Season stared at the ringing telephone as if it were an alien intruder. Her mind whirled with all that had transpired between them in the last few minutes. He was rejecting her . . . rejecting her love. He wouldn't even give them a chance.

The phone's third ring finally penetrated the pain enveloping her. With weary movements, she crossed the room and lifted the receiver. "Hello?" Her voice sounded strained and forced even to her own ears.

"Season, Riccitello here. Is Gard there?"

Riccitello. Beth's friend. No, Gard's friend. His detective partner. "Yes. Just a moment." Season refused to meet Gard's eyes as she held out the receiver. "It's for you."

Gard took the proffered instrument. "Kincannon!" he snapped. He was silent as he listened to what the other man had to say. He swore angrily. "You checked out the company? Right. Okay. I'll be there as soon as I can." He slammed down the receiver and ran his hand through his hair. "Damn!"

Season stood near the front door, staring out at the circular drive, unable to focus on anything through the film of tears blinding her.

"Season?"

She didn't turn. "Yes?"

"That was Rick. He thinks he's found something at the library. A small company that went under because of Victor's legislation. The company went bankrupt, and the owner lost everything. It's a slim lead, but all we have."

Season was silent.

"I have to go. We have to check this out. Beth's life could depend on it."

"I understand."

Gard went to her and placed his hands on her shoulders. She stiffened slightly at his touch. Ignoring her reaction, his hands stroked her shoulders through the sheer fabric of her robe. "As usual, the timing is hell. We need to talk more. You have to understand why I feel the way I do."

"I don't think there's anything else to say," she replied coolly. "You've made your feelings very clear. You've lumped me into the same category as your ex-wife and condemned me without giving me a chance. Without giving us a chance."

"Look, Season, I know what I'm talking about. I've seen it happen too often, and not just with Lynn and me."

Silence reigned, yet the sound of her heart breaking was deafening in Season's ears.

"Sweetheart, look at me."

Under the slight force of Gard's hands, Season's body was pivoted around until they stood face to face. With a regal dignity, she lifted her chin and met his eyes. He was surprised to see how emotionless hers were. Her face displayed neither anger nor pain, neither love nor hate. It was totally devoid of feeling, yet filled with a majestic nobility. It was as if she were two people: one, the loving woman he'd been in bed with only minutes before, the other, this cool, controlled woman who refused to listen to his reasoning. He couldn't believe the change, yet he accepted the fact that he'd brought it about. Still, he knew he was right. Statistics didn't lie. His blue eyes probed hers, searching for some hint of how she felt. She stared unflinchingly back. There was none. Gard felt his life crumbling around him for the second time.

"Can't you be happy with what we have?" he asked.

Could she? she wondered. Perhaps for a while. Yet, deep inside, she knew Gard had to offer her all of his life or nothing. She would settle for nothing less. She couldn't. "You'd better go," she said at last. "Rick is waiting."

"I'll call you as soon as I can."

"No!" The sharpness of her response was Gard's only clue that her emotions were very near the surface.

Their eyes met for long moments. Gard's bleak, unhappy; Season's unfathomable.

"Don't call," she repeated in a voice that trembled only slightly. "Not unless you can share your entire life with me. Forever."

She turned away from him and forced her attention to the front yard. A light breeze rippled the thin blades of monkey grass, and the birds sang of springtime love. Season was unaware of the beauty of the morning. Her world was suddenly gray. She prayed that he would hurry and leave— before she lost her tenuous hold on her tears.

Gard reached out to touch her rigidly held shoulders, but drew back before doing so. For the moment, she was lost to him. And in view of what had happened in the last half hour, and the unchanging style of his life, he realized sadly that she was lost to him forever. Now and forever.

The days following Gard's departure from Season's life were the longest, most miserable she'd ever lived through. She had only thought the time she'd spent before was agonizing. The uncertainty of his relationship with Beth was nothing compared to the anguish of knowing there was nothing she could do to bring him permanently into her life.

How could she fight for him? She couldn't. She couldn't fight Gard's old fears and hurts, and she couldn't begin to know how to compete with the work that was so important to him. More importantly, she didn't want to compete. If being a policeman was what he wanted to do with his life, then that was what she wanted for him. God only knew there were few enough dedicated law enforcers in the world.

He was good at his work; somehow she knew that. Gard would tackle his work as he did everything else in his life: with willingness and dedication. Maybe even pleasure. Yes, most certainly pleasure. He was one of the few people she knew who could find pleasure in small things, who could take something not so good and turn it into something special. Was that why she loved him so? He had taken her not-so-good life and turned it into something wonderful, unique. He had given her the love she craved. A man's love. The only other person who had ever loved her was her mother. Thoughts of Mary brought a fresh stream of tears. She needed to talk to her mother.

The older woman, who lived an hour away, listened to her daughter's woes with the patience only a mother can have with an unhappy child. She listened to the tears that in the past had been so untypical of Season and wondered what kind of man had wrought this change. She hoped fate granted her the privilege of meeting him.

"Oh, Momma! What can I do?"

"Season, do you remember what happened when your boyfriend broke the date with you to take another girl to the junior-senior prom?"

Season hiccupped. "I . . . I'm not sure."

"He told you he thought he liked someone else and wanted to take her to the dance. You told him you understood, that you wouldn't be mad if he took this other girl. Well, if I remember correctly, he took her and she smothered him. She demanded he spend every minute with her, dance every dance with her."

Season laughed shakily. "Tommy Gregory. And the girl was Charlotte Simpson. I remember. He couldn't wait to call me the next day so we could get back together."

"That's right."

"But what does that have to do with Gard?" Season asked.

"When you love someone very much, baby, you want his happiness above your own. And you love him enough to let him go. And you hope your love will be strong enough to bring him back to you. Just like you did with Tommy Gregory."

Season sat silently for a moment, struggling with her tears. "Oh, Momma," she choked at last, "I do want him to be happy. I do, but . . ."

"No buts. You're strong. I know how strong, but you don't yet. Now is the time you'll find out just who and what Season Clark Ashford is."

"But what if she isn't strong, Momma?"

"She is. Now dry your tears and go call Jim. He'll keep you so busy you won't have time to mope around."

Season smiled. "Maybe I will. Thank you, Momma . . . I love you," Season added.

"I love you too, baby. Take care."

"Take care," Rick told Gard as they started up the creaky staircase of the apartment building that should have been condemned years before.

Gard unbuttoned his jacket and unsnapped the holster of his gun. The cold metal of the Magnum felt as comforting as an old friend. And as smooth as Season's skin. Dammit! he chastised himself, forcing his attention back to his partner, who followed several paces behind him. "Where the hell is our backup?" he hissed over his shoulder.

Riccitello's answer mingled with the muted shufflings of two uniformed officers responding to their request for help. Help that might not be needed, but help that would be there if it was. Even as Gard watched, both men pulled guns from their holsters and followed the two detectives up the stairs. A thin film of dust fluttered at their movement, the tiny, playful motes dancing in the sunlight that was struggling to penetrate the layers of grime graying the broken and cracked windows. The powdery dust tickled Gard's nose, and for a moment, he toyed with the idea of sneezing.

Dammit to hell! This was no time to sneeze. Not when the slightest sound might alert the madman holed up in the room upstairs. Not when they were this close to the man who had killed Victor, threatened Beth, and hurt Season.

Reaching the top of the stairs, Gard motioned for the men to stop. Both he and Rick leveled their guns at the door that stood directly before them. Utter silence met their arrival. Was he in there? What if their informant had been wrong? What if it was a trap? What if the two days since Rick had called him at Season's had been spent searching for the wrong man? Gard cut his eyes to Rick's for a sign of readiness. At his partner's nod, he called loudly, "Open up! Police!"

Silence met silence. Gard felt a sudden prickling of alarm. The hair on the back of his neck bristled. Something wasn't right. The same inexplicable feeling that had saved his hide more than once caused him to shove Rick out of the way at the same time as he cried, "Get back!"

A single shot, fired through the cheap wood of the door, hissed past Gard, singing a death song in his ear. Without waiting, without thinking, acting only on the police training he'd received and on his own instincts, he rushed the door, kicked in the rusted hinges, and threw himself into a rolling ball onto the floor. Another shot screamed from behind the soiled and tattered sofa. From the corner of his eye, he saw Rick start to move into the room. At the same instant, a head and shoulders appeared over the back of the couch, a gun pointed directly at the movement in the doorway. Instinctively, Gard braced himself on his elbows and, aiming the gun, pulled the trigger. There was the ring of one shot, closely followed by another. Then silence.

The first sound that made its way into Gard's mind was his own heartbeat. He was alive. He had survived again. Adrenaline sent his blood coursing at a reckless speed throughout his body, giving him a feeling closely akin to intoxication. The happenings around him had a feeling of surrealism. Rick was bending over the injured man whose husky voice, already sounding like a death rattle, was rasping, "They deserved to die. They killed my father." One of the backup policemen was dialing the phone, the other was milling officially and efficiently around the apartment, riffling through papers and looking through drawers. Gard heard a montage of sounds—the sound of swearing, the sound of pain, the sound of excitement, and somewhere in the distance, the faint sound of a siren.

How much time passed he would never know. At some point, he had gotten up from the floor and reholstered his gun. He now found himself staring out the window into the beautiful afternoon sunshine that was totally incongruous with the grim scene just played out in the dingy room. Strangely enough, his thoughts flashed to Season. If ever there had been any doubt, he now knew he was right. He couldn't ask her to share this uncertainty. Couldn't expect her to share this hell. He loved her too much.

"It's over," Rick said, coming to stand beside him.

Gard's eyes flicked to his partner, then past him to the white-coated attendants carrying the white-sheeted body from the room. "Yeah," he replied in a tone that held absolutely no feeling, "it's over."

Season had barely changed from her work clothes when she heard the knocking at the back door. Her bare feet slapped against the tile floor as she crossed the kitchen. Dusk colored the sky outside, and the soft glow of evening, diffused through the sheer, beige and rust curtains hanging at the windows, seeped into the pristine whiteness of the kitchen. Season opened the door and saw Beth Galbraith standing on the porch. The older woman's face exuded an obvious relief.

"It's over," Gard's sister said. "Gard asked me to tell you." Season stared at her, not fully comprehending until Beth clarified the statement with the added words, "They got the killer."

Season absorbed the information. The threats on Beth's life were over. They had caught whoever was responsible. The same person was probably responsible for Victor's death as well. Gard had caught him. Gard . . . Season's mouth suddenly felt as if it was full of sawdust.

"Is Gard all right?" she choked out around the fear squeezing her heart and filling her chest with an agony of uncertainty.

Beth saw the almost wild look of fear in her young neighbor's eyes. Fear and hopelessness. The hopelessness she was familiar with. She'd seen it in Gard's eyes too often lately. "He's fine. May I come in?" she asked gently.

"Oh, yes. Yes, of course," Season stammered, moving aside so Beth could enter the dusky room. "Sit down. I'll put on some coffee."

She turned away and busied herself with filling the glass coffeepot with water and measuring out the required amount of fragrant, brown grounds, all the while longing to question Beth about what had happened. Her heart rejoiced in the one fact she did hold in her possession. Gard was alive. Her hands began to tremble in reaction as she pushed the button to *on*. Her task finished, she settled herself across from her guest and clasped her shaking hands tightly together on the table's polished oak surface.

Beth saw the tension in Season's body, noticed the palsy in her hands, and met her tortured eyes. She covered Season's hands with her own.

"It was all over around four this afternoon."

"Who was it?" Season's voice was hardly more than a whisper.

"His name was Max Witt," Beth explained. "His father owned one of the smaller companies affected by Victor's environmental protection bill. Evidently, the company didn't have the money to take care of the cleanup. When the penalties got so high the company couldn't pay them, the Witts were forced to shut their doors. The older Mr. Witt died less than a week later from a heart attack, and Max blamed his father's death on the stress he'd just been through. And to make matters worse, Max's wife left him."

"So he decided to do what? Punish you and Victor? That doesn't even make sense!" Season said.

"When you're dealing with mentally disturbed people, you find their way of thinking very rarely makes any sense, except to them," Beth told Season.

"How did they find him?"

"Something I said in a speech caught Gard's attention, and he decided to check the microfilm of back newspapers to see what people and companies were affected. It took a lot of hours at the library before they finally came to the Witt operation. When they learned the company had gone under, they checked more closely into the Witt family. When they discovered the tragedies occurring during the short span of time following the shutdown, they began to look more closely at Max Witt. When they learned he had rented a car the night you were run down, they were pretty sure they had the right man. They finally located him somehow through his mail. Gard said his apartment was filled with newspaper articles about Victor and me."

Season rose and poured two cups of coffee. She set the cups on the table and reseated herself. "Gard found him?"

Beth cradled the cup between her hands. "He and Rick went in after him. There was a shoot-out."

"Oh, God!" Season moaned. "And you're sure Gard's all right?"

"Yes. He's the one who . . . shot Max Witt."

Season's coppery skin paled. She took a sip of the hot coffee. Gard had shot a man! He had been shot at! The coffee refused to settle and nausea clutched her stomach. She forced her attention back to Beth, forced herself to remember he was alive. Alive and okay.

"He called me a little while ago from the station and said he and Rick were doing the paperwork on the case," Beth said. "He said he'd stay at his apartment tonight."

A long sigh escaped Season's slightly parted lips. She could picture him fixing himself something to eat in the tiny kitchen, see him sprawling on the beige sofa nursing a drink to relax himself, and imagine him sliding naked between the sheets to sleep while the moonlight poured through the French doors and spilled molten gold over him.

"Season?" Beth's voice interrupted the bittersweet daydreams. Season dragged her attention back to the woman before her.

"Yes?"

"You're in love with my brother, aren't you?" Beth's voice was gentle, knowing. Her eyes, peering from behind silver-framed glasses, were kind.

"Yes," Season admitted.

"He loves you, too."

"I know."

"Then what's the problem? I thought you had everything straightened out . . . after he told you about me." She laughed softly. "I never told you how flattered I was when I found out that you thought I'd snagged Gard for my companion." A feigned expression of hurt crossed Beth's features. "Come to think of it, why am I so flattered? You thought I had to buy him."

Season smiled wanly in return, Beth's attempt to lighten her mood failing miserably. "Things were good for a while. Then, I found out about Clay hiring him to watch me."

"Watch you!"

Season nodded. "Clay threatened to withhold his support from your campaign if Gard didn't. He also offered Gard a lot of money."

"That swine! I know Gard would never take money for something like that, but he did agree to keep an eye on you, didn't he?"

"Yes," Season agreed. "How did you know?"

"Because I know my brother. He'd want to do whatever he could to help me."

"That's what he said. I believed him, Beth." Her eyes filled with tears. It seemed she'd cried more tears the last few days than she had in all her life put together. She blinked back the suddenly forming moisture, a wry smile settling about her lips. "I asked him to marry me."

"And he obviously said no," Beth observed.

Season nodded, struggling with incipient tears.

"Oh, Season! That's so like Gard." She sighed heavily. "You know he was married before?"

"Yes. He told me a little about it."

"Well, Lynn was an hysterical woman looking for something to happen. Her father was a shopkeeper who was always home by five-fifteen on the dot. The most dangerous thing he ever did was cross the street. If possible, her mother was even more paranoid than she. She kept Lynn stirred up with horror stories all the time. There was never a policeman killed or injured that she didn't point out could have been Gard."

"And it could have been."

"Yes," Beth agreed, "it could have been. But her father could have been run down crossing the street, too. Season, listen to me. Gard is a good detective. A damn good detective. He has a mind capable of thinking as cunningly as the criminal he's after. He calls it gut instinct. I think it's because he's thorough and careful, a born cop. But whatever it is, it's brought him back from some pretty bad situations."

"I know. It wasn't me, Beth. I can handle the pressure, I know I can, but he can't. He won't. He doesn't believe I can take it, day after day, year after year, without coming to hate him and the job. He believes I'd wind up feeling as Lynn did. That I'd leave him the way she did."

Beth's face was a study in concern. "I was afraid he might feel that way. He loved her deeply and she hurt him just as deeply, but I don't think what he felt for her can even begin to compare with what he feels for you. As crazy as it may sound, Season, my big, hulking, macho brother is scared spitless of any sort of commitment." Beth smiled sadly. "And he's as stubborn as all get-out, so I don't know what to tell you."

"There's nothing else I can do. I've already done it, according to my mother."

Beth's dark eyes questioned her.

"I've loved him enough to give him what he wants. I've let him go."

The next morning as Gard sat glumly at his desk, finishing up the last report dealing with Max Witt's capture, Season was flying to Los Angeles for a three-day seminar. Speaking to a thousand would-be Sassoons was serious business. Big time. The goal she had dreamed of. Her mind should have been on her presentation or deciding exactly what she would do to the three women who were going with her as models. After all, as the main attraction at the conference, she would be lecturing on the new line of cosmetics she was backing and would be doing actual haircuts and makeup demonstrations. Instead, her thoughts centered on Gard.

Her talk with her mother had helped. She knew Mary was right, and there was a certain satisfaction in knowing she had done what Gard wanted. She hadn't pressured him. She hadn't flown into a frenzy when he'd rejected her offer of a life together. She had given him the freedom to pursue the work he loved, unfettered by the complications of a wife or any emotional entanglement. But those facts failed to lessen her heartache.

Season leaned her elbow on the armrest and stared unblinkingly at the sea of billowing white clouds stretching out below her. She missed him. Terribly. Desperately. But she functioned. She worked. She took care of her business. She immersed herself in whatever mind-occupying task was at hand. She proved her mother right. Life went on and so would she. She was learning, as Mary had predicted, of Season Ashford's strength. And she was beginning to see that although Gard had embellished her world with laughter and new frontiers, she would have survived without him if fate hadn't decreed that they meet. Just as she would survive life now without him. She was learning that she was one of life's survivors.

Rick breezed into Gard's office at the station with a smile on his face and a swagger in his gait. He stopped a few feet in front of Gard's desk, his smile petering out completely as he stared in astonishment at the man before him.

Gard sat slumped in his chair, his feet—shod in loafers—resting on the cluttered desktop. His left arm lay across his hard middle, his hand cupping his right elbow, while his right hand supported his chin. Rick sank into the chair across from Gard.

"What in the hell's the matter with you? You look like you just lost your best friend. Come to think of it, you haven't been yourself since we started wrapping up this case. What's going on, Kincannon?"

Gard shrugged, the action pulling the blue material of his shirt taut across his shoulders. He folded his forearms across his chest and resumed his morose expression.

"Look, Gard, you should be happy. The man who killed your brother-in-law and tried to kill your sister is lying in the morgue. That's reason enough to at least put a smile on your face. Besides, it's spring. The time for lovers.'' He grinned. "You know, *amour. La dolce vita.* All that stuff.''

Gard didn't answer.

Rick tried a new tack. "Okay, Kincannon, if you can't be happy for yourself, be happy for me, huh?'' He laughed suddenly, a smile smeared across the romanlike features of his swarthy face.

The sound of his friend's laughter caused Gard to look up in astonishment. Rick seldom laughed and never like this. Never as if he was really happy. "What happened to you, Riccitello? You get a raise or something?'' Gard's lips twitched in a semblance of a smile.

"Hell, no. Though I could use one. Especially now.''

"Will you stop with the little teasers and just tell me what happened to turn you into a laughing hyena?''

"I'm getting married.'' The words held a wealth of satisfaction.

Incredulity hit Gard's face with the suddenness of a slap. Rick married! After what his first wife had put him through? It was incredible! He thought his friend had more sense than to fall into the same trap twice.

"Hey, man, where are the congratulations?''

"Rick, do you know what you're doing?'' Gard asked in a voice tinged with disbelief.

The happiness slowly drained from Rick's face. "What is this, Gard? Be happy for me. Like I will for you when you and Season decide to tie the knot.''

"Season and I aren't getting married,'' Gard said coldly.

"What?!'' It was Rick's turn to look incredulous. During the weeks preceding the culmination of the Witt case, Rick had never seen his friend happier. He knew Gard loved Season. He had known there was something between them since the night she had been run down by Max Witt. So what had happened? He voiced his question out loud.

"Nothing really happened,'' Gard hedged. "I just knew she wanted more than I could give her.''

"Season wanted to get married?"

Gard ran a hand over his weary-featured face. "Yes."

Rick leaned forward, his face registering his sincerity. "But why not, Kincannon? If you love her and she loves you, why the hell not?"

"Because it would never work!" Gard yelled, swinging his feet from the desktop to the floor and rising from his swivel chair in one smooth motion. He plunged his hands into the pockets of his gray slacks and looked through the slats of the venetian blinds into the traffic snarling the streets. "It would never work," he said more quietly. "You of all people should know that."

"Why should I know that?"

Gard looked over his shoulder at his friend. "Because of what happened the first time."

"It isn't the same," Rick argued.

Gard whirled. "Of course it's the same! Nothing's changed! You moved from the East coast to Tulsa, but you're still a cop. You still have a dangerous job. The kind of job that makes kids and wives go bananas. Or leave you and find themselves a fifth of whiskey or another man to keep them warm and calm their fears. Is that what you're looking for for the second time?"

"It isn't the same, Kincannon," Rick repeated doggedly, his voice low, controlled. "Sally isn't Veronica. Just like Season isn't Lynn. Some women have something that others don't. It's that simple."

"That's a crock, Riccitello, and you know it!"

"Is it? Maybe so. But I don't want to believe it. I'm sick of going home to an apartment that isn't anything more than a place to sleep. I want someone to be there, and not to cook and clean and sleep with. Someone to just be there. Waiting. I'm tired of being alone, Gard. And I'm willing to take a chance with Sally. I'm willing to see if what we have isn't the stuff dreams are made of."

"But what if this falls apart, too? Man, I remember what

you were like when you first came here. Can you take that kind of beating again?"

"I don't want it to happen again, no. But I'm willing to chance it. Hell, we take chances every day in our work. Do you see what I'm driving at?"

"Not really." Gard leaned one shoulder against the windowframe, his brows drawn together in a frown.

"We exist, Kincannon. We don't really live. Dammit, we're so afraid we won't make it from one assignment to the next alive. Why? So we can go home to an empty apartment, drink a few beers, and indulge in a one-nighter occasionally just to prove we're alive, that's why. And that's not really living. There has to be more to it than that. I've been hurt. So have you, but we survived. They didn't bury us. You have a lot of courage when it comes to your work. Let's see some of that courage when it comes to your heart—your emotions. Take a chance, Kincannon. Take a chance on Season."

Without a word, Gard turned back to the window and raised his right arm, resting his forearm on the frame above his head. He leaned his aching forehead against his arm. Was Riccitello right? Should he try again? He pictured the newly married Lynn happy and smiling, then saw the smile turn to anger as she screamed that she wouldn't risk having his baby. He saw Lynn's features fade into those of Season. He heard her say she wouldn't bring a baby into the world without the relative assurance that its father would be around to help raise it. He felt an unfamiliar tightening in his throat. God, no! He couldn't bear to hear those words from Season. He couldn't bear to lose her. He felt sick. His head throbbed in synchronized rhythm with his heart. He knew if Season ever left him, he would die. Rick was right. He was existing, but just existing was better than the pain of watching Season walk away from him. He wasn't that strong.

Not even turning around, he said in a voice husky and

low, "Congratulations, Rick. I hope you and Sally will be happy."

Rick sat rooted to the chair for long moments while his partner continued to stare out of the window. He felt dejection sweep over him. Kincannon wasn't going to give it a go. Of all the people he knew who deserved happiness, Gard Kincannon was at the top of the list. Rick pushed himself out of the chair, suddenly feeling all of his thirty-eight years. He turned and glanced back over his shoulder for a final look at the man who had shared such a great part of his life the last few years.

Gard stood in the same position, looking like a piece of modern sculpture. It must have been some trick of the light, because just as Rick turned away he thought he saw the slight shaking of his partner's shoulders.

Chapter 13

GARD PUSHED BACK THE FOIL TRAY OF HALF-EATEN ENCHI-ladas and reached for the bottle of beer sitting beside his plate. He took a healthy swallow and rose from the table. His feet carried him to the living-room sofa. His mind, as it invariably did, went to Season and the night he had made love to her there. He tucked his weary body into one corner and lifted his feet to the scratched and cluttered surface of the coffee table.

It had been ten days since his talk with Rick. Ten long, agonizing days in which he'd weighed the pros and cons of the argument his friend had presented to him. Gard's mind felt numb . . . his body felt numb . . . except for his heart, which still throbbed with an aching need to see Season again or to at least hear her voice.

He had called her one night after the talk with Rick and the phone had rung time after time with no answer. She was gone and he didn't even know where she was. He'd driven to Beth's the next day and learned that Season was holding a one-woman seminar in L.A. and wouldn't be back for almost a week. He figured she should have returned three or four days ago, but he hadn't been able to get up the courage to call her again. Instead, he'd phoned one of his old, on-again-off-again girl friends and made a date. Just to see if he was still alive, as Rick said. He'd called the next afternoon and canceled the date on the pretext of work. He didn't want another woman. He wanted Season.

Gard took another long swallow of the beer and let his eyes roam slowly around his apartment. It was as sterile and lifeless as Rick had said. Worse. Even the new plants hadn't helped. Season's house was full of plants and he'd reasoned they were what made her house feel like a home. So, a few days ago he'd gone to a nursery and bought five green plants, hoping the life and color would help alleviate the utilitarian atmosphere of his living room. He'd looked and looked until he'd picked out an asparagus fern exactly like hers. Then he'd picked out a dieffenbachia, a schefflera, and a couple of philodendron. The woman running the joint probably thought he was a little crazy as he milled through the greenhouse looking for precisely the right plants. But he'd been wrong. Plants weren't what made a home. It was a person. Love. He didn't understand what was happening to him. Always before he'd been able to accept life's handouts . . . to adapt to whatever came along. He could file them away and go on with his life. Now, for the first time, he found his work wasn't enough to ease his mental turmoil. For the first time, he was afraid he'd never have peace of mind again.

Restlessly, Gard got to his feet and polished off the remainder of the beer. He couldn't sit in this lonely solitude any longer. He had to get out of the silent apartment. Find some people, some lights, some music, some . . .

He slipped his feet into his loafers and grabbed the keys to the Thunderbird from the coffee table. He couldn't get out of the apartment fast enough. The sound of the door closing behind him echoed hollowly in his heart.

Season rinsed out the cups she and Beth had used for their hot tea after they'd returned from a fund-raising dinner at the Civic Center. The evening had been a success, if numbers present was any indication, but both Season and Beth had felt the need to just sit down afterward and have a nice, quiet conversation before calling it a night. Beth had left only moments before, and Season straightened the kitchen out of habit. She filled the coffeepot for the morning and turned out the light.

She was barely into the hall when she heard a knock at the back door. She smiled. Beth must have forgotten something. Her mind was scattered in so many directions with the campaign, she complained of forgetting a lot of things lately. Turning, Season retraced her steps to the kitchen and flipped on the light. She unlocked the door and opened it, a smile curving her lips.

"What did you for . . . get . . ." The words trailed off into silence as she looked up into Gard's face. He looked terrible. Thinner. Older. Haggard.

Why now? she wondered. She was coping. She wasn't happy, but she didn't cry herself to sleep anymore. She hadn't in . . . two days now. Her dark eyes, full of questions and misery, held his. Neither spoke for endless, pregnant moments.

"What do you want?" she asked finally and in an almost breathless whisper.

The intensity of his narrow-eyed gaze held her in its grip. "You."

Season's eyes drifted closed. She felt herself swaying. She had never fainted in her life, but she felt perilously close to it at the moment.

"Season?" he asked, his hands closing over her shoulders.

His familiar and beloved touch started a quivering in her legs.

Gard looked down at the pallid face of the woman who meant more than life to him. He felt her iron control slipping. Her body trembled, and her breathing came shallowly and fast. "Season, are you all right?" he queried anxiously.

Season forced leaden eyelids upward. "Oh, Gard," she wailed, her hands gripping his arms, "what do you want? I can't take much more. I gave you what you wanted . . . didn't I?"

"Yes."

"Then what more can I do?! You took my love, my . . . my happiness. God! You almost took my sanity. I'm just now beginning to fill up the emptiness you left. I'm playing tennis and golf, and helping Beth with the campaign . . . and I'm working myself into the ground . . ." Her eyes filled with tears and her voice faltered. "I'm trying to make a new life for myself."

Gard saw the start of her tears, heard the edge of hysteria in her voice. He folded her unresisting body against the hard length of his and rested his chin on the top of her shining head. "Is there room in this new life for a tired, battered, disillusioned cop?"

Season was quiet in his arms. Very slowly she raised her head to look at him. What she saw in his eyes held her in riveted silence. Fear. His brow was etched with worry and harsh lines creased his cheeks . . . cheeks that were pale beneath his tan. He looked like a man who was scared to death.

"Oh God, Season, say something! Anything!" he begged through gritted teeth. His eyes glittered with an unusual brightness.

In that instant Season knew how much he loved her. He loved her, and he had been hurting just as she had. In the weeks since he had walked out of her life, she'd talked to Beth about him. She now felt she knew what made him tick even better than he did. She realized his just showing up at her door had been a major step for him. She was certain that reaching the decision to come to her must have been a journey through hell. He was so certain he was right . . . that a relationship could never work out. Coming here told her one thing: He was having doubts, serious doubts, about his convictions.

Season's hands lifted from their resting place against his chest to cradle his whisker-roughened cheeks. A tremulous smile tugged at the corners of her lipstick-free mouth, and her eyes began to smolder with the joy slowly building inside her.

"I love you," she whispered.

Gard's face paled even more. "Oh, God! Season!" he rasped. Then his mouth was on hers, drawing out all the hurt of the past weeks and replacing it with the never-to-be-forgotten ecstasy only he could create within her.

The next few minutes found only the sounds of harsh breathing and moans emanating from the kitchen before Gard swept Season up into his arms and carried her to the bedroom. From that room, with the door closed, hardly any sound could be detected at all.

Much later, the tickling of Gard's mustache against the swell of her breast roused Season from a light sleep. She wound her fingers through the vibrant softness of his hair, hair that looked as if it had acquired a few silver threads since she'd seen it last. He raised his head and looked at her, his eyes mapping the contours of her face, which was bathed in the gentle glow of the bedside lamp. What he saw was love and contentment.

"Marry me."

The words were a command, but held the entreaty of a question. Almost as if he was afraid she might refuse.

"Yes." She smoothed his eyebrow with a fingertip.

"It will work! We'll make it work!" he said fiercely.

"It will work," she repeated gently.

Gard swallowed. "She left one day while I was at work. Just packed and left." His voice still held a note of disbelief at his ex-wife's actions. "I know you love me now, but I can't help but wonder if . . ."

Season shook her head. "Never."

His eyes sparked with an almost feverish intensity as he captured her hand and kissed each finger one by one. "I love you so much it scares me."

"Why?" she murmured. "I love you the same way."

"Now. But what about . . ."

Season reached up with her other hand and silenced his words with her fingers. "Forever."

He gave a short, harsh laugh. "I'm paranoid, aren't I? Gard Kincannon. Twice-decorated hero of Vietnam. TPD Rookie of the Year. Several citations for bravery. He can look down the nose of a three-fifty-seven Magnum, but he's scared to death to give his heart to a woman. Afraid to risk loving." He trailed one finger along the curve of her bottom lip. "Do you think you can teach me how to trust?"

Season smiled at the seriousness in his voice. Loving him and having his love in return would be the easy part. She was awed and pleased to be its recipient. Proving that a life together could be good would take time, but with Gard at her side, she wouldn't mind the lessons. She would have the rest of their lives. "I'll try," she said, "if you'll smile for me."

It was forced, but it was a smile.

"Now," she said, wriggling beneath him, "I want *you* to teach me something."

"What? Anything," he promised, pressing his mouth to hers.

A sultry smile tilted Season's lips. "I don't know what you call it in the bedroom, but on the ball field, I think it's called a 'double play.'"

READERS' COMMENTS ON SILHOUETTE INTIMATE MOMENTS:

"About a month ago a friend loaned me my first Silhouette. I was thoroughly surprised as well as totally addicted. Last week I read a Silhouette Intimate Moments and I was even more pleased. They are the best romance series novels I have ever read. They give much more depth to the plot, characters, and the story is fundamentally realistic. They incorporate tasteful sex scenes, which is a must, especially in the 1980's. I only hope you can publish them fast enough."

S.B.*, Lees Summit, MO

"After noticing the attractive covers on the new line of Silhouette Intimate Moments, I decided to read the inside and discovered that this new line was more in the line of books that I like to read. I do want to say I enjoyed the books because they are so realistic and a lot more truthful than so many romance books today."

J.C., Onekama, MI

"I would like to compliment you on your books. I will continue to purchase all of the Silhouette Intimate Moments. They are your best line of books that I have had the pleasure of reading."

S.M., Billings, MT

*names available on request

If you enjoyed this book...

Thrill to 4 more Silhouette Intimate Moments novels (a $9.00 value)— ABSOLUTELY FREE!

If you want more passionate sensual romance, then Silhouette Intimate Moments novels are for you!

In every 256-page book, you'll find romance that's electrifying...involving... and intense. And now, these larger-than-life romances can come into your home every month!

4 FREE books as your introduction.

Act now and we'll send you four thrilling Silhouette Intimate Moments novels. They're our gift to introduce you to our convenient home subscription service. Every month, we'll send you four new Silhouette Intimate Moments books. Look them over for 15 days. If you keep them, pay just $9.00 for all four. Or return them at no charge.

We'll mail your books to you *as soon as they are published.* Plus, with every shipment, you'll receive the Silhouette Books Newsletter absolutely free. *And Silhouette Intimate Moments is delivered free.*

Mail the coupon today and start receiving Silhouette Intimate Moments. Romance novels for women...not girls.

Silhouette Intimate Moments